SOPHIA NIXON

The Mafia Boss Thinks I'm His Dead Wife

He Doesn't Just Want Me—He Believes I Belong to Him

Copyright © 2025 by Sophia Nixon

All rights reserved. No part of this publication may be reproduced, stored or transmitted in any form or by any means, electronic, mechanical, photocopying, recording, scanning, or otherwise without written permission from the publisher. It is illegal to copy this book, post it to a website, or distribute it by any other means without permission.

This novel is entirely a work of fiction. The names, characters and incidents portrayed in it are the work of the author's imagination. Any resemblance to actual persons, living or dead, events or localities is entirely coincidental.

Sophia Nixon asserts the moral right to be identified as the author of this work.

Sophia Nixon has no responsibility for the persistence or accuracy of URLs for external or third-party Internet Websites referred to in this publication and does not guarantee that any content on such Websites is, or will remain, accurate or appropriate.

Designations used by companies to distinguish their products are often claimed as trademarks. All brand names and product names used in this book and on its cover are trade names, service marks, trademarks and registered trademarks of their respective owners. The publishers and the book are not associated with any product or vendor mentioned in this book. None of the companies referenced within the book have endorsed the book.

First edition

This book was professionally typeset on Reedsy. Find out more at reedsy.com

To those who believe in second chances, in love that grows through trials, and in the strength to overcome our pasts. This story is for the warriors who fight not just with their fists, but with their hearts, and to the ones who never give up on love, no matter the darkness. May you find your peace, your redemption, and your own happily ever after.

For Victor and Elysia, and for everyone who dares to love fiercely.

Contents

Foreword		iii
Preface		iv
1	Prologue	1
2	Awakening	8
3	Victor's Obsession	21
4	A Dangerous World	32
5	Tension Rises	43
6	Doubts and Fears	56
7	The Bond Grows	69
8	Love or Fate?	81
9	Revelations	93
10	Unraveling the Past	105
11	Escalating Danger	117
12	A Family Divided	128
13	Secrets Unveiled	139
14	Betrayal in the Shadows	151
15	The Verrini's Grip	161
16	Under Siege	170
17	A Fragile Peace	181
18	Old Enemies Resurface	193
19	The Final Stand	205
20	The Choice	216
21	Unmasking the Truth	228
22	Crossing the Line	239
23	Rebirth	250
24	Moving On	262

25	Redemption	273
26	A New Beginning	284
27	The Final Test	295
28	Epilogue—A Love Rekindled	306

Foreword

In a world where power often comes at the price of loyalty, love is the one thing that refuses to be bought or sold. *A Love Rekindled* takes us deep into the heart of darkness, where betrayal and survival are daily truths, and redemption is the most elusive prize of all.

At its core, this is a story of love tested beyond its limits—love that is not just about passion, but about sacrifice, trust, and the courage to change. Victor and Elysia are not your typical heroes. They are shaped by their pasts, scarred by the violence and chaos of the world they come from, yet they fight for a chance at something pure—something lasting.

Through their journey, we see the true cost of power, the strength of vulnerability, and the undeniable pull of fate. But *A Love Rekindled* is not just a tale of bloodshed and betrayal; it's a story of transformation. It's about finding the strength to face our darkest fears and the courage to walk away from the very world that tried to destroy us.

I invite you to dive into this world of intrigue, danger, and passion. But more than that, I invite you to embrace the ultimate message of the story: no matter the darkness we've faced, the love we fight for is the light that can lead us into a new dawn.

— *Sophia Nixon*

Preface

Every story begins with a question—one that lingers in the mind, begging to be explored. For *A Love Rekindled*, that question was simple: Can love truly survive in a world where betrayal is as common as breathing, and where survival often means sacrificing everything you hold dear?

When I first envisioned this story, I wanted to dive into the complexities of love and loyalty, especially in a world that often forces us to choose between the two. Through Victor and Elysia, I wanted to explore the tension between what is and what could be, the constant battle between fear and hope.

Their journey is not just about falling in love. It's about the courage it takes to face our deepest flaws, to confront the darkness within and around us, and to fight not just for survival, but for a future built on trust and redemption. It is a story of healing, of understanding that no matter how broken we may seem, there is always a chance to start anew.

The world of the mafia, with all its brutality and twisted loyalties, provided the perfect backdrop to examine the high stakes of love, power, and choice. Victor and Elysia's path was never meant to be easy. There were moments of doubt, of fear, of decisions that would forever alter the course of their lives. But in the end, it is their strength and resilience—individually and as a couple—that carries them through the storm.

While *A Love Rekindled* is a work of fiction, the emotions that drive Victor and Elysia are very real. We all face moments when the past seems too heavy to overcome, when the weight of our choices threatens to crush us. But it is in those moments that we have the power to rebuild, to redefine who we are and what we stand for.

I hope this story resonates with you as much as it has with me. Whether you are drawn to the suspense, the romance, or the emotional depth of the characters, I invite you to join Victor and Elysia on their journey. I hope you find yourself rooting for them, questioning their choices, and ultimately, believing in the transformative power of love.

Thank you for letting me take you on this journey.

1

Prologue

The fog was thick that evening. A dense, suffocating haze that seemed to wrap the world in a blanket of despair. Elysia D'Alembert stood at the edge of the village, her gaze lost in the shadowy woods that stretched beyond the old stone walls of her family's estate. The wind carried whispers of ancient secrets, rustling through the branches of gnarled trees as though they were telling her something, something she couldn't yet understand. The dimming light of dusk clung to the earth like a last gasp of life before the cold darkness took over.

She had always loved the village—its quiet charm, the way it felt like time moved slower here, as if the world outside had forgotten about this corner of the earth. But tonight, there was a weight in the air, a heaviness that sat in the pit of her stomach. Something was wrong, and the sense of unease gnawed at her with a quiet persistence.

Elysia had never known betrayal could feel so real. Not until this moment.

The footsteps behind her were unmistakable. Frédéric—her betrothed, the man she thought she could trust. He was the one she had given her heart to, the one who had promised to stand by her side through everything. But his presence now, instead of bringing comfort, filled her with dread. She didn't turn to face him immediately. She couldn't.

The betrayal had been so carefully constructed. The soft-spoken words, the promises of loyalty, the assurances that everything would be alright—it had all been a carefully crafted illusion. She'd believed in him. She had believed in their love. But what was love if it could so easily be torn apart by lies?

"Elysia," Frédéric's voice broke through the fog, smooth and insistent, as he came closer, his silhouette emerging from the mist. She could hear the slight tremor in his tone, the one that hadn't been there before. But it was too late.

She turned to face him now, her expression unreadable. The moonlight caught in the silver of her eyes, casting them with an eerie, ethereal glow. There was a chill in the air, but it wasn't from the cold—it was from the sudden realization that the man she loved was not who he claimed to be.

"You're not the man I thought you were," she whispered, her voice fragile, like the last remnants of a dream slipping away.

His smile was faint, almost sad, but there was no warmth in it. "No," he admitted, taking a step closer. "I'm not. I never was."

In that moment, the fog seemed to grow thicker, as if the world itself were trying to hide the truth, to suffocate it. Elysia's heart raced, but she stood her ground, not allowing herself to step back, to show fear. She would not give him the satisfaction of seeing her falter.

"Why?" The question escaped her lips before she could stop it. She felt foolish, asking. She had always been careful, had always thought she knew him. But now, the truth was unraveling, and all she could do was stand there, helpless.

PROLOGUE

Frédéric's gaze softened, just a little. "You should have never trusted me, Elysia. But you were always too trusting, weren't you?" His voice was laced with an almost bitter nostalgia. "I never intended to fall in love with you, not at first. But I knew what you could give me. You were always more than just a pretty face, after all. You were the key to everything I wanted."

Elysia's heart dropped as she understood. She had been a pawn in his game. A tool for his ambition. Her father's wealth, her title, her influence—they had been the reasons behind his affection. Not her. Not her heart, nor her soul.

"I… I loved you," she choked, her throat tight, as if the very air was being stolen from her.

His face hardened, and he stepped closer still, until he was just inches from her. His breath was cold on her skin, a stark contrast to the warmth of the village behind them.

"I never wanted your love. I only needed what you could give me," he said, his words like a dagger plunging into her chest. His eyes gleamed with a coldness that sent a shiver down her spine.

But there was more. She could feel it. His smile twisted into something darker, more sinister. "You were never meant to be part of this world, Elysia. Your fate was always sealed. You just never saw it coming."

Before she could respond, before the words of disbelief could leave her lips, she felt it. A sharp pain—a searing agony that tore through her side, splitting her vision with red-hot fury. Her hand flew to her ribs, only to come away slick with blood. It spread fast, staining the pale fabric of her gown.

She tried to scream, but no sound came. The coldness of the night began to seep into her veins, numbing her, and the world began to tilt.

Frédéric stepped back, his face a mask of indifference. "I've done what I needed to do," he said softly, almost pityingly. "Goodbye, Elysia."

Her body crumpled to the ground, the fog now swirling around her like a dark, suffocating cloud. Her eyes fluttered shut, her last breath stolen by the cruel hands of fate.

The world seemed to freeze in that moment. The fog hung heavy in the air, as if it too mourned the end of an era. And yet, somewhere, deep within the layers of death, something stirred.

Elysia's body lay still, blood soaking the earth beneath her, the fog swirling like a living thing around her, thickening with each passing moment. The world seemed to press down on her, its weight suffocating, but there was something else. A pull, a sensation that was not of the physical world. It started as a whisper, a faint current that drifted into her consciousness like the flutter of a distant memory. It called to her with an eerie, soft insistence.

In her mind's eye, the earth seemed to shift. The fog, once dense and smothering, began to dissolve into a vast, endless expanse of light. It wasn't the warm, comforting light of dawn. No, this was something colder, more distant, yet powerful—untouchable. A realm between realms, where time seemed to stretch and bend like the very fabric of reality was being pulled taut by invisible hands.

Her vision blurred, then cleared, and she saw it—a door. It stood before her, black as midnight, surrounded by swirling shadows that seemed to dance in rhythm to an ancient song. The door was framed by two tall, imposing columns, their surfaces etched with symbols that were unfamiliar, yet deeply unsettling. A low hum vibrated through her bones, as if the very door itself was alive, waiting.

PROLOGUE

The pull grew stronger now, guiding her forward. She tried to move, to resist, but it was as though her body no longer existed. She was no longer Elysia D'Alembert, the woman who had once stood proud on the earth. She was something else—something untethered, floating in the great void between life and death.

Through the door, she glimpsed a world beyond. It was like nothing she had ever seen. The air shimmered with a soft, ethereal glow, and the ground below was a vast ocean of swirling lights—golden, silver, and violet streaks like a sky full of stars reflected upon water. It was beautiful, yet haunting, and Elysia felt a stirring deep within her—a tug of recognition, as if she had seen this place before.

The silence that stretched around her was overwhelming, broken only by the rhythmic hum that seemed to emanate from every corner of the universe. It was a silence that pressed in on her, demanding her attention, pulling her closer to the edge of the abyss. And in that moment, as she drifted toward the door, something stirred within the darkness behind it.

A voice, low and rich, called her name, its resonance vibrating through her very soul. The sound was familiar, yet foreign, as if it belonged to someone she had known long ago—or someone she was yet to become.

"Elysia," the voice whispered, its tone laced with sorrow and authority. "You are not yet finished."

Her heart, though it had no physical form, seemed to seize. She could not speak, could not move, but the voice—the presence—pulled at her, as if it were the very fabric of her being, fraying at the edges.

"You will return," the voice continued, this time stronger, more commanding. "You will walk again, but not as you once were. The path you must follow is already set, though you will not remember it yet. The one you seek is waiting, though he does not yet know your name. And he will be the one to bind you to the world of the living."

Elysia felt a shiver, though she no longer had a body to feel it. A sense of dread mingled with an undeniable pull toward something—someone. The world of the living seemed so far away, yet there was something waiting for her there, something that would define her journey. She had no choice but to follow.

"You must return," the voice urged once more, its tone filled with both sorrow and urgency. "There is no turning back, no escape from the role you will play."

A flash of something, a memory, surged within her—fragments of a life once lived, faces from a distant past, and one man, whose presence loomed large in her fleeting vision. But it was not yet clear. She saw only his shadow, his form blurred by the fog of time.

Before she could grasp it, the vision vanished, replaced by the overwhelming stillness once again. The door loomed ahead of her, black and unyielding. She could not see beyond it, but the pull was undeniable. It called to her, promising answers, but also demanding sacrifice. Her soul ached with a longing she could not understand, and with that ache came the painful clarity of one simple truth: she had no choice.

With the weight of fate pressing down on her, she drifted forward, crossing the threshold of the door, feeling the sensation of the world of the living slipping further away. As her consciousness passed through, she felt herself twist, bend, as though the very essence of who she was was being reshaped. And just before she lost herself entirely, she saw it—her new body, waiting for her.

The transition was sharp, almost violent, as though the very fabric of her soul were being torn and woven anew. The darkness that had once surrounded her faded, replaced by light—bright, blinding, and foreign. Her mind reeled, grasping for understanding as she tumbled into the unknown.

The next moment, she was no longer in the ethereal realm of forgotten souls. She was falling—falling through the veil that separated life and death, her body now taking shape in the world she had once known, but in a form that was not her own. The familiar weight of her existence returned, and with it came the crash of awareness, the painful, disorienting sensation of awakening.

And then, everything went dark.

2

Awakening

The faint scent of jasmine lingered in the air, but it was the overwhelming silence that first tugged at Elysia's senses. Her eyelids fluttered open, and she was met with the sight of thick velvet curtains swaying ever so slightly, as though moved by a whispering breeze. The room around her was far too grand for comfort—imposing, even. Dark mahogany walls encased the space, the opulent furniture arranged with a precision that felt almost predatory. A large, antique mirror framed one wall, reflecting the faint, fractured light that barely seemed to penetrate the heavy gloom of the room.

Where am I? Her mind was a maze of fog. The familiar pulse of panic began to creep along her spine, as if her body recognized danger before her thoughts did.

She tried to sit up but winced as a sharp pain shot through her side, causing her to fall back onto the silken sheets beneath her. Her limbs felt heavy, as though every part of her had been weighed down by some invisible force. The ache in her body was like a chorus of forgotten memories, each one too distant to grasp, too fleeting to understand.

She glanced down at her hands, the pale skin, smooth but trembling slightly.

They were trembling because they were alive. Alive… but how?

Then, it all came rushing back, but only in fragments—flashes of headlights, a screech of tires, a painful lurch. She remembered the cold metal of something sharp digging into her skin, the terrifying taste of blood as her throat constricted. But nothing after that. It was as if someone had pulled the plug on her consciousness, and now, all she could do was float in this strange limbo.

A figure entered her line of vision, casting a long, dark shadow against the floor, his presence immediately filling the room. Her breath caught in her throat as she caught sight of him for the first time.

He stood tall, the silhouette of a man who seemed to bleed danger with every movement. His dark hair was neatly combed, and his tailored suit spoke of wealth and power—each line and crease deliberate, calculated. His eyes, cold as ice, observed her from across the room, appraising, as if trying to decipher the very essence of her soul. There was something unnervingly intense about his gaze, something that made her skin crawl, and yet, inexplicably, it was impossible to look away.

Elysia's heart raced, not from fear alone, but from something deeper, something she couldn't explain. He was a stranger—yet there was an unsettling familiarity in the way he watched her. As if he had been waiting for this moment for far too long.

"You're awake," he said, his voice smooth, deep, and almost… too calm. The words seemed to slice through the heavy air between them, the weight of them pressing down on her chest.

"Where am I?" Her voice was hoarse, and for a moment, she wondered if she had spoken at all or merely imagined the words.

A small smile tugged at the corner of his lips, though it did little to soften the sharpness of his features. "You're in my home," he replied, his tone laced with something unreadable. "Victor Lupo," he introduced himself, though it was more of a statement than a greeting.

Her eyes narrowed slightly, struggling to make sense of the name. "Victor Lupo?" The name felt foreign to her ears, but there was something about it—something about the sound of it—that seemed to strike a chord deep inside her. A lingering sense of foreboding tightened her chest.

"Yes," he said, stepping closer. His gaze never left hers. "And you, Elysia, are no stranger to this place. In fact, you've been here before."

Elysia's brow furrowed as confusion clouded her mind. "What do you mean?" Her voice trembled despite her efforts to sound steady. She tried to sit up once more, this time with more force, but the dizziness swarmed her again, making her head spin. "Where… am I?" she repeated, her tone more desperate this time. "What happened to me?"

Victor's expression softened, but not in a comforting way. His eyes held a strange mix of compassion and possessiveness, as if he already knew her every fear and was patiently waiting for the moment she would come to accept the truth.

"You were in an accident," he said, taking another step toward her, his gaze locking onto her with an intensity that made her throat go dry. "A near-fatal one. I found you, Elysia. I saved you."

The word "saved" rang hollow in the air, and Elysia felt the edges of her disbelief slowly start to fray. A near-fatal accident? Saved by him? None of it made sense. She shook her head, disoriented, her thoughts fragmented like a puzzle that didn't fit together.

Victor studied her, his lips curling into a faint, almost imperceptible smile. It was the kind of smile that felt like a secret—an unspoken bond between them that she was not privy to, but which he seemed to know all too well.

"You don't believe me," he said, as if he had already expected this reaction, his voice laced with a hint of amusement. "But you will, Elysia. In time, you will remember."

Elysia recoiled slightly, trying to push herself further back into the bed, instinctively protecting herself from his advances. But the bed was large, and the space between them felt small. His presence encroached on her in a way that she could not ignore, an invisible force pulling her closer to him despite her every urge to retreat.

"What do you want from me?" she asked, her voice growing steadier, though still marked with confusion and fear.

Victor's smile widened, but it wasn't a reassuring smile. It was a promise—of something she didn't fully understand yet.

"I want you to remember," he said softly, his voice heavy with something deeper, something darker. "Because you are the one I've been waiting for. You are my Isabella."

Her heart stopped. For a moment, time itself seemed to freeze, and the room around her blurred. She had no idea who this Isabella was, but the name felt... familiar, like a forgotten dream hovering just out of reach. She swallowed hard, the air thick in her lungs.

Victor took a step closer, his presence suffocating, and for the first time, she truly noticed the intensity in his eyes—the kind of intensity that could either break you or consume you whole.

"You'll understand soon enough," he murmured, as if already knowing the path she was about to walk. "In time, Elysia... you'll remember everything."

But as his words settled in her chest, all she could feel was the icy grip of uncertainty tightening around her heart. What had she gotten herself into? And why did it feel like she was caught in the web of a story much older than she was?

Elysia felt a chill run down her spine as Victor's words settled into the heavy air between them. Isabella. Her name echoed in the silence, like a ghost she couldn't quite grasp, and it made her stomach churn. She pressed her hand against her forehead, as though the action would silence the growing noise in her mind, but the answer still eluded her. Who was Isabella? Why did that name claw at the back of her consciousness as if it belonged to someone she should have known?

Victor stood unmoving, his gaze fixed on her, and the air around him seemed to thrum with some unseen power—an energy that filled the room and made it feel smaller with every passing moment. He was waiting for something. But what? Her acceptance? Her understanding? She could feel the tension in her bones, each word he spoke wrapping tighter around her heart like a chain.

"You're not Isabella, but you are her," he repeated, his voice a low, hypnotic murmur, as though trying to coax her into a truth she wasn't ready to accept. "The same soul. The same spirit. But... in a new body."

Elysia recoiled, but the movement was so slight, so imperceptible, that it might have gone unnoticed had it not been for the sharpness of her own discomfort. She didn't understand him. This couldn't be real. It was too absurd. Too impossible.

"I'm not Isabella," she said, the words slipping from her lips with more force than she expected. She sat up fully now, despite the lingering pain in her side, pushing herself upright. "Who are you? What do you want from me?"

Her voice had become more steady, though the tremor in her hands betrayed her uncertainty. The room still felt cold, but now it was an unfamiliar cold—a cold that was nothing like the refreshing chill of a spring morning, but instead one that seemed to gnaw at her very being. She was lost in this labyrinth of confusion, her mind racing faster than she could process.

Victor, however, remained calm. Too calm. His eyes narrowed slightly, not in irritation, but in something else—something darker, more resolute. His next words were slow, deliberate, as though choosing them carefully would somehow reveal a deeper truth.

"I told you," he said softly, his voice curling around her like smoke. "I've been waiting for you, Elysia. For years. You were taken from me once, but now you've returned."

A sense of vertigo gripped her, and she fought the impulse to close her eyes against the storm of sensations that overwhelmed her. He couldn't be serious. He couldn't. Yet, despite the absurdity of his claim, something in his eyes—the intensity, the raw hunger—spoke of a truth she was unwilling to accept.

"But... why?" she whispered. The word came out as a breath, thin and fragile. "Why me? What happened to your wife?"

Victor's lips tightened, the smile vanishing from his face as quickly as it had appeared. The shift in his demeanor was instantaneous, like the sudden change of seasons—from the heat of summer to the biting cold of winter. He stepped back slightly, his posture stiffening, as though the mere mention of Isabella's name had brought forth memories too painful to bear.

"Isabella was everything to me," he said, the words dripping with an emotion Elysia couldn't quite place—love, grief, anger, obsession. "She was the light of my life, and when she died, I lost more than just a wife. I lost a part of myself. I could never let go of her. Not truly. I waited… I searched, and when you came into my life, I knew immediately. You're her."

Elysia's heart clenched at the rawness of his admission, but a wave of disbelief followed closely behind. She shook her head, disoriented by the tumult of emotions he had unleashed. "I'm not her," she repeated, her voice firmer this time. "I don't know who you are, but I'm not Isabella."

Victor's expression darkened, his jaw tightening. He took a step forward, the space between them closing in an instant, his presence looming over her like a shadow she couldn't escape. His eyes were cold—stone cold—and they held an edge of desperation that was impossible to ignore.

"You will remember," he said with finality, each word heavy with certainty. "Your memories are locked away, but they will return to you. In time."

Elysia felt the air around her tighten as though the walls were closing in, the claustrophobia pressing against her chest. "What if I don't want to remember?" she demanded, a sudden surge of defiance surging through her. "What if I don't want any part of this?"

For the first time, something flickered across Victor's face—something that looked almost like uncertainty. He hesitated for a brief, breathless moment, before his features settled back into their usual mask of control.

"You don't have a choice," he said, his voice devoid of warmth, yet there was something almost tender in the way he spoke. "You will remember because you must remember. Our love, our life together—it is inevitable. It's written in the stars."

The words felt like they should have been comforting, but instead, they chilled her to the bone. There was no room for doubt in his voice, no space for any alternative. He was convinced, and perhaps that conviction was the most terrifying thing of all.

Elysia leaned back against the bed, her fingers digging into the soft sheets as she tried to steady her breathing. Her thoughts were a whirlwind of confusion, panic, and something else—something unsettling that she couldn't quite identify. She had no idea how to process any of this, how to make sense of a man who spoke of reincarnation and soulmates and destiny as if they were facts, as if they had already been written into some ancient, immutable script.

Victor remained standing there, watching her with a patience that bordered on possessiveness. His silence spoke volumes, and Elysia couldn't help but feel the weight of it pressing down on her, suffocating her. There was something in his gaze—something that pulled at her like a magnet. The connection between them, the pull of his obsession, was undeniable.

For a moment, the room seemed to shrink, the oppressive silence wrapping around her, suffocating her. It was a stifling heat, and she struggled to find her breath, to find her thoughts.

Victor, sensing her struggle, seemed to soften. His gaze no longer carried the sharp edge of command, but something different—something almost like longing. He stepped back, giving her space, though the tension in the room remained.

"I'll leave you to rest," he said, his voice low, measured. "But remember this: you are mine, Elysia. You were always meant to be."

And with that, he turned on his heel and walked toward the door, leaving her alone in the heavy stillness of the room. The door clicked shut behind him, and for a long moment, all she could do was stare at the empty space where he had stood.

Her breath came in shallow gasps as the weight of his words sank in, like stones sinking deep into her chest. She was his. Was that her fate? Was that the truth of her existence? Or was she merely a pawn in some game she didn't understand?

The questions spiraled inside her, and the answers felt just out of reach, like a distant shore she could never quite swim to. All she had left now was the gnawing sense that her life had changed forever—and the sickening feeling that she might never find her way back to who she truly was.

Elysia couldn't remember how long she had been lying there in the vast, empty silence of the mansion. The hours blurred into one another like the slow drip of water against stone. The weight of Victor's words still pressed heavily on her chest, leaving her breathless and uneasy, but she tried to push them to the back of her mind, clinging to any semblance of reality she could hold onto.

Her thoughts drifted, and with them came the haunting visions that had begun to surface, unbidden and relentless. The images were fleeting at first—snippets of memories not her own. Faces she didn't recognize, places she couldn't name, but they all held one constant, a truth she couldn't escape. They felt real. Too real.

Victor's insistence that she was Isabella, his long-dead wife, echoed in the empty space of her mind, growing louder with each passing minute. She wanted to dismiss it. To deny it. But something deep inside her—a gut-wrenching instinct—told her that she couldn't.

The grand, oppressive silence of the mansion seemed to swallow her whole. She hadn't spoken to anyone since Victor had left her room, and the loneliness gnawed at her, amplifying her fear. The loneliness felt like a living thing, curling around her as she lay on the bed, her mind spinning in disorienting circles.

Suddenly, a sharp noise—like a door creaking open—cut through the stillness. Elysia jolted upright, her heart racing as her eyes darted toward the door. The faintest flicker of movement caught her eye, and her breath caught in her throat. Was someone there? She had thought she was alone, but now doubt crept into her veins, cold and insistent.

Slowly, her hand moved toward the edge of the bed, her fingers trembling slightly as she searched for a way to steady herself. The darkness of the room seemed to press in even closer, her mind whirling with questions she couldn't answer. What was happening to her? Who could she trust?

Then, in the midst of her growing panic, the vision hit her like a thunderclap.

It was like being ripped from her own mind and thrust into another. The world around her blurred, and she was no longer in the cold, dark room of the mansion. She was somewhere else entirely.

The air was thick with the smell of flowers—lilies, roses, something intoxicating. She could feel the sun on her skin, warm and gentle, but it was a distant warmth, like it belonged to someone else. The world around her was a blur of color and motion, but one thing stood out—him. The man standing before her, his expression fierce and possessive, holding her tightly by the wrist. His eyes—those cold, dark eyes—held her captive, but there was something in them, something desperate.

"Isabella," he whispered, his voice rough with emotion. The name felt wrong. It was like wearing a garment that didn't fit, but she couldn't escape it. "Isabella, you cannot leave me."

His grip tightened, and for a fleeting moment, she thought she could feel his pulse beneath her skin, his heart beating in sync with her own. And then the world fractured.

A vision of blood. Of darkness. A violent crash, and the sound of breaking glass. Her scream, echoing in the empty night, but there was no one to hear. She was falling—falling—into a void.

Suddenly, the vision snapped away, like a rope being cut in midair. Elysia gasped, her chest rising and falling rapidly as if she had been suffocating. Her hands trembled violently, and she gripped the bedpost, trying to steady herself. Sweat beaded on her forehead as the remnants of the vision swirled in her mind, teasing her with their fragments, leaving her shaken and breathless.

Her pulse raced, and her thoughts scattered like leaves in a windstorm. What was that? she thought, blinking rapidly as if trying to clear the fog in her mind. Was that me? Was that really me?

She couldn't make sense of it. The image of the man, his face so familiar and yet not, lingered in the back of her mind. His desperation. His grip on her wrist. And then, that sudden, violent end.

The terror of the vision still clung to her like a second skin, and she fought to steady her breathing, to hold onto something—anything—real. She couldn't afford to lose herself in the madness. But the doubt, the fear, was creeping in, making it impossible to ignore the growing sense that something—someone—was pulling her deeper into a life she couldn't escape.

Was this the past? Her past? Her past life?

The vision had been so vivid, so real. It felt as though the memory belonged to her, not to someone else. The more she tried to grasp it, the more it slipped away, like sand running through her fingers.

But there was one thing she couldn't deny. The name that had echoed in her mind, like a distant echo of some forgotten reality.

Isabella.

With trembling hands, she slowly rose from the bed, her legs unsteady as she made her way to the window. The cold glass felt soothing against her forehead as she leaned against it, staring out into the darkened courtyard below. The moonlight cast long, eerie shadows across the grounds, and she could feel the weight of the mansion pressing down on her, as though it were alive, watching.

A deep, unsettling feeling churned in her stomach. She wasn't alone. Not just in the room, but in the world. Something—someone—was always watching her. And that someone was Victor.

A thought flickered through her mind, sharp and sudden. Could he have been telling the truth?

The vision she had seen—the man, the blood, the overwhelming sense of loss—it felt like a message, a glimpse into something she wasn't ready to face. Yet, in that brief moment, she had felt it all. The fear. The pain. The love.

And the deeper, darker truth of her connection to Victor.

Elysia's heart clenched at the realization, and for the first time since her awakening, she truly understood the weight of the choice that lay before her. She could fight it, resist it, but the truth was there, like a shadow lurking just out of sight.

The realization settled deep within her like a stone, and she closed her eyes, drawing in a slow, steady breath. There was no turning back.

She had been pulled into this world, this fate, and now there was only one question left to answer.

What would she do with it?

3

Victor's Obsession

The faint aroma of roses lingered in the air, mingling with the scent of old leather and polished wood. Elysia stood in the center of the study, her fingers brushing lightly against the dark mahogany furniture that seemed to stretch endlessly across the room. The walls, adorned with portraits of men and women whose faces held secrets long buried in the past, seemed to breathe with the weight of forgotten histories.

She felt a shiver crawl down her spine, but she didn't understand why. She couldn't explain the growing sense of unease that gnawed at her, especially when Victor was just a room away. She glanced at the windows, where the darkening sky outside promised a storm—an eerie reflection of the tumultuous thoughts swirling in her mind.

Victor's footsteps echoed in the hallway, distant but unmistakable. He was close, and yet there was a profound distance between them. The sound of his approach made her heart race, a thudding beat that resonated within her chest as if her body were trying to fight against some unseen force. She turned her attention back to the portrait hanging above the fireplace—a woman with sharp features and deep-set eyes. The woman's gaze was haunting, almost familiar.

A soft knock on the door interrupted her thoughts. Victor entered without waiting for a response, his presence filling the room like a sudden storm. He stood there for a moment, eyes fixed on her with a mix of something unreadable—hunger, longing, obsession. He wasn't the man she remembered from her fleeting glimpses before the accident. He was something darker, something colder.

"You're staring at her again," Victor's voice was low, almost too soft, but it carried an edge. His eyes didn't leave hers as he crossed the room and stopped beside her. "You see her, don't you? Isabella."

Elysia's breath caught in her throat. The name—it was a whisper from a past she couldn't fully recall. Isabella. The woman in the portrait. Her mind raced as fragments of something long buried began to resurface.

"I don't…" Elysia started, her voice faltering as if she were drowning in a sea of forgotten memories. "I don't understand, Victor. Who is she?"

Victor stepped closer, his gaze unwavering. His eyes darkened, a storm raging behind them. "She was my wife. My love. My everything." His hand reached out, brushing a strand of hair behind her ear with a tenderness that didn't match the ferocity in his tone. "And you are her, Elysia. You are Isabella."

The words hung in the air like a fragile truth, but Elysia recoiled. His insistence, the intensity with which he spoke, was suffocating.

"I'm not Isabella," she said, her voice steady, though her insides twisted. "I'm Elysia. I don't even know how I ended up here."

Victor's lips curled into a sad, almost bitter smile. "You're more than just Elysia now. You are the reincarnation of her soul. You were brought back to me." He paused, his hand hovering near her cheek. "I know it's hard to believe. You'll remember. I'll make you remember."

A cold, inexplicable shiver ran through her body at the weight of his words. Reincarnation. Souls returning. It all sounded like madness, like the delusions of a man who refused to let go of the past. But there was something in the way he looked at her—something desperate—that made her question her own sanity. Was she truly who he claimed her to be? Was she, in some inexplicable way, bound to him by the threads of fate?

Her thoughts spiraled as her gaze flicked to the window once more. The storm outside was growing closer, and the wind howled, rattling the panes. She turned back to Victor, but his eyes were still locked onto her with the same intensity. He wasn't going to let her go. She could feel it in the air. His obsession was palpable, thick enough to choke her.

"You think I'm her," Elysia said, her voice small, her breath shaky. "But I'm not. I don't know who she was."

Victor exhaled a long breath, as if her words had wounded him in some way. "Isabella was everything to me," he said, almost to himself, his voice softer now. "She was my partner, my queen, my everything. We built this empire together."

Empire. The word struck her like a slap to the face. She hadn't fully grasped the extent of Victor's world, the power he wielded, the danger that lingered in the shadows. The Lupo family wasn't just a criminal organization; it was an empire that stretched its tendrils into every corner of the city.

"You and her… you were a part of this?" Elysia asked, her voice barely above a whisper.

Victor nodded, his expression darkening. "Yes. We controlled everything. The city, the streets, the people. But when she died…" His jaw clenched, his eyes flashing with a fury that sent a chill down her spine. "When she was taken from me, everything fell apart. And now, I've found you. You've come back to me."

Elysia couldn't breathe. His words seemed to suffocate her, tightening like a noose around her neck. A memory—faint, distant, like a dream on the edge of her mind—surfaced. She saw a woman, a woman with soft brown eyes and auburn hair, standing beside a man in the dim light of a grand hall. They were laughing, their hands intertwined, their eyes full of love. The image flickered, and she blinked, shaking her head.

"No…" she muttered, her hands trembling as the vision faded. "This isn't real. I'm not her."

Victor's hand reached for her again, his grip gentle but firm. "You are. You don't remember yet, but you will. I'll make sure of it."

Elysia felt her heart beat erratically in her chest. The past, her past, was slipping through her fingers like sand. She had no idea who she was anymore. No idea who he was. All she knew was that she was trapped in a world she couldn't understand, with a man who believed she was someone she wasn't.

And in the depths of her mind, a question whispered—one that haunted her more than any of the others: What if he was right?

The heavy curtains in the study were drawn tight, blocking out the last vestiges of daylight. Only the soft flickering light of a fireplace illuminated the dark room, casting long shadows that seemed to stretch across the walls like reaching hands. Elysia sat in a plush armchair near the fire, her hands clasped tightly in her lap as she stared into the flames. The warmth of the fire felt like a faint comfort against the coldness that had settled in her chest.

Victor stood across from her, a glass of dark amber liquid in his hand, swirling it idly. His presence was imposing, his silhouette sharp against the dim light, a man caught between power and loss. He hadn't said much since the earlier conversation—his obsession with Isabella still fresh in the air—but now, his expression was unreadable, his eyes shadowed with a kind of sorrow that seemed almost foreign to him.

Elysia shifted uncomfortably, her fingers tapping nervously against the armrest. The silence stretched, heavy and thick, until Victor finally broke it.

"I told you I would make you remember," he said, his voice low, almost a whisper. "I'll show you everything."

Elysia stiffened, her pulse quickening. "What do you mean by that?" she asked, though she was afraid of the answer.

Victor's eyes darkened, and he took a slow sip from his glass. "I mean I'll take you through the past. Our past. Isabella's and mine."

She recoiled inwardly at the mention of the name, but there was something about the way he spoke—so calm, so certain—that made her heart skip. His belief in her reincarnation was growing more intense by the day. She couldn't understand it. But it also made her question everything. How could he be so sure?

"Why?" she asked, her voice barely a whisper. "Why would you want me to remember? If I really am... if I really am her, how do I even begin to accept that?"

Victor set the glass down with a soft clink, then stepped closer, sitting across from her. His gaze was unwavering, intense, as though he were trying to look straight through her.

"Because," he said slowly, "I loved her. I still do. And I will do anything to bring her back to me. Even if it means waiting for another lifetime."

Elysia's heart lurched. She didn't want to believe it, but there was something so raw in his voice, so desperate, that it tugged at a part of her that she couldn't explain.

Victor's hand reached for hers, his fingers brushing lightly against her skin. Elysia flinched, but he didn't pull back. Instead, his touch seemed to tighten around her, grounding her in place, as if she were an anchor to something he could never let go of.

"The night she died," he began, his voice low and haunted, "we were supposed to leave together. Run away from the chaos. But something happened. Someone betrayed us. Someone close to me." His eyes glinted with something dangerous. "Isabella was killed, Elysia. But not just by anyone. By someone who knew everything about us, about me. A person I trusted."

The words hung in the air like a deadly promise, and Elysia felt the room close in around her. The shadows in the corners of the room seemed to deepen, taking on new shapes, forming specters that whispered in her ears. Her pulse quickened.

"Who?" she asked, her voice trembling.

Victor stood abruptly, pacing before her. He was suddenly a man on fire, his emotions igniting like a blazing inferno. "It doesn't matter. The point is, she's gone. And you," he paused, turning back to her with a piercing gaze, "you're the only piece of her I have left. The only person who can fill the hole she left behind."

Elysia shook her head, the reality of his words crashing down on her like waves. She was the reincarnation of someone who had been murdered. His wife. The woman in the portrait. Isabella. A past that she couldn't grasp, but a past that was now haunting her with each passing moment.

"But I don't remember anything," she protested, her voice shaky. "I don't feel like her. I don't even know what she was like. How can I be her?"

Victor's jaw tightened, his gaze unwavering. "Because you will. Over time. It's all buried in your soul. You'll remember the way she smiled, the way she laughed, the way she loved me."

He moved toward her again, his steps measured, deliberate, like a predator stalking its prey. Elysia could feel the tension crackling in the air between them. He was so close now, the heat of his body radiating toward hers.

"I will make you remember," he repeated, his voice rough, as if every word was a desperate plea. "I will make you remember the way she loved me."

Elysia's heart fluttered painfully in her chest. The weight of his words was suffocating, but at the same time, there was something in the way he spoke, something in the depth of his eyes, that made her wonder... what if he was right? What if she was more than just Elysia?

The thought was a poison, creeping its way through her thoughts, twisting them into something she couldn't control. She recoiled, pushing the thoughts away as if they were something she could physically cast aside.

"I'm not her," she said firmly, though her voice lacked conviction.

Victor's gaze softened, and for a moment, it was as if she could see the man he used to be—the man before the pain, before the obsession, before the grief.

"You will be," he said simply, his voice almost tender. "I'll show you how."

Elysia didn't know what to think anymore. Her mind was a battlefield, each thought pulling her in different directions. Victor's obsession was consuming him, and yet... there was something about him that she couldn't deny. He believed what he was saying. And in a twisted way, she found herself believing it, too.

But the question lingered in the air between them, unspoken yet undeniably there: Who was she really?

The mansion was deathly quiet in the stillness of the night. A cool draft filtered through the cracks in the grand windows, whispering against the thick curtains that lined the walls. Elysia lay in the massive four-poster bed, the rich silk sheets tangled around her legs as she stared at the ceiling, her mind a whirlpool of thoughts she couldn't control.

Victor's words echoed relentlessly in her head, chasing her into the realms of fevered dreams and whispered doubts. You will remember. You are Isabella. The more he spoke of it, the more the idea took root in her, worming its way into her thoughts until she couldn't tell where Elysia ended and Isabella began.

It was ridiculous, she knew. She couldn't be someone else, not really. She had memories, fleeting and disjointed, but they were hers, weren't they? Yet, at times, she swore she could feel the faintest pulse of someone else's life running beneath her skin, like a current that wasn't her own. She shivered, hugging the pillow tightly to her chest, trying to block out the sensation.

The moonlight spilled through the window, casting long, jagged shadows across the floor, stretching and twisting into grotesque shapes. Elysia's breath hitched as a sudden flash of memory gripped her—an image so vivid it almost burned her mind. A woman, pale and beautiful, her eyes filled with grief and regret. Blood stained the floor, and the sound of a gunshot echoed in her ears.

Isabella, she thought, and with that thought, her breath caught in her throat.

In that instant, the room seemed to close in around her, the shadows crawling toward her, pressing in as if they were alive. The sense of dread was suffocating, tightening around her chest like a vice. She gasped for air, but her lungs felt heavy, as though they were filled with the weight of an ocean.

The door to her room creaked open, and Victor's silhouette appeared in the doorway, framed by the dim light from the hallway. He stepped in silently, his presence filling the room like smoke, thick and suffocating. His gaze found hers immediately, his dark eyes studying her with the intensity of a man who had already claimed her, body and soul.

"Elysia?" His voice was soft, almost cautious, but there was something darker in it, something she couldn't quite name.

"I… I had a vision," she whispered, her voice trembling as she tried to sit up. The fear that had clutched her chest was now threatening to spill over into her words. She wasn't sure if the vision was real, if it was a memory, or if it was just a fragment of a nightmare. "It was her. It was Isabella. I saw her die."

Victor didn't move, his gaze never leaving her. There was no shock in his expression, no surprise, only a quiet, knowing sadness.

"I told you," he said, his voice low and filled with a quiet urgency. "You'll remember. It's all coming back to you."

Elysia shook her head violently, the panic welling up inside her. "No! This isn't real. This isn't happening." She pressed her hands to her temples, as though trying to hold the pieces of herself together, afraid they would slip through her fingers. "I can't… I can't be her."

Victor's gaze softened, and he took a step closer, his feet silent on the thick carpet. "I know it's hard, but you have to trust me. This isn't some random coincidence, Elysia. This is fate."

She looked up at him, her heart pounding as though it might break free from her chest. The man who had saved her, who had brought her into his world of darkness and obsession—he wasn't lying. Not to her, at least. He believed every word he said. The question was, did she?

"I'm not Isabella," she said, the words feeling heavy as they left her lips. "I'm not her, Victor."

For a long moment, Victor didn't respond. He only stared at her, his expression unreadable, his mouth set in a hard line. Then, slowly, he knelt beside her bed, his eyes never leaving hers.

"You're more her than you realize," he said quietly, almost tenderly, his fingers brushing a strand of hair away from her face. "You're not just Elysia anymore. You're both."

The words were like a weight around her throat. She felt as though she might suffocate under them, drowning in the unrelenting pull of the past and present colliding. She wanted to scream, to run away from the terrifying truth that was taking shape, but she couldn't. She was trapped in this mansion, in this life, in this madness.

"I don't know who I am anymore," she whispered, her voice cracking.

Victor's gaze softened, and for the first time since she'd met him, there was a flicker of something approaching vulnerability in his eyes. "You will. In time, you will remember everything. And when you do… when you finally see it all clearly, you'll understand why I did what I did."

Elysia swallowed hard, tears welling up in her eyes. She had to leave. She had to escape, but the idea of leaving him, of leaving this strange, obsessive world, terrified her. Because deep down, beneath the fear and confusion, something in her wanted to stay.

Victor seemed to sense the turmoil within her. He stood and moved toward the window, turning his back on her for a moment. The moonlight illuminated his figure in stark contrast, casting him as a shadow in the night. He spoke softly, his words carrying the weight of a promise.

"Sleep, Elysia. Tomorrow, we'll talk more. I'll help you remember."

With that, he turned and left the room, his footsteps fading into the silence of the mansion. Elysia lay back against the pillows, her chest tight, her mind racing with a thousand questions she couldn't answer. She closed her eyes, but the images of Isabella, of death and betrayal, haunted her, drifting just beyond the veil of her consciousness like a whispering ghost.

The line between past and present had blurred, and she wasn't sure which world she was living in anymore.

But as she drifted into an uneasy sleep, she knew one thing for sure: the life she had known was gone. She was no longer just Elysia. She was becoming something else, something she didn't understand. And that frightened her more than anything else.

4

A Dangerous World

Elysia's breath caught in her throat as she stood on the balcony of Victor Lupo's grand mansion, her eyes drifting across the sprawling cityscape below. The moon hung low in the sky, casting a pale light over the endless maze of streets. The city was alive with energy, but to her, it felt suffocating. It wasn't just the heavy silence of the mansion that made her uneasy; it was the weight of what she had learned about the Lupo family—the empire that Victor ruled.

The air was thick with the scent of fresh-cut roses from the garden beneath her. Her fingers tightened on the stone railing, the coolness of it doing nothing to soothe the warmth spreading through her body. Her heart pounded in her chest, and though her body was no longer bruised and battered from the accident, her mind was just as fractured, a jigsaw puzzle with too many pieces missing.

She had thought Victor's mansion would be a sanctuary, a place where she could recover, but it was quickly becoming a gilded cage. The walls, adorned with ornate gold mirrors and towering bookshelves filled with dark, leather-bound tomes, felt less like luxury and more like the inside of a fortress. She felt as if she were being watched even in the stillness. Every whisper of movement in the halls, every creak of the floorboards, made her jump, reminding her of the ever-present danger that hung over this place.

But it wasn't just the mansion that unnerved her—it was the revelation she had been forced to face. The Lupo family wasn't just a wealthy, influential family. They were an empire. And Victor wasn't just any man. He was a kingpin in a world of shadows, his power stretching across the city like a web, ensnaring anyone and everyone who came too close.

Victor Lupo wasn't simply the man who saved her life. He was the man who owned it.

Her mind whirled with questions, questions that she had yet to voice, questions that lingered on the tip of her tongue like poison. Why had he chosen to save her? What did he want from her? He claimed she was the reincarnation of his wife, Isabella, a woman who had died in a tragedy years ago. Yet, every time she looked into his eyes, those eyes that were as dark and calculating as the night itself, she felt the truth slipping further away from her grasp.

A soft voice broke through her thoughts. "You shouldn't be out here alone."

Elysia turned to see Victor standing in the doorway, his tall figure outlined against the warm light spilling from the hallway behind him. His dark suit, immaculately tailored to fit his broad shoulders, was a stark contrast to the shadows that clung to the edges of the room. He stepped forward, his movements deliberate, as though every step he took was part of a larger plan.

"Why?" she asked, her voice strained. The question came out more bitter than she had intended, but the truth was, she was exhausted—exhausted from the weight of his words, exhausted from the strange connection she couldn't explain, exhausted from the life she no longer recognized.

Victor's lips quirked up in a smile, but it didn't reach his eyes. "This world isn't kind to those who don't understand its dangers."

The hairs on the back of her neck prickled as he closed the distance between them. His presence was imposing, yet there was an undeniable magnetism to him. The closer he got, the more she could feel the pull, like gravity itself was working against her, trying to draw her into his orbit.

"I'm not afraid of you," she said, though the words tasted like a lie. She wasn't afraid of him—at least, not in the way she should have been. There was something about him, something that both terrified and intrigued her. It was as if his very essence radiated power, and the closer she got to him, the more she realized just how much she didn't know about the world he ruled.

Victor studied her for a moment, his gaze sharp and calculating. "You should be."

The weight of his words hung in the air, suffocating. Elysia took a step back, her eyes darting toward the mansion's grounds below, but the view did nothing to calm her nerves. She could still feel him watching her, as though every movement she made was being scrutinized. She was a pawn in a game she hadn't yet learned the rules to.

Victor's voice broke through the tension once more. "I understand this is difficult for you, Elysia. But you are part of this world now. My world." His words were almost a whisper, yet they carried the weight of a command. "And I won't let you leave. Not when you've returned to me."

The implication of his words slammed into her chest like a physical blow. Her heart skipped a beat, and for a moment, she could have sworn she heard the faintest echo of a voice—her own voice, but not from this life. It was distant, almost drowned out by the noise in her mind, but it was there. The memory of a life lost.

"Returned?" she repeated, the word slipping from her lips without her consent. "What are you talking about?"

Victor stepped closer, so close that she could feel the heat emanating from his body. His eyes were dark, unreadable. "You're Isabella. You don't remember it yet, but you will." His voice was low, tinged with a reverence that unsettled her even more than his words. "I've waited for you to come back to me."

She felt a surge of anger—of frustration. "I'm not her!" The words were sharp, desperate, and they made her heart ache in a way she couldn't explain. She wasn't Isabella. She was Elysia. She didn't care about his delusions or his obsession. She wanted to return to the life she had, the one she couldn't even remember fully.

Victor's expression softened, but it was no less intense. "You will remember, in time. I know you will."

The certainty in his voice made her stomach twist. She wanted to run, to escape, but the truth was, she didn't know where she could go. This was a world unlike anything she had ever known, and somehow, in some unfathomable way, she was bound to it. The walls around her were closing in, and she had no choice but to let them.

Elysia felt as though the very air had shifted since Victor's revelation. The mansion had once seemed like a place of solace, a quiet refuge where she could recover from her injuries. But now, each room seemed to pulse with a quiet menace, the walls closing in on her in ways she couldn't explain. The luxurious furnishings—the polished marble floors, the gilded frames adorning every wall, the soft velvet curtains that cascaded down from the windows—felt less like signs of wealth and more like a gilded prison.

Victor's words from the night before haunted her, echoing through her mind like a melody she couldn't shake. You are Isabella.

He believed it. That much was clear. The way he had looked at her, the reverence, the obsession. He wasn't just a man grieving the death of his wife. He was a man who believed that his wife's soul had returned to him. Through her.

The very idea of it was maddening. It wasn't possible. Elysia had no memories of this so-called past life, no flashes of another woman, another love. Her life had been her own. Or so she thought.

Still, she couldn't ignore the strange pull she felt whenever Victor was near. It was more than the physical attraction that simmered between them, more than the magnetism that seemed to draw her in every time he spoke. It was as if something deep inside her soul was responding to his presence, awakening something she couldn't fully understand.

She didn't want to think about it. Not yet.

The mansion felt eerily quiet as she walked through the darkened hallways, the soft echo of her footsteps accompanying her as she wandered aimlessly. She passed the grand staircase, its steps winding upward to the upper floors where Victor had led her on the first night, and made her way into a large, opulent sitting room. The room was vast, a cavernous space filled with rich mahogany furniture, and the air seemed to shimmer with an unspoken tension.

A soft rustle of fabric reached her ears, and she turned to find a woman standing near the doorway. She was tall, with sleek black hair and dark eyes that seemed to observe everything with sharp intelligence. Her attire, a tailored black dress that clung to her frame, screamed power. But it wasn't the woman's presence that made Elysia's stomach twist—it was the coldness in her gaze.

"You must be Elysia," the woman said, her voice smooth, yet laced with something hard and dangerous.

Elysia stiffened, trying to mask the unease bubbling up in her chest. "Yes, and you are?"

"I'm Adriana," the woman said with a cool smile. "Victor's sister."

Elysia's mind raced. Victor has a sister? She hadn't seen or heard anything of her in the few days she'd been here, but the sudden introduction made sense. Adriana's aura was just as commanding as Victor's—just as powerful.

"I'm surprised Victor hasn't told you about me," Adriana continued, her gaze appraising Elysia with a detached curiosity. "We don't often entertain guests, but you seem to have… captured his interest."

There it was again. The unmistakable undercurrent of something darker in her words. Elysia was no fool. She could feel the tension between them, the unspoken challenge in the air. Adriana was sizing her up, and the weight of it settled heavily on Elysia's shoulders.

"I'm not here to stay long," Elysia said, trying to keep her tone even, though the uncertainty she felt was seeping through. "I just need time to figure things out."

Adriana's smile didn't falter, but it became colder. "You're already part of this world, Elysia. You'll learn that soon enough."

Before Elysia could respond, Adriana turned on her heel and walked toward the windows, pulling back the curtains to reveal the sprawling garden below. She stared out into the darkness, as if lost in her own thoughts.

Elysia took a cautious step toward her. "What do you mean by that?"

Adriana glanced over her shoulder, her expression unreadable. "You're not just the reincarnation of Isabella. You're the key to Victor's past, his obsession. The more he believes in you, the more he's willing to protect you. But don't fool yourself." She paused, the words hanging in the air like a warning. "Victor's world isn't a safe place. It never was."

Adriana's voice had softened, almost pitying, as if she knew something Elysia didn't. It was clear that the relationship between Victor and his sister was fraught with tension, and whatever Adriana's motives were, she wasn't about to make Elysia's situation any easier.

"I'm not interested in being anyone's obsession," Elysia shot back, her temper flaring. "I don't even know what you're talking about. I don't know this world, and I don't want to."

Adriana gave her a long, scrutinizing look before walking away from the window. "It doesn't matter what you want. You're already in it. And trust me, Elysia—leaving isn't an option."

As Adriana's figure disappeared into the hallway, Elysia was left standing in the room, her thoughts churning. There was something unsettling about the way Adriana spoke, as if she already knew Elysia's fate had been sealed the moment she stepped into this mansion.

Elysia crossed the room, reaching for the door, but the sound of Adriana's words kept echoing in her mind. Victor's world isn't a safe place. What did that mean for her? What had she stepped into? And how much of it was true?

She felt a sudden pang of frustration, her hands gripping the doorknob so tightly her knuckles turned white. She needed answers, but the more she asked, the more tangled her thoughts became. She could feel the pull of Victor's world tightening around her, the invisible strings that kept her bound to him, to the dark empire he ruled.

The deeper she went, the harder it became to escape.

Elysia sat in the expansive library, the scent of old leather and polished wood filling her senses as she scanned the rows of books. There were hundreds—thousands, it seemed—of texts lining the walls, their spines worn from years of use. Some of them were in languages she didn't recognize, others old enough to have been passed down through generations. She ran her fingers over the ancient tomes, feeling the weight of the history embedded in the room.

It was a stark contrast to the quiet emptiness that had settled in her heart. The mansion, with all its grandeur, still felt like a gilded cage. And now, as she dug deeper into the layers of this world, she could feel the invisible chains tightening around her.

Victor had been unusually silent that morning. He hadn't come to check on her, as he often did, and she hadn't seen him in hours. It gave her time to think, to gather some semblance of control over her thoughts. But instead of clarity, all she found was more confusion. The questions that plagued her mind only grew louder, like an incessant drumbeat she couldn't silence.

Was Victor really right? Was she Isabella, his long-lost wife, reincarnated?

Her hands trembled slightly as she reached for a book on the shelf. It was leather-bound, the edges embossed with gold, the title worn beyond recognition. She opened it at random, the pages yellowed with age, the ink faint but still legible. The words blurred as her mind drifted, thinking of the strange and unsettling moments that had defined her time here. The fragmented visions of her past life that felt so familiar yet so foreign.

It wasn't just the visions. It was the way Victor's touch made her skin burn, the way his voice seemed to fill the void inside her in a way she didn't understand. She couldn't explain it. She didn't want to feel it.

Her thoughts were interrupted by the sound of footsteps, heavy and deliberate, growing louder with each passing second. She looked up to find Victor standing at the doorway, his dark eyes locked onto hers with a quiet intensity that made her heart skip.

She didn't trust him. Not entirely. There was something off about his obsession, something dangerous. But there was also something in the way he looked at her, something that spoke of a lost love he couldn't let go of. Something that stirred a buried longing inside her, a desire to understand what it was, and why it felt so important.

"Elysia," Victor's voice was deep, calm, as he stepped into the room, his presence filling the space like a storm gathering on the horizon. "I've been looking for you."

Elysia's heart gave a brief, traitorous flutter, but she quickly pushed the emotion aside. "Why?" Her voice came out sharper than she intended, but she couldn't stop it. The words felt like a challenge, a line she was unwilling to cross.

Victor's lips quirked into a smile, but it didn't reach his eyes. There was no humor in that smile, no warmth. "I wanted to show you something," he said, his tone smooth and enticing, like velvet wrapping around steel. "Something that might help you understand."

He moved toward her, his steps slow, calculated. For a moment, she was reminded of a predator circling its prey, and an instinctive fear clutched at her chest. She stood, backing away slightly as she crossed her arms over her chest in an attempt to protect herself.

"You think showing me something will make me believe your story?" she said, her voice cold. "That I'm your wife reincarnated? You can't just make me believe that."

Victor's gaze hardened, the fleeting softness in his eyes vanishing in an instant. His jaw clenched, but his voice remained steady. "I don't need to make you believe, Elysia. I need you to remember."

She swallowed hard, unsure of what to say. The tension between them crackled, thick with unspoken words and unresolved emotions. It was becoming harder to maintain the distance she had built around herself.

Victor stepped closer, and for a moment, she felt a rush of heat from his proximity. The magnetic pull was undeniable. She couldn't look away from him, and that frightened her. Why does it feel like this?

"There is a reason you're here," Victor said, his voice lowering, turning almost possessive. "A reason the accident happened. A reason you came back to me."

Elysia shook her head, trying to clear the fog that clouded her thoughts. She wanted to push him away, to reject everything he was telling her. But part of her—the part she couldn't ignore—whispered that maybe, just maybe, there was some truth to it.

"I don't remember anything, Victor," she said, her voice small but defiant. "And even if I did, even if I was Isabella, that doesn't make me her. It doesn't make me yours."

Victor took another step forward, his gaze never leaving hers. "I understand your confusion, Elysia. But that's why I'm here. I need to help you remember, to bring you back to me. To bring us back together."

Elysia felt a pang in her chest at the sincerity in his voice, but she quickly suppressed it. This wasn't real. It couldn't be. She was trapped in a nightmare that she couldn't wake up from.

"I don't want your help," she said, though her voice trembled ever so slightly. "I want my own life back. I want to know who I am, not who you think I am."

Victor's eyes flashed with something dark, something predatory, but when he spoke, his voice was calm, almost tender. "You're already mine, Elysia. In this life, and the next."

A chill ran down her spine as his words settled into the room. For a moment, neither of them spoke. It was as if time had stopped, leaving only the unspoken weight of his claim hanging between them.

"I'm not yours," she whispered, more to herself than to him.

Victor's lips curled slightly. "We'll see about that."

The room felt suddenly smaller, the air thick with tension. Elysia's heart was racing, her pulse quickening with the intensity of the moment. But as he turned and began to walk toward the door, she couldn't shake the feeling that something—something deep and dangerous—was about to consume her.

5

Tension Rises

The city sprawled beneath the looming mansion, a sea of lights and shadows stretching to the horizon like the shifting tides of an ocean. Inside, the mansion was as dark as the world it inhabited, its walls lined with cold, polished marble, and heavy curtains that swallowed the weak rays of the setting sun. The air was thick with the weight of secrets, whispered conversations, and the sound of distant thunder threatening to break the silence. Elysia could feel it—the growing tension in the house, in the very air she breathed, curling like smoke into her lungs.

She stood at the large bay window, staring out at the city that sprawled endlessly before her, a place she was beginning to know too well, yet too unfamiliar to truly understand. Her fingers pressed lightly against the cool glass, her reflection merging with the darkened cityscape outside. It was a mirror of her own confusion—caught between the light of her past life and the shadow of her new reality.

Victor's voice broke the stillness, rough and commanding, as always.

"You can feel it, can't you?"

She turned, her heart catching at the cold, detached way he spoke. He was leaning against the doorframe, his silhouette a dark figure in the soft glow of the chandelier. His piercing eyes, always intense, were trained on her, studying her every movement. In his gaze, there was a fire that didn't flicker but burned with a constant, unyielding heat.

Elysia didn't answer right away. Instead, she glanced down at her hands, as if they could offer her the answers she sought. She had only been in this house for a few days, but already, she could feel the weight of the place—a heavy, suffocating presence that clung to her like a second skin. The mansion was more than just a building; it was a fortress, one built on a foundation of power, deceit, and danger. And Victor, the man who controlled it all, was as much a part of the house as the stone that held it up.

The tension in the air was palpable, like the storm clouds that loomed in the distance, and Elysia knew that it wasn't just about the weather. Something was coming. She could sense it in her bones.

"Something's off," she said, her voice barely above a whisper, though she knew he could hear her.

Victor stepped forward, the sound of his shoes clicking against the floor echoing in the quiet. His gaze never wavered from hers, his expression unreadable, as if every word she spoke was being measured, weighed, and calculated.

"It's not just you. The Verrini family is making their move." He paused, his jaw tightening. "They're trying to destabilize everything. Every move I make, every breath I take—they're watching."

The name Verrini rang in her ears like a warning bell. A powerful family, a rival to Victor's own. Elysia had heard of them, of course—who hadn't? But hearing the name from Victor's lips, in such a cold, measured tone, made her blood run colder.

The Verrini family was known for its ruthlessness. They were a force to be reckoned with in the underworld—a family of criminals who played their cards with deadly precision, and if Victor's words were anything to go by, they were about to play a dangerous game. And she, unfortunately, was now a piece on that board.

"I don't understand," Elysia said, turning to face him fully. "What do they want with you? Why target—" She broke off, not knowing how to finish the question. Why target me? Why am I here? These questions had been swirling in her mind ever since she woke up in this mansion, disoriented and confused, with only Victor's cryptic explanations to anchor her. But she couldn't bring herself to voice the fears she had buried deep inside. Not yet.

Victor took another step closer, his presence overwhelming, his dark eyes scanning her face like a predator examining its prey. There was something about him that unsettled her, something that both terrified and fascinated her in equal measure. She could feel the weight of his gaze on her skin, tracing the line of her jaw, lingering on her lips before pulling away with deliberate slowness.

"They want power," he said softly, his voice lowering, as though sharing a dark secret. "And they know that if they take me down, they take everything. The empire I've built, the family that's under my protection… it all falls. And they'll stop at nothing to make sure that happens."

His words were calculated, but there was an edge of something raw beneath the surface. Something that hinted at a deeper, more personal animosity between Victor and the Verrini family—something that went beyond business and power struggles.

Elysia swallowed, feeling the knot of unease tighten in her chest.

"And where do I fit into all of this?" she asked, her voice barely a breath. "What do they want from me?"

Victor's gaze shifted then, a fleeting moment of vulnerability breaking through the cold, impenetrable mask he wore so effortlessly. "You," he said, his tone firm, as though making a promise he was bound to keep, "are the key to it all."

Elysia frowned, her heart racing as the weight of his words pressed down on her. "What do you mean? I don't understand."

His lips curved into a small, almost imperceptible smile, but there was no warmth in it. "They know who you are," he said. "And they know who you were. The past is never as buried as we think."

For a moment, time seemed to stretch and hold its breath. Elysia's pulse quickened, a flutter of memories she couldn't quite place rising within her. She had heard these words before, she was sure of it. Not from Victor—no, these words felt older. They were echoes from a life she couldn't remember, but that was beginning to resurface in fragments—fragments that made her question everything.

Victor stepped closer still, closing the distance between them, his presence overwhelming. He reached out, his hand brushing lightly against her arm, and in that touch, Elysia felt something—something unspoken, something that neither of them could deny.

"You are my past, Elysia," he murmured, his voice low and raw, like a promise laced with desperation. "And you are my future."

A chill ran down her spine, and for the first time since she woke in this mansion, Elysia wondered if she would ever escape the web Victor had already woven around her.

She pulled her gaze away from his, staring once more out the window. The storm was closer now, the clouds dark and heavy with impending rain. The city below her—no, the world she was about to step into—was a battlefield, and she was caught in the crossfire.

As the first drop of rain fell against the glass, she knew her life would never be the same again.

The night had swallowed the mansion whole, its vast halls now bathed in shadows. Elysia sat alone in the grand dining room, the long oak table stretching before her, its polished surface gleaming faintly under the soft, ambient light from the chandelier overhead. The heavy silence pressed down on her, an oppressive weight that seemed to follow her wherever she went. Her fingers absently traced the rim of her wine glass, but her mind was far from the luxurious setting around her.

The mansion felt more like a prison with each passing hour.

She wasn't supposed to be here—she had no place in this world. This world of power, deception, and danger, where Victor Lupo was the king, and she was nothing more than a pawn in his obsessive game. Yet, despite her resistance, she couldn't help but feel the pull of him. She couldn't ignore the strange, undeniable connection that seemed to bind her to him—one she neither understood nor could escape.

Elysia stood abruptly, the chair scraping against the floor as she pushed herself to her feet. Her restless energy was rising again, that insistent need to know more, to understand this twisted web she'd been thrown into.

The door creaked open behind her, and her pulse quickened. She didn't need to turn around to know who it was. She could feel him—Victor—his presence as unmistakable as the weight of a storm looming overhead.

"Elysia," he said, his voice a smooth, dark drawl, as if the very sound of her name was a caress. His steps were deliberate as he crossed the room, but his eyes never left her face. "I told you not to leave the room."

She couldn't stop the small laugh that escaped her lips, bitter and hollow. "I didn't leave. I just... I needed a moment to breathe."

Victor stopped a few feet away, watching her with that same intense gaze, as if every movement, every flicker of emotion was a puzzle he was intent on solving. His eyes, dark and fathomless, held a certain coldness, but there was something else buried deep within them—a simmering, ferocious desire that made Elysia's skin crawl.

"Breathe, huh?" His lips quirked up into a smile, but it didn't reach his eyes. "You're not the only one who needs to breathe, Elysia. We all do. But this... tension between us? It's suffocating. I know you feel it."

She stiffened at the unspoken accusation in his words. "I don't feel anything for you."

He took a step closer, and the air around them thickened. "Liar," he murmured, his voice dropping low. "You're lying to yourself, Elysia. I can see it. You feel it. The pull between us. And you know as well as I do that it's not just a coincidence. You're not here because of some twist of fate. You're here because you belong here. With me."

The words stung more than she cared to admit. How could he be so sure? How could he believe that she—someone with no memory of the past, someone lost in a life that wasn't hers—could possibly belong in his world?

Elysia crossed her arms tightly over her chest, her heartbeat quickening with both frustration and fear. "Stop. I don't care about your theories. I don't care about the past. I'm here because you've trapped me in this place,

Victor. And I want out."

The words hung in the air, suspended by the tension between them, and for a moment, Victor didn't move. He didn't flinch. He simply watched her, his gaze calculating, unwavering.

Then, he stepped forward again, closing the space between them with dangerous grace. He reached out, but instead of touching her, he took the wine glass from her trembling hand, setting it down on the table beside them.

"You think you want out?" His voice was eerily calm, but there was something in the way he spoke that made her heart race. "You're here because I saved you. You're here because I've made it my mission to protect you. Don't mistake my protection for imprisonment. You're in a cage, yes, but I built it for you, to keep you safe. From them."

Elysia's throat tightened. The truth of his words stung, even as she tried to deny them. She had no memory of the accident. No recollection of how she had gotten here, how Victor had found her, or why she had survived when others had not. All she had were fragments of memories—fragments that didn't make sense—and a nagging feeling that told her she wasn't meant to be here.

"No one asked for your protection," she snapped, her voice shaky but defiant. "I didn't ask for this—this life, this… this cage you've put me in."

Victor's eyes darkened, his lips pulling into a thin line. For a moment, Elysia thought he might lash out, but instead, he did something unexpected. He reached out and touched her cheek, his fingers brushing against her skin with a gentleness that felt foreign.

"I'm not asking you to thank me," he said softly. "I'm asking you to accept it.

You're the reincarnation of Isabella, my wife. You belong with me, Elysia. Whether you like it or not."

Her breath hitched in her throat, and she pulled away from his touch, her eyes wide with panic. "I don't remember her! I don't remember you. I don't even remember my own life!"

Victor's gaze softened, but there was a steeliness to it that she couldn't ignore. "You will," he promised, his voice low and intimate. "It's only a matter of time. And when you do, you'll see that I was right. You are mine."

The way he said it—the certainty in his tone—sent a shiver down her spine. She wanted to scream at him, to tell him he was insane, but she couldn't. Because somewhere deep inside, in a place she refused to acknowledge, she wasn't so sure he was wrong.

The silence stretched between them, thick and uncomfortable, until the sudden, sharp ring of her phone shattered it. Elysia jumped, startled, as she reached for her phone on the table, the screen lighting up with an unfamiliar number.

Without a word, she answered, her heart pounding in her chest.

"Elysia," a gruff voice said on the other end, "we need to talk. Now."

Her pulse quickened, and she glanced at Victor. His expression had changed, the protective mask slipping into something more dangerous, more calculating.

"Who is that?" he asked, his voice low and threatening.

Elysia ignored him, pressing the phone closer to her ear. "What is it?"

"You're in more danger than you realize," the voice on the other end warned. "And so is he. Watch your back. The Verrini are making their move."

A cold shiver ran down her spine as the call ended abruptly, and she turned to face Victor. His eyes were dark with fury, the promise of violence simmering just below the surface.

"I told you," he muttered, more to himself than to her. "They're coming for us."

The storm outside had finally arrived, the rain pouring down in sheets against the windows. Inside the mansion, however, the storm was just beginning.

And Elysia realized that there was no escaping the chaos that had just entered her life.

The air in the mansion felt thick with tension, heavy and suffocating. Elysia stood by the large windows in the grand living room, staring out at the torrential downpour, her thoughts swirling as wildly as the storm outside. The flashing lights from the occasional thunder seemed to pierce the otherwise darkened world, casting long, twisted shadows that seemed to reach out for her.

Victor's voice echoed in her mind, unrelenting. "You are mine." The words clung to her, reverberating in her ears as if they were carved into her very soul.

She pressed a hand to her forehead, trying to block out the thoughts, the confusion, the fear. The phone call—the warning from the mysterious voice—still lingered in her mind. The Verrini. The threat. The storm was not just outside. It was closing in, and she had no idea how to escape.

Behind her, she could hear the sound of Victor's footsteps, deliberate and steady. He had not yet spoken since the call ended. There was a coldness in his silence now, something far more dangerous than the anger she had seen in him before. She turned slowly, meeting his gaze.

His face was set in a hard, implacable mask, but there was a flare of something in his eyes—an emotion she couldn't quite place, but it was unmistakable. Fear. Fear, and something darker. Something possessive.

"They're coming," he said, his voice low, the words thick with a dangerous promise. "The Verrini think they can take what's mine. They've underestimated me. They've underestimated us."

Elysia swallowed, her throat tight. "What do you mean, us?"

Victor didn't answer immediately. Instead, he took a step closer, closing the distance between them in a fluid motion. His presence was overwhelming, his aura commanding and intense. She could feel the heat radiating from him, like an inferno threatening to consume her.

"They're not just after me," he continued, his voice darkening, a note of finality creeping into his words. "They want you. They want you as leverage. They want to destroy what I've built, what I've protected."

His gaze softened for just a moment, his lips barely twitching as if fighting a painful memory. "And I won't let that happen. Not again."

Elysia's heart raced in her chest as the weight of his words sank in. Her thoughts were a tangled mess, racing faster than her ability to comprehend. She wanted to scream at him, to tell him this wasn't her fight, that she was just a woman caught in the middle of a war she didn't belong to. But as Victor's presence loomed over her, she felt something shift within her—a strange pull, like an invisible thread tying her to him. It was inexplicable, terrifying, and yet, it felt… inevitable.

The vulnerability she had tried so hard to suppress flooded her, a flood of emotions crashing over her, threatening to drown her. She couldn't ignore the connection, the pull toward him, even though everything in her screamed to run. But she wasn't running. She was standing here, in this mansion, in this dangerous world that had become her reality.

"You don't understand, Elysia," Victor continued, his voice becoming more urgent, his eyes burning with an intensity she had never seen before. "They killed Isabella, my wife. She—" He paused, his breath hitching for a moment, and then he shook his head, as if to clear the memory that threatened to choke him. "She died because of them. Because of betrayal. And I will make them pay. I will destroy anyone who dares to touch what's mine."

His hands gripped her shoulders, holding her steady, as if trying to ground her in this storm of emotions and revelations. Elysia could feel the heat of his hands through the fabric of her dress, the pulse of his power, and despite herself, she couldn't tear her gaze away from his.

"I'm not Isabella," she whispered, her voice barely audible, the words feeling like a desperate plea.

Victor's grip tightened slightly, and his gaze became more intense, more searching. "No," he said softly, but there was no denial in his voice, only an undeniable certainty. "But you are her. You are the reincarnation of the woman I loved. And I will never let you go again."

Her breath caught in her throat as he pulled her closer, his presence enveloping her like a dark storm. The connection between them was undeniable now, pulsing in the air around them, drawing her in despite her resistance. She could feel it in every fiber of her being, that nagging sensation, the haunting memories that tugged at her mind—memories of a life she couldn't remember, of a love that felt both foreign and familiar.

"I can't do this," she said, her voice cracking as she pulled back slightly, breaking his grip. "I can't be the woman you want me to be. I don't even know who I am."

Victor stared at her, the raw intensity in his gaze never wavering. For a moment, the room felt as though it had fallen into complete silence, the only sound the pounding of her own heart in her ears. And then, slowly, he nodded, his eyes softening.

"I know it's not easy," he said quietly. "But I'll make you remember. I'll help you remember, Elysia. You're not alone in this. Not anymore."

A sudden explosion of noise from outside shattered the fragile moment between them. The windows rattled as gunfire erupted in the distance, followed by the unmistakable screech of tires.

Victor's eyes flared with fury as he turned toward the sound, his entire posture shifting into something far more dangerous. "They've made their move," he muttered under his breath.

Before Elysia could react, he grabbed her by the wrist, pulling her towards the door. "Stay close," he commanded, his voice sharp with authority. "We're not safe here. Not anymore."

They rushed through the darkened halls of the mansion, the sounds of chaos growing louder. She could hear shouts, the thunder of footsteps, and the distinct click of weapons being loaded. The Verrini weren't just threatening them. They were here.

Victor's grip on her wrist tightened as they reached the main foyer. His eyes scanned the room, calculating, assessing, as if waiting for the next move.

His entire being radiated danger, and Elysia couldn't help but wonder if she had made a terrible mistake by staying.

But it was too late for doubts now.

The front doors burst open with a force that shook the entire building. The storm outside had nothing on the ferocity that had just entered her life.

And she realized, with a cold, sinking feeling in her gut, that there was no turning back.

This was her reality now. The world of the Lupo family, the world of danger, obsession, and death, had swallowed her whole.

6

Doubts and Fears

The rain whispered against the glass dome of the garden like a thousand secrets begging to be heard.

Outside, the world remained shrouded in a watery gray, but inside the Lupo estate's private greenhouse, the air was thick with the perfume of roses. They bloomed wildly along iron trellises and stone statues—untamed, clawing at the glass like they longed to escape. Red. Crimson. Blood-bright.

Elysia stood barefoot on the cold marble floor, arms wrapped around herself. The silk robe Victor had gifted her barely clung to her skin, dampened by the mist curling through the broken windows. Morning had not yet arrived, but sleep had abandoned her hours ago, chased away by dreams that felt too real to dismiss.

The third-person eye drifted through the lush solitude, catching the flicker in Elysia's gaze—the haunted look of a woman caught in limbo. Not quite prisoner, not quite lover. Just… lost.

Her fingers traced the edge of a rose petal, soft as a sigh and just as fleeting. The thorns below pricked her thumb. She did not flinch.

In the silence, memory and imagination blurred, spinning through her mind like windblown leaves. Flashes. Whispers. A woman's laughter. The scent of lilacs. A gunshot. Pain. And then—Victor's voice, low and reverent, calling her Isabella.

She was not Isabella. She was Elysia Monroe. And yet…

"Why can't I stop thinking about him?" she whispered to no one, her voice brittle with exhaustion. The question dissolved into the mist, unanswered.

From afar, the third-person gaze shifted—beyond the vines, beyond the dripping stone archway, to where Victor Lupo stood, hidden in the shadows. His presence, as always, was a storm waiting behind a calm sky. Unseen but felt.

He watched her like a man haunted by both devotion and madness.

To Victor, she was more than a woman. She was the echo of a vow never fulfilled, the second chance born from ash and time. And that belief, unshakable as the earth beneath his feet, had grown into obsession.

Yet now, in this moment, he did not approach. He merely observed, the silence between them thick with unspoken truths and restrained longing.

The narrative lens returned to Elysia, the way her breath fogged the glass before her, the way her shoulders trembled—not from cold, but from the war raging inside.

She remembered Victor's hands—steady as granite, lethal as wolves. The way he held her after the nightmare. How his fingers brushed her cheek like she was made of something breakable. And still, beneath the tenderness, there was the ever-present shadow of who he was.

A mafia king. A man carved from violence and vengeance. A man who believed her soul belonged to him.

Could love grow in such dark soil?

She closed her eyes. And the greenhouse seemed to close in with her, its greenery no longer inviting, but overgrown. Wild. As if the roses were listening. As if they understood.

"Even now," she murmured, "part of me wants to trust him."

Her voice cracked on the word trust, like a mirror fracturing from pressure too long ignored.

From his hidden vantage, Victor took a single step forward—but stopped when she turned. Her eyes scanned the garden, not seeing him, but feeling him.

"I know you're there," she said softly. "You always are."

And like the inevitable pull of gravity, he emerged.

Victor Lupo. In all his tragic glory.

The rainwater clung to his dark hair, his silk shirt slightly unbuttoned, revealing the line of a scar across his collarbone—a memory etched into flesh. He walked slowly, each step echoing through the mist-laced silence.

"I didn't mean to intrude," he said, voice low as thunder before a storm. "But you looked like you were somewhere else."

"I was," she answered. "I'm always somewhere else these days."

A beat passed. Then another. Between them hung the tension of a thousand unsaid things.

"Are you remembering more?" he asked carefully.

She laughed bitterly. "I don't know what I'm remembering. Maybe it's your stories getting into my head. Maybe it's madness. Or maybe…" Her eyes narrowed. "Maybe it's something else entirely."

Victor said nothing.

A butterfly, ghost-white, fluttered between them and vanished into the vines.

"I don't know who I am anymore," Elysia admitted, her voice a breath, not a statement. "And you—Victor, you make it so much harder to figure that out."

He stepped closer. Not too close. Just enough for the heat between them to rise like steam from stone.

"I only want you to remember," he said, and in his voice was something fragile. Hope.

"But what if I don't want to be her?" Elysia asked.

A pause. Rain drummed louder above them.

"Then you'll still be mine," he said. "Elysia or Isabella. Soul or stranger. I'll protect you either way."

The vow hung in the air like incense—sweet, heady, suffocating.

She looked away. Her gaze found a rose—blooming perfectly, red as sin.

"And what if I need protection from you?"

That hit him like a blade, though he did not flinch. But the omniscient eye saw the flicker in his expression—the fracture beneath the iron mask.

"I would never hurt you," he said.

"No," she whispered. "But you might love me until I disappear."

Silence.

The rain thickened into a downpour, blurring the glass, turning the garden into a world apart.

Victor reached into his coat and pulled out an old silver key. He set it on the stone pedestal beside her.

"A gift," he said. "For when you're ready to open what's hidden."

She didn't take it. Not yet.

He turned and walked away, vanishing into shadow once more.

Elysia stared at the key. Rain slid down the glass behind her like tears on a face. Somewhere deep inside, something shifted. A lock turning. A door creaking open.

The roses rustled, as if in approval.

The mansion slept.
    Midnight had painted the Lupo estate in hushed shades of navy and ash.

Outside, the storm had passed, leaving only the faint hiss of wind against the ivy-covered walls. The chandeliers were dimmed, casting golden pools of light across velvet carpets and oil-painted ancestors who watched from their frames with unblinking eyes.

But the library pulsed with quiet life.

Firelight flickered in the grand hearth, dancing along mahogany shelves that stretched from marble floor to coffered ceiling. The scent of old paper and pipe smoke lingered—ghosts of stories, long told and long hidden.

Elysia stepped inside barefoot, her robe drawn tight as she hugged herself. Her hair clung damply to her neck, and her thoughts swirled more chaotically than the storm clouds that had just passed. Her bare feet made no sound across the carpet, but the weight of her presence pressed into the room.

Books were scattered across the nearest table—thick tomes in Italian, French, Latin. Names she didn't recognize. Symbols she didn't understand.

But one book caught her attention. It was older than the others, leather-bound with curling gold filigree. No title. Just a faint imprint of a wolf's head, almost worn smooth from time.

She opened it.

The pages were a patchwork of handwriting, faded ink, and glued-in letters. Newspaper clippings. Photographs yellowed with time.

The omniscient perspective narrowed in—on her hand trembling slightly as she turned a page. On her breath catching in her throat as a name reappeared.

Isabella Lupo.

Her image was there, in a photograph pressed into the page. A wedding photo, taken in black-and-white. The bride's face was her own.

No—Isabella's.

But the resemblance was uncanny, enough to raise goosebumps across Elysia's skin. They could have been twins. Or mirrors.

And Victor… he looked the same. Not younger. Just colder.

The page crackled beneath her touch. Her mind recoiled from the impossible truth.

Suddenly, a slip of paper fluttered free, landing at her feet like a whisper fallen from time.

She picked it up.

The paper was delicate, ivory with edges curled like petals scorched by fire. The writing was elegant, unmistakably feminine, written in blood-red ink.

> "If I disappear, it will not be an accident. Trust no one—not even him."

No signature. But the letter was tucked into Isabella's page. Intentionally. Carefully. A warning.

Elysia's heart thudded once, hard enough to make her sway.

The narrative shifted, pulling outward, showing the tremble in her jaw, the storm rekindling behind her eyes. Her breath shallowed, fogging the page in her hands.

Could Victor have—?

No. She didn't finish the thought.

But the seed had been planted.

A creak behind her.

Elysia whirled, the letter crushed in her fist.

It was Emilio—Victor's consigliere. The family's cold-eyed lawyer and shadow-scribe. Always watching. Always quiet. His suits were darker than midnight, and his expression rarely shifted from unreadable.

"You shouldn't be here," he said evenly, stepping into the firelight.

Elysia didn't flinch. "Neither should you."

His mouth twitched—half-smile, half-sneer. "Curiosity is a dangerous habit in this house."

Her fingers tightened around the letter. "Why was this hidden?"

He tilted his head. "What have you found?"

"You know exactly what I found."

There was a pause—measured and weighted.

Then he stepped closer, eyes never leaving hers. "There are truths Victor refuses to speak aloud. About Isabella. About the night she died. He believes silence is mercy. I believe silence is betrayal."

Elysia swallowed. Her voice was low. "Did he kill her?"

Emilio said nothing.

The fire hissed. The air grew heavy.

"I asked you a question."

"You're asking the wrong person," he said softly. "The only person who knows what happened that night is Victor. And he'll never tell you the whole truth… not unless you leave him no other choice."

Her heart twisted. "And what would that cost me?"

"Everything."

The word fell between them like a dagger.

Emilio stepped back into the shadows. "You should burn that letter. For your own sake."

He disappeared, his footsteps swallowed by silence.

Elysia stared after him, the weight of the letter growing heavier in her hand.

She looked down at Isabella's photo again—at the familiar stranger wearing a haunted smile beside Victor.

"Who were you?" she whispered. "And what did you see before the end?"

The fire popped behind her.

Somewhere in the walls, the old pipes groaned.

The third-person lens captured her—small, alone, standing in the center of a room filled with secrets. A woman caught between two lives. A future tangled in shadows.

And as the flames flickered over Isabella's warning, the echo of her words seemed to reach across time.

Not even him.

It was the quiet moments that betrayed her most.

After days shadowed by Victor's intense presence, nights thick with questions and half-remembered dreams, Elysia found herself retreating to the one place in the mansion that didn't feel haunted—the greenhouse.

By day, it was filled with citrus trees, orchids, and climbing roses that kissed the vaulted glass ceiling. But tonight, silver moonlight filtered through the panes, turning every leaf into stained glass and every breath into a whisper of mist.

She sat on the stone bench nestled between potted lemon balm and jasmine, her thoughts louder than the world around her.

Victor had been… gentler that morning. Almost human. He had brushed a curl from her cheek with such reverence, she'd almost forgotten her fear. But it lingered, coiled like a snake beneath her skin. Every soft touch. Every quiet word. They were petals hiding thorns.

"I'm falling for a man who might have buried his wife," she muttered aloud.

The omniscient perspective widened. The roses heard her confession, the stars bore witness. Yet, she remained unburdened. The truth was still buried deep.

Until she found it.

It began with a scent—lavender and cedarwood, an old perfume she didn't recognize but felt in her bones. It lured her back inside, up the staircase, past the portraits with eyes that followed.

She hadn't entered Isabella's old room before.

Victor kept it locked, and no one spoke of it. But tonight, the door was ajar.

Drawn by something unspoken, Elysia stepped inside.

DOUBTS AND FEARS

The room was preserved in time, like a breath held too long. Dust floated in the air, disturbed by her arrival. The wallpaper had faded, but not the sadness embedded in the furniture. A vanity sat untouched, bottles of perfume still perched like sentinels. Silk curtains hung heavy over tall windows, moonlight slicing through in silver ribbons.

A music box rested on the nightstand. Carved with roses and wolves. Ornate. Familiar.

She reached for it.

Click.

The lid lifted with a sigh, and a lullaby drifted into the room—a gentle, aching melody that pried open something inside her chest. Her fingers hovered over the tiny spinning ballerina inside. She wasn't sure if it was memory or déjà vu, but tears welled in her eyes.

Then she saw it—folded neatly beneath the velvet lining. A letter.

Another letter.

Her hands trembled as she unfolded the aged parchment, the scent of perfume rising like a ghost.

"My love, if you are reading this, then something has happened to me. I feared it would. There is betrayal in this house, closer than Victor dares to believe. I no longer know whom I can trust—not even him. He loves fiercely, but his obsession blinds him."

Elysia sat down hard on the edge of the bed, her breath gone.

"They told me to be quiet. That if I said a word, it would destroy him. But I cannot keep silent if it means my life, or yours. Someone in this family—someone close—wants me gone. Wants to erase what we were. If I vanish, promise me this: you will look deeper. You will not believe the first story you're told."

There was no name. No date. Just smudges of ink where tears had once fallen.

The omniscient lens zoomed out to show her now—a woman seated in a dead woman's room, reading a letter written from beyond the grave, her identity crumbling under the weight of truths too long buried.

Elysia gripped the letter in both hands, her knuckles white.

"Why didn't he tell me?" she whispered.

Victor, who swore to protect her. Victor, who said she was his salvation. Victor, who looked at her with reverence—but kept her in the dark.

Was it grief? Guilt? Or something darker?

She stood, her shadow dancing on the walls like a warning.

A noise behind her.

She turned.

Victor stood in the doorway, his shirt unbuttoned at the throat, sleeves rolled to the elbow, moonlight casting his face in silver and shadow. His expression was unreadable—neither fury nor sorrow. Just stillness.

"I didn't mean to—" she began.

"You found it," he said softly.

Her fingers curled around the letter. "Did you know?"

He stepped into the room slowly, like approaching a wounded animal. "I knew she wrote something… I didn't know where she hid it."

"And what about what she said?" Her voice rose, sharp with fear and fury. "That someone wanted her gone? That you might've had something to do with it?"

His jaw clenched. The omniscient view dipped close to his eyes—storms of rage, regret, and something too human to define.

"I loved her," he said. "But I couldn't protect her."

"That's not an answer."

"It's the only truth I have left."

Silence fell like snowfall.

She looked at him—really looked—and didn't see the monster she feared or the lover she longed for. She saw a man made of cracks and shadows, clutching at the only piece of the past that hadn't burned.

Elysia stepped past him without another word.

The letter was still in her hand.

And as she descended the stairs, one thought echoed louder than the lullaby still playing upstairs:

If Isabella had been silenced… who else in this house wore a smile with a knife behind their back?

7

The Bond Grows

The rain whispered against the tall windows of the Lupo estate, a persistent hush that threaded through the sleeping halls like a lullaby for the damned. Inside Victor's private library—his sanctum—shadows danced along the walls as firelight licked the shelves of ancient books and secrets too old to speak aloud. The storm outside had cloaked the manor in a brooding silence, but within, tension simmered beneath the quiet.

Elysia stood near the hearth, the silk of her borrowed robe clinging to her as though it feared the air between them. Her eyes traced the spines of tomes she couldn't name, yet some titles triggered a sense of eerie recognition, like whispers half-remembered in a dream. Her fingertips grazed the edge of a carved table, her skin cool to the touch, and still—there it was again.

That ripple.

Not fear. Not curiosity.

Recognition.

She didn't know why she'd come here tonight. Perhaps it was the weight of the storm or the way Victor's voice had lingered in her memory hours after dinner, rough and haunted, yet tethered to something tender. She wasn't sure if she hated that feeling or yearned for it.

"Couldn't sleep?" came his voice, low and velvet-dark, from the corner chair where he sat cloaked in shadows.

She turned. He was part of the room, a shadow among shadows. His suit jacket lay abandoned on the floor, his white shirt open at the collar. The fire painted him in gold and scarlet, a Renaissance prince dipped in blood and longing.

"I didn't know you'd be here," she said, her voice barely above the storm's murmur.

A lie.

Victor studied her, eyes a molten silver that pierced through the flickering light. "Yes, you did."

There was no accusation in his tone—only certainty. The kind of certainty that men didn't earn, but were born with. Or perhaps cursed with.

Elysia exhaled, brushing her hair back from her temple. "Sometimes, it feels like the walls here breathe. Like they remember things. Things I shouldn't know."

He stood, slow and deliberate, as though his movements were part of some ritual. "That's not the house remembering, Elysia."

The way he said her name—soft, reverent, as though he were recalling a hymn—made her pulse stutter.

"You believe I'm her," she said.

"I don't believe," Victor said, stepping toward her. "I know."

A log cracked in the fire, sparks shooting up like dying stars. Outside, thunder rumbled—a deep growl that shook the foundations.

Elysia folded her arms across her chest. "You said Isabella was… kind. Gentle. I don't feel like her."

He came close enough that she could smell him—amber, spice, and something darkly masculine. "Because you're still remembering how to be her."

She looked up at him, meeting the truth in his face. And God help her—she wanted to believe it. She wanted to believe that her confusion had meaning, that the strange flashes—of a piano, a garden in bloom, a silver blade glinting in moonlight—were not madness clawing at her mind, but fragments of another life. Her life.

"I'm not sure if what I feel is real," she admitted. "Or if I'm just… falling into your obsession."

Victor touched her cheek, his hand feather-light, reverent. "Obsession dies. What I feel for you—has survived death itself."

There it was again—that unrelenting pull. Like gravity had changed its axis, and he was its new center.

"But what if I'm not her?" she asked, her voice cracking, betraying more than she wanted. "What if I'm just a girl who looks like a ghost?"

His eyes burned brighter in the firelight. "Then I will love the ghost. And the girl."

Elysia swallowed. Her throat felt tight, her chest crowded with emotion she hadn't named. "You speak like this is fate."

"Isn't it?"

For a moment, the world stilled. The fire no longer cracked. The rain no longer whispered. Even the wind seemed to hold its breath.

She stepped back, needing air, needing space—but her fingers brushed the corner of a book. The moment she touched the worn leather, a flash burst behind her eyes.

A scream.
   The scent of roses and gunpowder.
   Blood on silk.
   A ring tumbling into darkness.

Elysia gasped and staggered, catching herself on the edge of the table.

Victor was at her side in an instant. "What did you see?"

Her lips trembled. "I don't know. A memory… or a dream."

"A piece," he murmured, guiding her to sit. "Another piece."

Elysia pressed a hand to her temple. "I'm losing my mind."

"No," he said firmly. "You're reclaiming it."

The room swirled around her. Was this what madness felt like—soaked in longing, laced with grief, scented with roses blooming in winter?

THE BOND GROWS

Victor knelt before her, his voice low. "Let me show you something tomorrow. Something that might help you remember."

She didn't nod, but she didn't say no.

Outside, the storm eased, its fury spent. Inside, another storm had only begun to brew—one between love and memory, between truth and illusion.

Elysia's hand trembled where it rested in her lap.

Victor placed his over it, and together, the trembling stilled.

The fire hissed softly, as if offering a secret neither of them dared say aloud.

The next morning unfolded like a well-dressed lie—sunlight filtered in through tall windows, casting gilded stripes across the marble floors of the Lupo estate, as if nothing dark had ever walked its halls. The staff moved like whispers, avoiding eye contact, but alert, as though anticipating an aftershock that hadn't yet come.

In the breakfast room, the porcelain clink of fine china was the only interruption to the silence between Victor and Elysia. He sat at the head of the long mahogany table, half-shadowed beneath a Renaissance portrait of one of his ancestors, a wolfhound at the man's feet like a sentinel from another lifetime.

Elysia picked at the edge of her toast. Her fingers felt numb despite the warm tea, and her appetite had been stolen sometime between memory and morning. Across from her, Victor had barely touched his espresso. He watched her with the unshakable patience of a man used to playing long, dangerous games.

"You said you'd show me something," she said, her voice soft but steady.

Victor inclined his head, setting his cup down with quiet precision. "Come."

No guards. No fanfare. Just her and him, walking through the house like two phantoms retracing the same steps they might've walked in another life. Elysia didn't know what she expected—the basement, perhaps. A bloodstained journal. A hidden room of relics. But what she got was the garden.

Victor led her past the formal rose beds and into the overgrown back garden, a place left untamed, as though time had forgotten it. Ivy curled up the sides of cracked statues. Wild lavender burst from the earth in defiance of symmetry. And in the middle of it all: a white marble bench with a name carved into it.

Isabella Valezzi Lupo.

The sight of it struck her like cold water across the soul.

She stepped forward, her heart in her throat, fingertips brushing the carved letters. Her skin tingled.

"I buried her here," Victor said quietly, standing beside her. "Not because it was proper. Because it was sacred."

The words caught in her chest. "This… this is what you wanted to show me?"

Victor's expression didn't change, but something shuttered behind his eyes. "Look closely."

Beneath the name was a date. Her supposed death. And above it—Elysia's breath stuttered—a symbol. Two entwined moons and a thorned rose. The same symbol that had been haunting her sketches. The same one she'd dreamed about days ago.

Her fingers trembled over the engraving. "I've seen this before."

"I know," Victor replied. "You used to wear it around your neck."

A necklace. The one she woke up with in the hospital. Lost. Or stolen.

Elysia turned to face him. "Who else knows about this? The symbol, the grave, all of it?"

Victor's jaw tightened. "Just me. And now… you."

It was too much. The fresh scent of lavender. The name etched in stone. The feeling blooming in her chest that her entire life had been a curtain—and someone had just yanked it open.

Her voice cracked. "I don't want this to be real."

"But it is," Victor said gently. "And part of you already knows that."

Elysia backed away, breath ragged. "You buried your wife. And now you're in love with her shadow."

Victor didn't move. "I'm not in love with a shadow. I'm in love with the soul that never left me."

Silence stretched long and taut.

The wind shifted, carrying the scent of honeysuckle and secrets.

Elysia turned her face to the sun, as though it could burn away the confusion inside her. But it didn't. Instead, it illuminated something deeper—a fragile thread of memory tugging at her from beneath her skin.

She remembered running barefoot across this garden. Laughter. A voice calling her *bella mia*. And the feel of Victor's lips brushing her wrist, reverent, like a man worshipping something more divine than flesh.

"I remember this place," she whispered.

Victor closed his eyes for a beat. "Then you remember us."

No. Not yet. Not fully. But the bones of her soul did.

Her hands clenched at her sides. "That doesn't mean I'm her. It doesn't mean I forgive this life. The violence. The danger. The obsession."

Victor stepped closer, his voice quieter than the wind. "I'm not asking for forgiveness. I'm asking for truth. For you to follow it to the end."

Their eyes locked. Fire and ice. Memory and fear. A heartbeat balanced on a razor's edge.

"I don't know if I can," she said.

"Then let me help you," he answered.

Elysia turned back to the marble, tracing the final line of the inscription.

"Love, even in death, is not undone."

The bond between them was no longer just emotional— it was elemental. Air. Fire. Bone. Memory.

And still, she wasn't sure if it was love… or a beautifully orchestrated curse.

Nightfall came cloaked in thunder.

It wasn't the gentle kind of rain that soothed the skin and lulled the soul. This storm came howling—wind clawing at the windows like a beast starved for blood, lightning stitching scars across the clouds. The sky itself seemed angry, as if the heavens, too, were tangled in the storm of truths Elysia had unearthed that day.

Inside the Lupo estate, the walls felt heavier, as if burdened by the weight of the past clawing its way to the present.

Victor was gone.

He hadn't said where. Only a note left beside her bedside glass of water: "Stay inside. Lock the doors. Trust me." Four words that begged for her obedience—and betrayed his need for control.

Elysia paced the library now, surrounded by aged volumes and the flicker of dying firelight. Her heart was a metronome gone rogue, skipping with every gust of wind that rattled the windows. She wasn't afraid of ghosts anymore. No. She was afraid of what the living might do to chase them.

She pressed a hand to the bookshelves for balance. That symbol—the entwined moons and thorned rose—haunted her still. A family sigil, perhaps? A secret society? Or maybe something far older, more arcane. She didn't know. But deep in her marrow, something ancient stirred in response to it. Like an echo across time.

Then, from the shadows—a noise.

A whisper of movement. Too soft for footsteps. Too sharp for coincidence.

Elysia froze, her breath catching like a ribbon in the wind.

She turned slowly, scanning the library's darkened corners. "Victor?"

Silence.

Then—glass shattered.

The sound came from the eastern corridor. Not a dropped cup. A window, broken with force.

Instinct overruled logic. She didn't scream. Didn't run. Instead, she moved—fast but silent—across the Persian rug, grabbing the antique fireplace poker from its brass holder. Her grip trembled, but she refused to be a porcelain girl anymore. Not in this world. Not in this life.

As she stepped into the corridor, lightning flooded the hallway in white-blue brilliance, revealing a figure cloaked in black by the shattered window.

A man. Armed. Masked.

Not Victor.

She ducked behind a column just as the intruder stepped forward, sweeping the hall with the practiced efficiency of someone trained to kill without pause. The gun in his hand gleamed like a promise of death.

She had seconds. Maybe less.

Adrenaline surged. Her mind raced—not with fear, but calculation.

Think, Elysia. Victor said trust him. Trust the house.

She remembered something Victor had shown her in passing days ago—a panel near the stairs that disguised a narrow servant's passage. Her feet moved before her mind caught up.

She darted down the corridor, praying the man hadn't seen.

Another crash behind her.

He had.

She reached the panel, found the latch, shoved it open—and slipped into darkness just as a bullet punched through the wood beside her.

The passage was narrow and pitch-black, the air thick with dust and memories. But it offered cover. And perhaps—if luck was kind—salvation.

She pressed her back against the cold wall, fighting the tremble in her limbs. Her ears strained for sound. Footsteps. Breathing. Anything.

Silence.

Then, a whisper in Italian: "Trovatela. Ora."

Find her. Now.

There was more than one.

Elysia's blood iced. The Verrini. It had to be. The timing wasn't coincidence. Victor's absence. The letter he left. He knew something was coming.

But he hadn't expected them to strike here. Not this soon.

She crept forward in the dark, feeling her way along the walls until she reached the hidden exit that opened into the music room. She pushed the panel with slow, careful pressure—and stepped out just as the lights flared back on with a snap.

THE BOND GROWS

Victor stood in the center of the room, soaked in rain and rage, a gun in one hand, his other bloodied.

Behind him, two masked men lay on the floor—unmoving.

For a beat, everything was silent but the thunder outside and the sound of their breathing.

Elysia dropped the fireplace poker with a metallic clatter. "Victor—"

"You're hurt?" His voice cracked like a whip, eyes scanning her for wounds.

"No. I—Victor, they were in the house."

"I know." He stepped forward, grabbing her by the arms. Not rough, but urgent. "They weren't here for me this time. They were here for you."

The words hit like shrapnel.

"They knew I'd be gone," he muttered. "They waited. Timed it perfectly. Someone… someone close fed them this information."

The taste of betrayal clung to the air like smoke.

Elysia's hands clenched into fists. "Then we're not safe here anymore."

Victor shook his head, the fury in his expression replaced by something colder—resolved. "No. We're not. But I'll burn this city to the ground before I lose you again."

His words were fire. His touch, lightning.

And something in Elysia's soul—something buried deep and aching—

responded.

She wasn't sure if it was fear or fate she felt in that moment.

Only that her world had tilted.

And there would be no turning back.

Later that night, while Victor conferred with his men, Elysia wandered the estate alone, unable to sleep. She found herself drawn to the west wing—where the locked doors remained.

One was ajar.

Inside: a velvet-lined box, hidden beneath a loose floorboard. Inside it—a letter, yellowed with age.

Addressed in familiar handwriting.

To my dearest Victor…

The final line stopped her heart.

"If I die… it will be by someone we both trust."

8

Love or Fate?

The rain had ceased, but the echo of thunder still haunted the air like a forgotten hymn. Pale dawnlight filtered through the sheer curtains, painting soft golds and bruised violets across the walls of Victor Lupo's bedroom. Elysia sat at the edge of the bed, a silk robe draped around her shoulders, the hem fluttering like a hesitant whisper.

The room was too still.

Behind her, the bed bore the indentation of a restless night—pillows overturned, sheets twisted like the remnants of a fevered dream. Her gaze was fixed on the antique mirror in front of her, its gilded frame ornate and wolf-carved, curling with baroque thorns. Within it, her reflection shimmered uncertainly. Not entirely Elysia. Not entirely Isabella.

Her fingers traced her collarbone, as if searching for a scar left by a memory she couldn't quite recall. Last night's adrenaline still pulsed in her blood, ghostlike. The sound of gunfire, the sharp cry of Victor's voice, the way her body had moved on instinct to shield him—it all played in her mind like a scene she hadn't rehearsed but somehow knew by heart.

"Who am I?" The question, silent on her lips, floated in the morning hush.

Victor's voice stirred the quiet like a breeze through tall grass. "You didn't sleep."

She didn't turn. She could see him in the mirror—shirtless, a long scratch across his chest half-healed. The wound looked like a mark carved by fate itself. He stepped forward, barefoot, moving with the predatory grace of a man born to shadows.

"I didn't want to dream," she answered softly.

The mirror flickered again, and for a heartbeat, the reflection shifted. A woman with dark red lips. Longer hair. The same eyes—haunted and bold. Isabella?

She stood abruptly, the hem of her robe whispering across the marble floor. "Why does it feel like I've been here before?" she murmured, more to herself than to him.

Victor's gaze darkened. "Because you have."

Lightning cracked behind his words. Not in the sky, but in the air between them—charged, dangerous, inevitable.

Elysia turned to face him. "Don't say that."

"But it's the truth," he said, closing the distance between them. His hand brushed a strand of hair from her cheek. "You remember something. Don't you?"

A flicker. Blood on her hands. Roses crushed under booted heels. A silver locket clutched tightly as she fell.

"I don't know what I remember," she confessed, voice quaking like a violin string stretched too tight. "But something inside me recognizes you. And that terrifies me."

Victor's jaw clenched, but he didn't pull away. "It terrifies me too."

Outside, the wind moaned against the glass—a mournful sound that might have been mistaken for a cry. Time stood suspended as Elysia returned to the mirror, this time stepping closer until her breath fogged the glass.

"Sometimes," she whispered, "I see her."

"Isabella," he said without hesitation.

Her fingers grazed the mirror's surface. "Was she happy, Victor? Or just yours?"

A heavy silence settled. One of those rare silences thick with things unsaid.

"She was both," he said finally, though his voice carried the weight of a lie—or at least, an omission.

Elysia's reflection stared back at her like a puzzle half-assembled. "And how did she die?"

Victor's reflection stilled. A shadow passed through his eyes, like a storm cloud chasing the sun. "Too violently. Too soon."

"You said I died in your arms."

"You did."

"And you didn't save me?"

The question was a blade dressed as silk.

Victor moved behind her, his hands gently encircling her waist. "I didn't get there in time," he said against her ear. "But I never stopped trying."

There it was again—the dichotomy of him. Gentle hands, violent world. Tender words, dangerous truths. He was a man at war with himself, and she was standing on the battlefield.

Her gaze locked with his in the mirror. "So what am I now? A second chance? A replacement?"

"No," he said firmly. "You're the beginning I never thought I'd have again."

The air pulsed. The room felt smaller, as though memory itself was pressing in from all sides.

But Elysia pulled away, walking to the open balcony doors. The wind swept into the room, tangling her hair, lashing against her bare calves like some restless spirit come to remind her she didn't belong here.

She stared down at the garden below—rows of blood roses Victor had planted in Isabella's honor. They swayed now, dancing in a breeze heavy with memory.

"You buried her beneath those roses, didn't you?"

He didn't answer. But his silence was confirmation.

Elysia turned to him once more. "And you wonder why I'm afraid?"

"I don't wonder. I understand. But I need you to understand something too." He crossed to her in three strides, cupping her face, his voice a low vow. "Whatever you were before, whatever you become again—you are mine, Elysia. And I will protect you this time. Even from myself."

His words sank into her like rain into thirsty soil. And yet, part of her screamed to run. Because love this consuming… it had the power to save. But it also had the power to destroy.

Her heart beat wildly in her chest—like it remembered the night it had stopped.

Victor had retreated to his study, leaving Elysia alone in the vastness of his mansion. The soft hum of silence wrapped itself around her like a cloak she couldn't quite shed. In the stillness, the questions she had buried deep inside her began to claw their way to the surface.

She moved through the rooms like a ghost, unable to escape the pervasive weight of Victor's world that seemed to seep into the very walls—golden chandeliers, heavy curtains, the scent of expensive wood polish and cigar smoke lingering in the corners. It was a life of excess, of power, and yet, none of it made her feel safe.

The hallways twisted in a maze, each turn leading her deeper into the labyrinth of her own confusion. She had trusted him once. She had thought, for a fleeting moment, that his obsession might be a reflection of love—an impossible bond that had defied time. But now, it was different. Every word he spoke, every touch, felt like it carried the weight of a past she wasn't sure she could bear.

She paused before a large window, gazing out at the sprawling grounds below. The mansion sat on a hill, overlooking a city bathed in the soft blush of early afternoon. The beauty of it was suffocating, a stark contrast to the violence and betrayal that lingered just beneath the surface.

"What do I do now?" she asked herself. The words felt hollow in the vast silence of the room.

Her thoughts were interrupted by the sound of footsteps approaching. She didn't need to look to know who it was. His presence filled the space long before he spoke.

"You're still here."

Victor's voice was a low rasp, like the soft rumble of thunder before a storm. He stood in the doorway, framed by the dim light spilling from the hallway. His eyes—always so intense, so calculating—seemed to soften for a fraction of a second, a crack in the wall he'd built around himself.

"I don't know where else to go," she replied, her voice betraying the exhaustion that had taken root in her bones. "This place… it's all so much."

Victor stepped closer, the silence between them thick with unspoken truths. He was a predator, born from a world of shadows, but there was something human in the way he looked at her now—a tenderness that made her wonder if he could ever truly understand the cost of what he demanded.

"Elysia, I know this isn't easy for you," he began, his tone more careful now, as if choosing his words with the same precision he used in his business. "But you're not alone here. I know you're afraid, but trust me. Let me help you."

The words were familiar—too familiar. He'd said something similar the night before, when she had saved him, instinct driving her to shield him from the gunfire that had come from nowhere. She had done it without thinking. In that moment, her body had moved on its own, her mind clouded by an emotion she couldn't name. But now, in the quiet aftermath, it felt like a mistake.

"I don't need saving," she said sharply, turning away from him. Her eyes caught the reflection of herself in the polished glass—a woman caught between two worlds. She had never felt so out of place, so trapped by her own memories and the weight of Victor's expectations.

Victor's sigh was heavy, laden with a frustration she didn't want to acknowledge. He stepped closer, his presence filling the space behind her. He didn't touch her this time, though his proximity was enough to make her pulse race.

"You're wrong," he said softly, his voice dark with the weight of everything he hadn't told her yet. "You do need saving. From yourself, from the lies you've been told, from the family that's waiting to claim you again. I know you're afraid of what's inside you. But I'll help you understand it."

Elysia's hands gripped the windowsill, her knuckles white. She wanted to believe him, she really did. There was a part of her—deep down—that recognized the truth in his words. She had always felt like an outsider, like something was missing, but now she was beginning to wonder if that missing piece had always been Victor.

But then there was the other part of her—the part that screamed in rebellion, that reminded her of the violence that followed him, of the blood that stained his past. How could she trust a man who lived in a world of deceit and danger? How could she trust him when everything in her screamed that he was dangerous, that he would destroy her if she let him?

"I'm not the woman you want me to be," she said, her voice barely above a whisper.

Victor moved even closer now, his breath warm against her ear. "You don't have to be. You don't need to be Isabella. You're Elysia. And I'll make sure no one can ever take you from me again."

His words were wrapped in a promise, but it felt like a chain being wrapped around her heart. She could feel the tension in his voice, the desperation in his touch. It was all-consuming, this pull between them, and she was powerless to resist it.

Elysia turned slowly, meeting his gaze. Her heart pounded painfully in her chest. She wanted to ask him the questions that had been gnawing at her—about Isabella, about his past, about his dark deeds—but the words were trapped in her throat, suffocated by fear.

"I'm scared," she admitted, her voice trembling. "Victor, I'm scared of what this is. What you want me to be. What I might become."

Victor's expression softened for a moment, the hardness in his eyes giving way to something raw, something vulnerable. For a brief second, he was just a man—a man in love, afraid of losing the one person who could save him from the ghosts of his past.

"I know," he said quietly, the words like a broken promise. "But I'm not letting you go. Not this time. No matter how hard it gets."

And in that moment, Elysia realized something that terrified her even more than the violence of his world—she didn't want to leave. Not yet.

The air between them was thick with tension, as if the very atmosphere of the mansion had been woven into a delicate thread that could snap at any moment. Victor's words had both soothed and unsettled her, and Elysia felt the weight of the choices that now loomed over her. Was she destined to repeat the mistakes of her past life? Was she simply a pawn in a game she had no control over?

Her heart hammered against her ribs, and despite the quiet of the room, she could hear the thunderous roar of her own doubts. The attraction, the undeniable pull toward Victor—it was a force she couldn't escape, even if she wanted to. And God, how she wanted to escape.

But Victor wasn't giving her that option. His presence was an ironclad certainty, wrapping itself around her every waking thought.

"Elysia," Victor murmured, his voice breaking through the storm of her thoughts, "there's something I need you to understand."

She turned toward him, her eyes narrowing, instinctively bracing for the weight of his next revelation. What more could he say? What could he reveal that would change the truth of what she had already seen—the violent, twisted world he lived in?

Victor took a slow step toward her, his gaze dark with something that bordered on regret. His presence seemed to fill the room as he closed the distance between them, his form casting a shadow that loomed larger than life.

"I never meant for this to happen," he said, his voice tight, almost strained. "You were never meant to be caught in the crossfire. Not this time. Not again."

The words hung in the air, vibrating with unspoken implications. Elysia felt her heart skip a beat, and for the first time in what felt like forever, she allowed herself to look deeper into his eyes—into the vulnerability that lay beneath the impenetrable mask of power he had so carefully constructed.

"Then what do you want from me?" she asked, the words coming out sharper than she intended. "What is it you're asking of me?"

Victor's jaw clenched, the tension in his body palpable, before he spoke again, his tone softening. "I'm asking you to trust me. I'm asking you to stop running from the truth of who we are, of what we are."

His words were a challenge, a proposition that she didn't know how to answer. He was right, of course. She had been running for so long, hiding from the truth of her past life, from the dangers that surrounded them both. But how could she trust him? How could she trust herself when everything about their connection screamed of inevitability—of fate?

Her pulse quickened as she stared at him, the pull between them undeniable. She had never felt anything like this before. It was as if the very earth beneath her feet trembled in response to his proximity, urging her to give in, to surrender to the inevitable.

But she couldn't. Not yet.

She stepped back, shaking her head, the words that had been building in her chest finally spilling out. "You say you never meant for this to happen, but you've made me a part of a world I never wanted. I don't know what I'm supposed to do with all of this, Victor. I don't know if I can ever accept who I was… who I am."

The pain in her voice was raw, unfiltered. It was the sound of a woman torn between the past and the present, between the reality of what was and the terrifying uncertainty of what might be.

Victor didn't move, didn't speak for a long moment. His gaze never wavered from hers, as though he was searching for the right words, the words that could finally bridge the gap between them.

Then, in a voice that was barely above a whisper, he said, "You think I don't know what this feels like? You think I don't carry the weight of our past? I've spent years wondering if I was the one who was meant to be punished for what happened to Isabella… if I was the one who should have died instead of her."

Elysia felt a tremor run through her, her resolve faltering for just a moment. She had never seen him like this—raw, unguarded. She had always known him as the powerful, ruthless mafia boss. But now, in the quiet of the room, she saw something else—a man who had loved and lost, a man who was haunted by the ghosts of the past.

"You didn't kill her," Elysia said, her voice trembling, as if she were trying to convince herself as much as him.

Victor shook his head, his eyes filled with something dark, something regretful. "No, but I might as well have. The guilt is the same. I failed her. And now, here you are—Elysia, the woman I've spent years searching for, believing I could make it right, believing I could fix everything."

The words crashed over her like a wave, and for a moment, she couldn't breathe. The reality of it settled over her like a heavy cloak. Victor wasn't just a man obsessed with a past love—he was a man carrying the weight of guilt and remorse that she hadn't understood until now.

Her heart ached for him. But her head... her head screamed that she couldn't get lost in this. She couldn't lose herself in him.

"You need to stop this," she whispered, almost pleading. "You need to let go of whatever this is. I can't be your salvation."

Victor's expression hardened, but there was a flicker of understanding in his eyes. He didn't say anything for a long time, just watched her, as if he were memorizing the way she stood, the way her defiance radiated from her.

"I can't stop," he said finally, his voice low, steady. "I won't stop. I won't let you go."

The finality in his words echoed through her chest. Elysia's heart raced as she felt the bonds of fate tightening around her, pulling her back into a life she didn't want, a love she wasn't sure she could survive.

9

Revelations

The mansion stood before Elysia like a dark sentinel, its towering presence casting long, jagged shadows across the garden. She had always thought of it as beautiful—a labyrinth of marble and gold—but now it felt more like a cage, gilded and impenetrable. Each time her gaze swept over the sprawling grounds, a chill ran down her spine. There was no escaping the shadows of this place, the secrets it held. And none more dangerous than the man who haunted its halls.

Inside, the silence was suffocating, a heavy stillness that matched the weight in her chest. She paced slowly through the long corridor, her footsteps muted against the polished stone floor. The room ahead held Victor, as it always did. But today, there was something different in the air—something thick and volatile, like the calm before a storm.

She paused outside the door, hesitating for just a moment. Her hand lingered on the handle. Her heart pounded in her chest, each beat seeming to echo in the stillness. It was the same sense of foreboding that had clouded her thoughts for days, the same nagging feeling that had taken root ever since the truth about her past life began to surface. She could no longer deny the connection between herself and the woman Victor had once loved, the woman who had died tragically—the woman he believed her to be.

But what did it all mean? Was she truly Isabella reincarnated, or was this just some twisted fantasy in Victor's mind? And why had she suddenly begun to remember flashes of a life she never lived—memories of love and loss, of betrayal and vengeance? The questions twisted in her mind like a maze, each turn leading to more confusion.

With a deep breath, she pushed open the door.

Victor stood by the window, his back to her. His silhouette was framed by the soft glow of the evening sun, the light casting a halo around him. He looked every bit the dangerous kingpin he was—his broad shoulders taut with tension, his jaw set in that grim line she had come to know all too well. The air around him crackled with an intensity that made it impossible to breathe.

"Elysia," he said, his voice low, rich with an almost unbearable weight. His back remained to her, but she knew his eyes were on her. He always knew where she was, what she was thinking, even before she spoke. He had always been like that—controlling, omnipotent in his own way.

"Victor," she replied, her voice sounding smaller than she intended. She took a hesitant step forward, feeling the distance between them stretch, despite their physical proximity. "We need to talk."

Victor turned then, his expression unreadable, a mask of stone. His eyes, dark and intense, locked onto hers. For a brief moment, the world seemed to disappear—there was only the two of them, suspended in time. The air between them was thick, heavy with the tension of unspoken words and unacknowledged truths.

"I know what you want to ask me," he said, his lips curling into a half-smile that did nothing to ease the heaviness in her chest. "You want to know about Isabella."

She swallowed hard, nodding. "I need to know," she said, her voice barely a whisper. "The truth. About her. About me. About what happened."

Victor's eyes darkened, a flicker of something painful flashing across his face before it was quickly masked. "What if I told you that the truth is more than you can bear?" he asked, stepping closer, his presence suffocating.

Elysia held her ground, despite the pounding of her heart. "I want to know," she repeated, her voice stronger now, determined. "I have to know."

Victor sighed, his gaze softening, if only for a moment. He seemed to battle with himself, as though torn between the man he had been and the one he was trying to become. "Very well," he said, his voice low but steady. "You deserve the truth, even if it shatters you."

He took a seat in the chair by the window, motioning for her to join him. Elysia hesitated before sitting across from him, the space between them feeling vast, even though the physical distance was small. She knew this conversation would change everything. She could feel it in her bones.

"Isabella was my wife," he began, his voice thick with sorrow. "She was everything to me. My world, my anchor. And when she died, part of me died with her."

Elysia's heart fluttered at the mention of Isabella's name. She had always known she was linked to the woman in some way, but hearing Victor speak of her with such intensity, such devotion, made the connection between them undeniable. She could feel the weight of his words in her chest, the grief that lingered in his voice like an old wound that had never healed.

"You loved her," Elysia said softly, more to herself than to him. "You still do."

Victor looked at her, his gaze unwavering. "Yes," he replied, his voice heavy with the confession. "But I don't think I ever stopped loving her. Even after everything that happened. Even after she was gone."

Elysia swallowed, her throat dry. "What happened to her? How did she die?"

Victor leaned forward, his fingers curling into the armrests of his chair. "She was betrayed," he said, his words laced with bitterness. "By someone within my own family. Someone I trusted. Someone I thought was loyal."

The words hit Elysia like a blow to the chest. Betrayal. She felt the sharp sting of it, deep in her gut, as though it were a part of her own history. The memories—no, the flashes—of her past life, began to flood her mind. Isabella's betrayal, her own death. The knife in her back. The family she had once trusted.

"I don't understand," Elysia murmured, her voice breaking. "Why would they betray her? Why would they betray you?"

Victor's eyes narrowed, his jaw tightening as the old pain resurfaced. "It was about power," he said, his voice cold now, distant. "There are no loyalties in my world. Only power. And when Isabella died, the power shifted. But I couldn't let go of her. Not then. Not now."

Elysia's mind reeled. The pieces were starting to fall into place, but there was still so much missing. "And what does that have to do with me?" she asked, her voice barely above a whisper.

Victor stared at her, his eyes searching hers as if looking for something—something only he could see. "Everything," he said, his voice thick with emotion. "You're the key to everything. The reincarnation of my lost love. Isabella's soul has returned to me. And I won't lose you again."

REVELATIONS

Elysia's breath caught in her throat. The truth—the one she had been avoiding—was now undeniable. She was bound to this man, bound to his past, and to the betrayal that had shaped his entire existence.

Victor leaned closer, his voice dropping to a whisper. "You may not believe it now, but you will. And when you do, we'll face the world together. We'll make them pay."

The weight of his words pressed down on her like a suffocating force. Elysia knew she was standing at a precipice, torn between the man who claimed to love her and the shadow of a past that threatened to swallow her whole.

The air in the room had shifted—what was once heavy with tension now felt thick with unspoken promises. The silence stretched between them, a living thing, pulsating with the weight of the truth that had just been laid bare. Elysia's mind swirled with a thousand thoughts, each one more jumbled than the last. Victor's words had carved a path through the fog in her mind, but the more she thought about them, the deeper the questions grew.

She was Isabella, he said. Reincarnated. But she couldn't reconcile that with the person she was today—the woman sitting in this room, fighting the strange pull toward the man who held her heart, despite everything.

Victor stood in front of her now, his broad figure towering, casting a long shadow across the room. His presence was as commanding as ever, but the distance between them had widened—emotionally, if not physically. He had given her the truth, but it felt like he had given her a blade to hold, its edge razor-sharp and gleaming in the dim light.

"I didn't mean to hurt you," Victor's voice was softer now, his usual steel masked with a vulnerability that Elysia had never heard from him before. The shift was subtle but undeniable. "But you deserve to know the whole story. Every piece of it."

Elysia shook her head, the confusion still thick in her chest. "I don't know what to believe anymore, Victor. What if I'm not her? What if this isn't real?" Her voice trembled at the end, betraying the storm brewing within her. She could almost taste the bitter, metallic edge of panic on her tongue.

Victor's gaze softened as he knelt in front of her, taking her hand gently in his. His touch, though tender, held a force behind it—a promise of something unyielding. "You are her," he said, his voice quiet but sure. "And I know this is hard to understand. But the connection we share—it's not something I can explain easily. I just know, Elysia. I know you're the one."

She pulled her hand back instinctively, her pulse quickening, but his eyes followed her every move. There was no escape from him—not physically, and certainly not emotionally. She felt as though the walls of the mansion were closing in around her, the dark history of Victor's world creeping up at the edges of her vision.

"How can you be so sure?" she whispered, almost to herself, as the memory of her previous life flickered at the edge of her consciousness. The fragments of a life she never lived seemed to reach for her, urging her to remember things she hadn't consciously known. She saw Isabella's face—fragile and haunted, the same eyes that stared back at her in the mirror now.

Victor's expression hardened, the mask slipping for just a moment. "I know because I never stopped searching for you. When you died, I lost a part of myself. But when you reappeared, when I saw you again, I knew—I could feel it in my soul—that you were Isabella. I never gave up on you, Elysia. I couldn't."

Elysia closed her eyes, a bitter laugh escaping her lips. "You never gave up on me? But what about everything else? The betrayal? The lies?"

Victor stiffened at the mention of betrayal, his eyes darkening once more.

He stood abruptly, pacing the room, his hand running through his dark hair in agitation. The vulnerability that had once softened his face was now replaced with a sharp edge, as though he were bracing himself for a fight.

"I didn't betray you," he said, his voice low, barely controlled. "The ones who killed you—those are the ones who betrayed you. And I…" His voice faltered for just a moment, and for the briefest of seconds, the mask slipped. "I couldn't stop it. I couldn't save you. And that's something I've had to live with every day."

His confession hit her like a wave, crashing through her defenses. She knew he had been haunted by his past, but hearing him admit to the weight of his guilt, the deep remorse he carried—it made her question everything she thought she knew about him.

"You couldn't save me," Elysia repeated, the words lingering in the space between them. There was a strange echo to them, as if they had been spoken by someone else before her. She could almost hear Isabella's voice whispering them, the same resignation in the words.

"I couldn't," Victor confirmed, his tone almost a plea. "But I will never stop trying to save you now, Elysia. Not again. I promise you that."

The promise hung in the air, heavy and irrevocable. But Elysia's heart, battered and torn, couldn't reconcile the man before her with the man from her past—the man whose love had been both a gift and a curse. The man who had once betrayed her.

"You don't understand," Elysia said, her voice rising, a note of panic creeping in. "You think I'm just supposed to forget the pain, the betrayal, and pretend like everything's fine? Like I'm just supposed to fall back into this… this life we shared before?"

Victor's gaze turned cold, his jaw tight. "This isn't just about you and me," he snapped. "This is about survival. The moment you stepped into my world, you became part of it. You can't just walk away from that, Elysia. Not without consequences."

Elysia's heart clenched at the harshness in his words, but it was the truth, wasn't it? She could try to run, to escape this world, but it would always pull her back. The ties that bound her to Victor were too strong—too deep. And as much as she wanted to deny it, she felt the pull of those ties, stronger than ever.

Victor took a step closer, his voice softening once again, his hand reaching out as if he couldn't help but touch her. "You were the best part of my life, Isabella. I'll do whatever it takes to make sure you're safe this time."

But the safety he promised wasn't the safety she needed. Elysia's heart thundered as the pieces of her past life collided with the present, a maelstrom of conflicting emotions threatening to drown her.

"I don't know if I can trust you anymore, Victor," she whispered, her words trembling as they left her lips.

Victor's eyes flared with something close to desperation, but Elysia had already turned away, unable to meet his gaze any longer. The truth was a heavy burden, and she didn't know if she could carry it.

But as she stood there, in the suffocating silence of the room, she realized that she wasn't just struggling with Victor's betrayal. She was struggling with her own fears—fear of the truth, fear of what it meant for her future, and fear of the man who had once held her heart.

The mansion's vast, empty hallway stretched before them, its cold marble floors reflecting the dim light from the chandeliers above. Elysia walked ahead of Victor, her footsteps echoing through the silence, but there was no distance she could create between them that would ease the heaviness in her chest. The walls seemed to close in around her, mirroring the suffocating feeling inside her as she grappled with the truth that had been thrust upon her.

Victor was silent behind her, the weight of his gaze like a physical presence, pressing against her back. She could feel him, as if the bond that tethered them was too strong to break, too strong to ignore. But she wasn't ready to face him again—not yet. Not when the very foundation of everything she had thought was real had crumbled in an instant.

Isabella... The name clung to her thoughts like a forgotten melody, repeating over and over, a haunting refrain that refused to fade. She had been her. She had been the woman who had once loved Victor—who had died for him, or because of him, she still couldn't decide.

Elysia reached the large window at the end of the hall, the glass cold beneath her fingertips as she stared out into the dark night. The world beyond the mansion was a blur, shadows dancing in the moonlight. She felt untethered, adrift in a sea of uncertainty. What had Victor meant by betrayal? And why did it feel like she was being pulled into a web of lies—woven by her own past life, tangled with the threads of Victor's family and the mafia that controlled everything?

Victor's voice broke through the stillness, low and strained, a ghost of pain lingering in each word. "Elysia, please," he said, his footsteps growing closer. "I need you to understand. What I did—what I allowed to happen—it wasn't my choice. I was forced into a corner. And when I found out who was responsible, who had orchestrated everything... I lost myself. I couldn't stop it."

She turned to face him then, her heart twisting in her chest. His eyes were darker than she had ever seen them, haunted by a memory that weighed far too heavily on his soul. He wasn't just asking for her forgiveness—he was asking for her trust.

"You never had a choice?" Her voice came out cold, more biting than she intended, but it was the only shield she had left. "Then what choice do I have, Victor? What am I supposed to do with all this? You say you love me, but how can I trust you? How can I believe you when everything about this world—about us—is built on lies?"

Victor stopped just a few feet away from her, his gaze locked onto hers with a fierce intensity. His jaw clenched as though holding back something more—something darker, something raw.

"I didn't lie to you," he said, his voice rising slightly, his control faltering. "I've never lied to you about what I feel. The rest of it? Everything that happened before... It's all a part of this damned world I live in, Elysia. A world that's destroyed everyone I've ever loved, including you. But I swear to you, I never stopped loving you. Even after everything. I never stopped searching for you."

Elysia swallowed hard, the taste of his words bitter and sharp in her mouth. "And what if I can't love you back?" she asked, her voice barely above a whisper. "What if I can't let go of the fact that you were the reason I died? What if that betrayal... it haunts me too much to move forward?"

The air between them crackled with tension. She had said the words aloud, the truth of her fears now hanging in the air, too heavy to ignore. His face twisted with a mix of frustration and sorrow. He reached out to her, but this time, she didn't pull away. She stood there, her breath shallow, waiting for him to speak—waiting for him to explain it all.

"I can't change the past," Victor said, his voice thick with regret. "But I can change the future, Elysia. I can make sure you never have to suffer again. I'll protect you. Always."

Her heart was a battlefield, torn between the desire to believe him and the gnawing fear that his world—the world that had consumed her once—would pull her back in and swallow her whole. She was no longer just Isabella. She was Elysia, and the woman she had been was dead. The woman she was now was scared—of Victor, of the truth, and of the darkness inside the world he controlled.

"I don't want to live in your shadows, Victor," she said, her voice trembling, but firm. "I can't be the woman you need me to be if it means sacrificing who I am. I can't do this again. Not after everything."

Victor's eyes darkened with something unreadable. His hand shot out, grabbing her wrist with a force that left no room for escape. "You think you have a choice?" he asked, his voice low, dangerous. "You think you can walk away from this? From me? From us?"

Elysia's heart raced in her chest as she pulled against his grip, but his hold tightened, not in anger, but in desperation. "You don't understand," he whispered fiercely. "You're already a part of me. You always have been."

Her pulse quickened, and for a moment, everything around them faded—the mansion, the night, the uncertainty. It was just the two of them, locked in this moment of truth and emotion, where the past collided with the present, and the future seemed to hang in the balance. She was Isabella, and yet, she wasn't. And the man before her, though he had changed, still carried the weight of a past they could never outrun.

She searched his face, looking for something—anything—that would tell her he wasn't lying. That this wasn't all some twisted game. But all she saw was the raw, broken man who had once loved her, a man who still craved her—still needed her.

And in that moment, a part of her wanted to believe him. Wanted to trust that the man he was now could be the man she needed him to be. But fear clung to her, suffocating and cold.

"Victor," she whispered, her voice trembling with the weight of everything she couldn't say. "I don't know if I can forgive you."

His grip loosened slightly, his thumb brushing across her wrist in a gesture that was almost tender. But the silence that followed was louder than any words they could have spoken. Elysia closed her eyes, feeling the pull of the past and the present, a dizzying force that threatened to tear her apart.

"I'll never give up on you," Victor vowed quietly, his voice rough with emotion. "But you have to decide, Elysia. Do you want me? Or do you want to walk away?"

Her heart pounded in her chest as she looked up at him, the uncertainty of the moment swirling around her like a storm. She had no answers, no solutions. Just the knowledge that whatever decision she made, it would change everything.

And she wasn't sure she was ready for that.

10

Unraveling the Past

Elysia's pulse hammered in her throat as she stood at the edge of the darkened alley, the night air thick with the scent of rain and exhaust fumes. The city around her buzzed with life, oblivious to the storm of emotions churning within her. She had to get away. The walls of Victor's world were closing in, their cold, suffocating presence pressing against her chest, making each breath feel like a battle.

Her hands shook as she tightened her grip on the worn leather bag slung over her shoulder, its contents light—too light for a journey of escape, but it didn't matter. She couldn't carry the weight of all that she had left behind. The blood-stained memories. The weight of Victor's gaze. The intensity of his obsession. She didn't need it.

Victor had promised to protect her, to keep her safe within the fortress of his mafia empire. But how could she feel safe when every step she took seemed to drag her deeper into his world—a world of power and violence she could never escape? He had already started to blur the lines between love and possession, between safety and captivity. Every kiss felt like a chain being fastened, every whispered vow a silken thread that wound tighter around her throat.

She had to leave.

But as Elysia moved, the heavy thud of boots against concrete echoed behind her. Her body froze, every nerve igniting as if she'd been struck by a jolt of electricity. She didn't need to turn to know who it was. The low, dangerous presence—Victor's scent, a mixture of expensive cologne and something darker—was unmistakable.

"Running again?" His voice was a low growl, the kind of sound that rumbled in the chest and vibrated through the air like a threat. She didn't answer. She couldn't.

Turning her back on him, she began walking faster, the sound of her boots slapping against the wet pavement mingling with the faint rhythm of her frantic heartbeat. She wasn't sure where she was going. Somewhere far from him. Somewhere far from all of it.

But Victor was faster, always faster. Within moments, he was beside her, his long strides easily matching her pace. His presence pressed in on her like the shadow of a thunderstorm, dark and foreboding.

"Don't do this, Elysia." His hand shot out to grab her wrist, and she flinched, her body tensing, every muscle screaming to break free. But his grip was firm, unyielding.

She yanked her wrist out of his grasp, spinning around to face him. "Don't you get it?" Her voice was sharp, her throat tight with emotion. "I'm not yours. I don't belong here. I can't live like this. I can't—"

Her words were cut off by the cold, calculating gleam in his eyes. He stepped closer, not out of aggression, but something worse—a possessive calm. It made her stomach twist, as though the air had grown thick with some invisible force she couldn't escape.

"You think you can run from me?" he asked softly, his voice like velvet, but laced with the unmistakable weight of authority. "You think you can run from us?" He gestured vaguely to the city behind him, to the empire that he controlled, the empire that was as much a part of him as the blood running through his veins. "There is no 'away' for you, Elysia."

His words sliced through the fragile bubble of resolve she had been clinging to. How could she run when the very city itself seemed to be woven into the fabric of her fate? The mafia had its fingers in every corner of this place, a dark, invisible web that would never let her go.

"You don't understand," she whispered, her voice raw with fear and something else—something she couldn't quite name. "I'm not who you think I am. I'm not Isabella."

Victor's eyes darkened, his jaw tightening as if her words were a physical blow. For a brief moment, the mask of control slipped, and she saw the vulnerability beneath—the raw, aching need that simmered just below the surface. But then it was gone, replaced by the cold, impenetrable steel that had defined him since the first moment they met.

"You think I don't know that?" he asked quietly. "But you are her, Elysia. I feel it in my bones. The way you move, the way you look at me, the way you—"

He stopped himself, clenching his fists at his sides. She could see the conflict in him, the battle between his love for the woman he had lost and the twisted, obsessive desire he had for her. It was suffocating, this unholy bond between them.

"I'm not her!" she cried, shaking her head, the tears she had been holding back threatening to spill over. "I don't remember anything about her. I'm not your dead wife, Victor. I don't want to be."

Victor's gaze softened for the briefest of moments, his hand reaching out as though to touch her face. But she stepped back, her chest heaving with desperation.

"You don't understand," she whispered again, her voice breaking. "I can't live in the shadow of a woman who's dead. I can't—"

But Victor's expression hardened once more, and in that instant, she realized something: He wasn't going to let her go.

With a swift motion, he reached for her, pulling her into his embrace with a force that left her breathless. His lips brushed against her temple, the touch almost gentle, as if he were trying to anchor her to him.

"I'm not asking you to be her," he murmured. "I'm asking you to be with me."

Elysia's heart pounded in her chest as she closed her eyes, her mind racing with a thousand thoughts—each one a war between the woman she was and the woman Victor saw in her. The past and the present blurred together, and she didn't know which was which anymore.

"I can't," she whispered, her voice trembling. "I can't do this."

But even as she said the words, she knew they were futile. The pull between them was too strong, the ties of fate too tangled. And no matter how far she ran, she knew she would always be tethered to him.

Victor didn't speak. He didn't need to. His silence said everything she already feared.

The mafia world wouldn't let her go. And neither would he.

Elysia couldn't sleep. The bed was too large, the silence too heavy. Every time she closed her eyes, the shadows of the past seemed to creep into her dreams, mingling with the present. She had tried to push them away—the memories of Isabella's life, her death—but they clung to her like a second skin, each fragment of a life she hadn't lived before filling her with an unease she couldn't explain.

She turned restlessly, the cool silk sheets sliding off her skin, leaving her exposed. The moonlight filtered in through the heavy curtains, casting pale slivers of light across the room. She stared at the ceiling, counting the cracks in the paint as if they could offer her some sort of comfort, some explanation for why her life had unraveled so suddenly.

In the distance, the soft hum of the city reached her ears. But the city no longer felt like home. No, it felt like a prison.

The sound of footsteps interrupted her thoughts, slow and deliberate. Her breath caught in her throat, and her heart quickened, as if it knew what was coming before her mind could catch up.

Victor.

He appeared in the doorway, his silhouette framed by the dim light. His presence filled the room, the air thickening with his intensity. There was no mistaking it: He was still watching her, still haunting her every move. The thought should have terrified her. But instead, it anchored her, like a force she couldn't break free from.

"You're awake," his voice was low, almost a murmur, yet it resonated in the quiet of the room, vibrating through her chest.

Elysia didn't answer immediately. She couldn't. The words she wanted to say—about needing space, about needing freedom—died in her throat.

Instead, she shifted on the bed, sitting up, wrapping her arms around herself in a futile attempt to ward off the chill creeping over her skin.

"Why are you still here?" she whispered, her voice thin, fragile. She wasn't sure if she was asking him or herself.

Victor stepped inside, his eyes never leaving her, his gaze dark and unreadable. He walked toward the bed with a quiet confidence, as if every step he took in this world was a claim to the space he inhabited. He was always in control, always so sure of everything, while she… she felt lost.

"I'm not going anywhere," he said softly, his tone steady but filled with something she couldn't quite place. "Not until you stop running from me."

She shuddered, the words burrowing deep into her chest, churning a mixture of fear and something else—something dangerous, something like longing.

"I'm not running," she replied, but the tremor in her voice betrayed her. She wasn't even sure if she believed herself. How could she be running when she was already tangled up in the very web she tried to escape?

Victor sat down beside her, too close. His presence was overwhelming, and yet there was something strangely comforting about it. She didn't know how to make sense of it—how could the same person who terrified her also be the one who seemed to hold the power to make her feel safe?

"You think I don't understand?" he asked, his voice softer now, almost gentle. "That you're afraid?" He paused, his hand hovering near hers, the slightest movement, like a question in itself. "Elysia, I'm not the enemy here."

She turned to him, her chest tight, her mind racing. She didn't know how to answer him. She wanted to scream, to lash out at him for trapping her in this world she never asked to be a part of. But the truth was, she was just as trapped in her own emotions, caught between the pull of her past life and the uncertainty of her present.

"I can't—" she began, but her words broke off as she met his gaze. For the briefest moment, she saw something in him that surprised her—something raw and vulnerable, a side of him she had never seen before.

"I know you're afraid of me," he continued, his voice now softer, almost pleading. "Of what I've done, of what I am. But you don't have to be afraid of me, Elysia. Not anymore."

She swallowed, the lump in her throat growing larger with each passing second. "I don't know who you are anymore, Victor." The words hung in the air between them, a chasm of doubt that neither of them could cross.

"I'm still the same man you met," he said, his voice thick with emotion. "The man who will protect you, even if it means breaking every rule I've set for myself. I would destroy anyone who tries to hurt you, Elysia."

She pulled her legs up to her chest, hugging her knees tightly, as if physically distancing herself from him would somehow make it easier to breathe.

"I don't want to be protected," she whispered. "I just want the truth. About Isabella. About my past."

Victor's jaw clenched, his eyes flashing with a mixture of anger and something else—regret, perhaps.

"The truth?" he echoed, his voice hardening. "The truth is that you're not just a reincarnation of Isabella. You're a part of me—whether you want to accept it or not."

The words hit her like a punch to the gut, and she recoiled, her pulse spiking. "I don't want to be part of you!" she shouted, the force of her voice surprising even herself.

Victor's expression softened, a flicker of sadness crossing his features before he quickly masked it. "Then what do you want, Elysia?" he asked, his voice barely above a whisper. "What do you want from me?"

Her chest tightened as the weight of his words settled over her. She didn't know what she wanted. What she wanted was to escape, to run far away from all of this—but every step she took felt like it led her straight back to him.

"I want to know who I am," she said, her voice trembling with the raw honesty of it. "And I want to know why my past life ended the way it did."

Victor didn't answer immediately. Instead, he reached out, his hand resting lightly on her arm, a gentle, unspoken plea for her to understand.

"I'll tell you everything," he said softly, his voice rough with emotion. "But you have to trust me first."

Elysia's breath caught in her throat as the weight of his words settled in. Trust him. Could she? Could she ever trust him again after everything that had happened?

The room seemed to grow colder, the walls pressing in around her. She felt as though she were caught in an inescapable whirlpool, torn between the desire to break free and the undeniable pull of a man who seemed to hold the very threads of her existence in his hands.

"I don't know if I can," she whispered, her voice barely audible.

Victor didn't respond, but the look in his eyes—intense, vulnerable, and filled with a silent promise—spoke volumes. He wouldn't give up. Not on her. Not on them.

And that, Elysia realized, was the most terrifying part of all.

The city outside was a blur of light and shadow as Elysia stared through the floor-to-ceiling windows of Victor's penthouse, watching the streets below. She felt distant, removed from everything—her own body, the world, even the man standing behind her. The feeling of being watched, of being caged, had never been more suffocating.

Victor's presence lingered like a shadow, and for a moment, she wished it would all fade away, that she could return to a life untouched by the mafia, untouched by this endless pull between past and present. But every time she closed her eyes, she saw Isabella's life—her death—and the question burned in her chest like a brand: Why had it happened?

Victor had promised to tell her everything. He'd said he would reveal the truth, but she knew better than to take him at face value. There was still so much he kept hidden, so much he wasn't willing to share. She could feel it—the quiet walls of his guilt, of his anger at himself, woven through his every word and movement.

"I'm leaving," she said suddenly, her voice steady but laced with a quiet defiance.

Victor's steps faltered behind her. "You're not leaving," he replied, his tone not commanding, but certain, almost final.

"I need to," she said, her hands trembling as they gripped the edge of the windowsill. "I can't keep doing this. I can't keep living in a world where I don't even know who I am anymore."

The words felt like an explosion inside her chest, ripping apart everything she'd thought she understood. She had tried, tried so desperately to hold onto a sense of herself, but how could she when every corner of her world was saturated with memories of a life that wasn't hers?

Victor's voice softened, and when he spoke again, there was a vulnerability to it that she hadn't expected. "You don't have to leave, Elysia. You're not alone in this."

She turned to face him, finally looking him in the eyes. The emotions swirling between them were like a storm, pulling her in every direction. There was anger—so much anger—but also pain, raw and untamed.

"I am alone in this," she replied, her voice breaking. "You have no idea what it's like to wake up and be told you're someone else's reincarnation. To carry the weight of their life on your shoulders, their death, their betrayal." She stepped forward, her chest tight with frustration, with confusion. "You think I can just accept this? That I can live in this world, trapped by it, knowing that nothing will ever be mine again?"

Victor's eyes darkened, and for a moment, she saw the flicker of the man he used to be—a man who had been consumed by guilt and rage, someone who had burned everything around him in a desperate attempt to keep control. But it wasn't that man she feared now. It was the new Victor—the one who made her believe, for a fleeting moment, that she could be more than a pawn in a game she never wanted to play.

"You don't have to accept it," he said, his voice dangerously soft. "You never have to accept anything you don't want. But you can't leave, Elysia. You don't know what they'll do if you do."

His words hit her like a physical blow. The threat was there, looming in the background, unspoken but clear. The mafia world had no place for escape, no room for those who tried to run from it. She had learned that quickly.

And yet, as her heart raced, as the weight of her choices pressed down on her, she couldn't help but feel a sense of resolve. Maybe leaving wasn't an option, but neither was staying—at least not in the way she had before.

"I don't care," she whispered, her voice stronger than she'd expected. "I'm not going to let you control me. I won't be your prisoner, Victor."

The silence that followed was thick and heavy, like the calm before a storm. Victor's eyes flickered with something unreadable, his expression hardening as if he had finally reached the breaking point.

"Don't make me choose for you," he warned, his voice low and dangerous, the air around them suddenly charged with tension.

Elysia squared her shoulders, taking a deep breath as she looked at him. She was done being afraid. She was done being caught between the past and present, done being the pawn in someone else's game.

"I'm not asking for your permission," she said, her voice firm now. "I'm making my own choice."

Victor's gaze darkened, the air crackling with the dangerous force of his emotions. For a moment, neither of them moved, as if the world itself had held its breath, waiting to see what would come next.

And then, without another word, he turned and left the room.

Elysia stared after him, the knot in her chest tightening. She wasn't sure what was worse—the fact that she had chosen to stay or the fact that she knew, deep down, that she had just sealed her own fate.

The door clicked shut behind him, leaving her standing alone in the silence. Her heart pounded in her ears, but this time, there was no fear—only a quiet determination. She would learn the truth, no matter the cost.

As she stood there, staring at the door, she knew one thing for sure: The game had changed. And now, it was her turn to play.

11

Escalating Danger

Elysia sat by the window, her gaze unfocused as the city lights flickered beneath her. The rain had started falling heavily just moments before, a slow rhythm that drummed against the glass, blurring the lines between reality and the fog inside her mind. Her reflection in the pane was distorted, the woman who stared back at her a shadow of someone she was struggling to recognize. Victor's mansion loomed around her, a gilded cage dressed in opulence, but all she could feel was the ever-tightening grip of entrapment.

Her thoughts were interrupted by the creak of the door. Victor entered, his presence as commanding as it was suffocating. His sharp, dark eyes fell on her immediately, the intensity in them unmistakable.

"You've been staring out that window for hours," he said, his voice low but carrying an undercurrent of something more dangerous. "What are you thinking about?"

Elysia hesitated, unsure of how to answer. There was a time when she could have told him the truth—back when they were strangers, when he was just a man whose name haunted her dreams. But now? Now, every word that passed between them felt like a delicate dance of deception.

She turned slowly, glancing over the room—its luxurious surroundings, the heavy silence that felt oppressive rather than peaceful. "I was thinking about how I ended up here," she said, her voice barely above a whisper. "About how everything in my life has changed."

Victor didn't move closer, but his presence seemed to fill every inch of the room, making the space feel smaller, more confined. He stood at a distance, studying her, as if weighing her every word. His lips parted, but before he could speak, a sharp, distant sound echoed through the corridors. A muffled noise, something akin to a slamming door.

His eyes narrowed. "Stay here," he ordered, his tone now colder, harder.

Elysia didn't argue, though her heart quickened with a sense of impending danger. The unease that had been festering for days now felt real, pressing against her chest like a heavy weight. It wasn't just the mafia world she feared—it was him. Victor. His protectiveness, while seemingly caring, often felt like a leash, tightening with every passing moment. She had no way of knowing what tomorrow would bring, but she knew one thing for certain: the walls of the world he controlled were closing in around her.

As Victor disappeared through the door, Elysia stood, her legs unsteady beneath her. She moved toward the door, her footsteps quiet, almost as if she were trying not to disturb the fragile balance of their relationship. The mansion was silent once more, save for the low hum of voices from down the hall. Her curiosity piqued, she edged toward the door, trying to listen for any clues.

But the moment her fingers brushed the cold handle, it was as if the air around her shifted—charged, palpable. A presence behind her. She froze.

"Don't," Victor's voice came, thick with warning. He had returned, his eyes burning with intensity. His gaze flicked to her hand on the door, then to her face, tracing the flicker of indecision that crossed her features.

"Why do you always do that?" she whispered, more to herself than to him. The question hung in the air, heavy with meaning. Why did he always prevent her from leaving? Why did he keep her tethered to this place, this life she couldn't escape?

His jaw clenched, and his fingers reached out, curling around her wrist. His touch was firm but not cruel, though there was something in it—something possessive that stirred unease in her gut. "Because you don't know what's out there," he said quietly, his voice laced with both authority and something softer, more urgent. "You don't know the danger you're in. Not yet. And you're not going to."

Her pulse quickened as he stepped closer, invading her space, his presence swallowing her whole. The scent of him—cedar and leather—was suffocating, overpowering. She could feel his breath on her skin, his warmth pressing against her as though he were trying to anchor her to him.

She jerked her wrist out of his grasp, but it was too late. The damage had already been done. The grip on her heart had tightened.

"I'm not afraid of you," she said, trying to steady her breath, to mask the vulnerability she could feel rising like a tidal wave.

Victor smiled—small, almost imperceptible—but there was something about it that unsettled her more than anything else. "You should be."

The door to the hallway swung open once again, and a figure appeared—tall, imposing, and wearing the same cold air of authority that Victor did. But unlike Victor, there was no warmth in this one's eyes.

"Victor," the man said, his voice smooth, calculating. "We have a problem."

Victor's attention shifted immediately, his eyes hardening as he assessed the newcomer. But it was the look on his face, the subtle flicker of concern that passed through his usually controlled demeanor, that caught Elysia's attention. This wasn't just business—it was something deeper, something that went beyond the normal tensions of the mafia world.

Victor turned toward her then, his gaze sharp. "Stay here. Don't go anywhere."

She watched him leave, the finality in his words settling in her chest. There it was again. The control. The assumption that she would stay behind, that she would wait, like a good little prisoner in his gilded cage.

But Elysia wasn't sure how much longer she could be the obedient little captive. A piece of her—no matter how small—longed to break free, to see the world beyond these walls, to find out what had happened to her, to her past. But the world Victor was trying to shield her from was closing in, faster and faster, and she wasn't sure if there was any escape at all.

The mansion was eerily quiet now. The muted sound of distant conversations echoed faintly from the hallway, but the living room where Elysia stood seemed almost deserted—abandoned in the silence that settled like a heavy blanket around her. She'd barely noticed how much time had passed since Victor had left. Her heart was still racing, her skin tingling with the memory of his touch, the possessiveness that seemed to seep through every word he spoke.

It was as if the walls themselves were closing in on her.

She couldn't stand still. Her feet seemed to move on their own, pacing back and forth in the plush carpet, her mind swirling in a fog of confusion. How had she become a part of this world? How had she let Victor pull her in so completely, so deeply, that escape felt like an impossibility?

The house had always felt like a gilded cage, but now, it felt like a tomb.

She reached for the glass of water on the table but stopped short when the sound of approaching footsteps reached her ears. She didn't need to turn to know who it was. His presence was unmistakable, suffocating, wrapping itself around her like an unspoken command.

Victor's footsteps stopped just behind her, and she could feel the weight of his stare. She didn't turn around. There was nothing he could say now that would erase the feeling in her chest—the fear, the helplessness, the growing dread that she had become a pawn in a game she could no longer control.

"Elysia," Victor's voice was low, but there was an unmistakable tension to it, a thread of something she couldn't quite place. He reached out to touch her shoulder, but she pulled away sharply, an instinctive reaction to the way he always made her feel like an object, something to be controlled rather than someone to be trusted.

"You didn't answer my question," he said, his voice softer now, though there was still an edge to it. "What were you thinking about?"

Elysia closed her eyes, her throat tight. "I was thinking about how dangerous this life is," she said, her voice trembling with a mix of fear and frustration. "How I don't belong here. I never wanted any of this."

Victor's hand tightened on her arm before she could pull away. His grip was gentle, but there was something unmistakably possessive in the way he held her. He was trying to pull her closer to him, trying to make her understand. Trying to trap her further.

"You're wrong," he said, his voice smooth, soothing even, as though he were speaking to a frightened animal. "You belong with me. You always have."

Elysia's chest tightened, her breath coming in shallow gasps. The way he said it—the certainty in his voice—struck a nerve. He'd said the same thing when they first met, when she thought it was just an obsession, a fleeting need to claim what he thought was his. But now, after everything they had been through, after everything she had learned, she couldn't help but wonder if he truly believed it. If he believed that he had a right to her—body, mind, and soul.

Her heart ached with the impossible weight of his words. "I don't belong to anyone, Victor," she whispered, her voice trembling as she pulled away from his touch. "Not even you."

Victor's face hardened at her words, the mask of control slipping just enough to reveal the storm underneath. His eyes flashed with something darker—something dangerous. The air between them thickened, charged with unspoken tension.

For a moment, Elysia thought he might lash out—might reach for her, drag her back into his arms, force her to see reason. But instead, he took a step back, his hands clenched at his sides, his breath slow and steady, as if he were trying to master the fury that flickered behind his eyes.

"You're not ready to understand," he said, his voice colder now. "But you will be."

Before Elysia could respond, there was a sudden, sharp knock at the door.

Victor's eyes flicked toward it, his jaw tightening. The moment passed in a heartbeat, but the unease in the air lingered. He turned back to Elysia, his expression momentarily softening.

"Stay here," he ordered, his voice clipped but still laced with that undeniable authority.

She watched him leave, her mind a swirling mess of confusion and defiance. How much longer could she endure this, this constant push and pull, this dance between desire and fear? The walls were closing in faster than she could breathe.

When the door closed behind Victor, Elysia exhaled a shaky breath, staring at the darkened hallway. The faintest sound of voices echoed from behind the door—Victor speaking to someone. She couldn't make out the words, but the tension in his voice was palpable, like a storm just waiting to break.

Instinctively, she moved to the window again, her eyes searching the rain-slicked streets below. But instead of the city lights she had once found so calming, all she saw was a world full of shadows, a world where danger lurked in every corner, and she wasn't sure where she fit.

The thought of leaving crossed her mind again, stronger this time. But as she stood there, torn between the desire for freedom and the fear of what would happen if she tried to run, her chest tightened. She couldn't leave. Not while she still had questions, not while her past—her previous life—remained a mystery she had yet to unravel.

Victor's world had become her prison, but it was the only world she knew now. And the more she tried to escape it, the more dangerous things became.

And she feared that one day, she might not have a choice.

The tension in the mansion thickened, coiling like a spring on the verge of snapping. Elysia paced the hallway, her mind refusing to settle, each step a beat in the frantic rhythm of her racing heart. The sound of Victor's voice, muffled through the walls, blended with the distant roar of a thunderstorm that seemed to reflect the turmoil inside her. She couldn't stay still any longer. The walls were suffocating, every corner of the mansion a reminder of the life she was trapped in.

Victor's words still echoed in her ears, reverberating like a chant, insistent, commanding. "You belong with me."

But that wasn't the truth, was it? She didn't belong here, not in this world of darkness and bloodshed. She didn't belong to him.

Elysia's eyes flicked to the door. She had told herself over and over that she would leave, that she would run from the dangerous pull of the mafia's grasp, but every time she tried, something pulled her back—Victor, his world, his promises. The promises that felt more like chains than freedom.

Her fingers curled into fists as she stared out of the large windows, the rain hammering against the glass. The view was blurred, indistinct—much like her future now. Her feet carried her toward the door, her hand already on the doorknob when a voice froze her in place.

"Where do you think you're going?"

Victor's voice, low and dark, sent a shiver down her spine. It was a command, wrapped in the calm of someone who knew exactly how to control her. He stood at the top of the stairs, his silhouette framed by the dim, flickering light of the chandelier.

Elysia's breath hitched as she turned to face him. His gaze was piercing, his stance unyielding, and the tension in the air between them crackled like static. "I'm going out," she said, her voice sounding too weak even to her own ears. She fought to steady her nerves, but the reality of his presence, his unrelenting control, threatened to undo her. "I need to get some air."

Victor took a step down toward her, his eyes never leaving hers. His footsteps were silent, but his presence filled the room, overwhelming her. "You think you can just leave?" His voice dropped to a whisper, but the threat in it was clear, like a blade being sharpened.

"I'm not asking for permission," she snapped, frustration bursting through her carefully controlled exterior. "I need space. I can't breathe in this damn house anymore."

Victor's jaw tightened at her words, the tension in his body coiling tighter. "You don't get to walk out that door, Elysia. Not when I've already told you how dangerous it is out there."

Her heart thundered in her chest, and for a brief moment, she considered stepping forward and confronting him—truly confronting him. "And what if I don't care?" she retorted, her voice trembling with the rawness of her emotions. "What if I don't care about the danger, about the mafia, or about you? What if I'm just done?"

There was a long, heavy pause, and Elysia felt the weight of his gaze pinning her in place. His eyes were stormy, a mix of fury and something darker, something unreadable that seemed to twist inside him.

"You're not done with me," he said, his tone low and controlled, but his grip on the railing tightening. "You're mine, Elysia. And I'll make sure you never forget that."

A pulse of fear swept through her, a cold rush that hit her like a bucket of ice water. But there was something else, something buried deeper within the pit of her stomach—anger. A rage she hadn't allowed herself to acknowledge until now.

"I'm not anyone's possession, Victor." Her words felt like they were tearing through her chest as she forced herself to speak, her voice low but steady. "I didn't ask for this. I didn't ask to be here, to be tied to you. But I'm not your pawn."

His gaze darkened, his expression shifting from anger to something far more dangerous, more intense. "You think you can walk away from me? You think you can just throw this all away?" His steps were deliberate now, closing the space between them in a way that made her heart stutter. "I've been protecting you, trying to keep you safe, because I promised I would. But I won't let you destroy this, destroy us."

Elysia recoiled slightly, her breath shallow. She didn't know if it was the suffocating weight of his words or the pressure building in her chest, but she could feel the walls around her beginning to crumble. His possessiveness, his control—it was smothering her, and yet, she couldn't bring herself to completely push him away.

She was trapped.

"Why?" she whispered, the question slipping from her lips before she could stop it. "Why can't you just let me go? Why can't you let me breathe?"

Victor's eyes softened just slightly, the intensity in them faltering for a heartbeat. But before she could allow herself to believe that perhaps he truly understood, he stepped closer, his presence swallowing her whole.

"Because I can't live without you," he said, his voice a soft rasp against her ear, his breath warm on her skin. "You're the only thing that matters to me, Elysia."

The words felt like a double-edged sword, cutting through her defenses and leaving her raw and exposed. She wanted to fight, to reject him, but there was a part of her—one she couldn't ignore—that ached to believe him. To let herself believe in the love he claimed to feel.

But she couldn't. Not like this.

"I don't know who I am anymore," she said, her voice barely above a whisper.

"I don't know what I'm supposed to feel. But I can't live in your world, Victor. I can't live like this."

For a moment, Victor's expression faltered, the hardened exterior cracking, showing a flash of something that resembled vulnerability. But it was gone in an instant, replaced by that familiar, impenetrable mask.

"You're not leaving," he said, the finality in his tone making it clear that no matter what she said, no matter what she wanted, she wouldn't be allowed to walk away.

Elysia stood frozen, her heart torn between the desire for freedom and the crushing reality of the situation. The storm outside raged on, and inside, the storm in her heart was far more dangerous.

She wasn't just caught in his world. She was drowning in it.

12

A Family Divided

The air in Victor's study felt thick, a storm cloud hanging above the heavy mahogany desk. Elysia sat in the plush chair, her fingers lightly tracing the rim of her glass, the whiskey inside catching the soft light from the chandelier. But she wasn't drinking it. Her mind, a battlefield of emotions, was far from the amber liquid.

Victor's presence filled the room like a dark shadow. His broad shoulders were tense, his jaw set in that unforgiving line that usually signaled a storm was coming. She had seen that look before. It was the face of a man on the edge. And he didn't even notice how the weight of his own world was crumbling around him, piece by piece. How could he, when his eyes were always on the horizon, chasing a power that now seemed as fragile as glass?

The door opened with a soft creak. Antonio, Victor's most trusted lieutenant, stepped in, his expression unreadable. He had been one of the few men Elysia trusted implicitly in this dark underworld. But trust, like everything else in Victor's world, was fragile.

"Boss," Antonio's voice was steady, but there was a flicker in his eyes that betrayed the storm that was about to break. Elysia's heart stuttered. Something was off.

Victor didn't look up from the papers scattered across his desk. His hand brushed them aside with a flick of impatience, his mind lost in the labyrinth of plans he was always weaving. "What is it, Antonio?"

Antonio's gaze flickered toward Elysia before he turned back to Victor. "It's about Luca... he's been in contact with the Verrini family. I—"

The words stopped abruptly, and Elysia's breath caught in her chest. She met Antonio's eyes, searching for a trace of a lie, a flicker of hesitation. But there was nothing. Only cold, hard truth. Her chest tightened, the space around her growing suffocating.

Victor's eyes, those dark, stormy eyes, finally lifted to meet Antonio's. His voice was low, but the anger behind it was unmistakable. "You're sure?"

"Yes, boss," Antonio replied, his voice unwavering. "We've intercepted messages. It's all here." He placed a thick envelope on the desk, the seal of the Verrini family staring up at them like a challenge.

Elysia could feel the tension crackle in the air. A betrayal of this magnitude would tear apart everything Victor had built. Everything she had reluctantly become a part of.

Victor's gaze hardened as he picked up the envelope. The harsh lines of his face softened for a brief moment, but the flicker of vulnerability in his eyes was gone as quickly as it had appeared. He ripped the envelope open, his fingers moving with mechanical precision. The silence that followed was unbearable.

"Luca..." Victor muttered under his breath, his voice tinged with disbelief, like he was trying to come to terms with the reality of it. He stood up abruptly, his chair scraping harshly against the floor. "What do you mean, he's working with the Verrini?" His voice rose now, raw and unforgiving.

Antonio stood his ground. "It's been going on for months. The Verrinis have promised him control of the western territories in exchange for his loyalty."

Elysia could see it now—the cold fury in Victor's eyes, the storm that had been building for weeks finally crashing over them. She should have been afraid, but instead, there was a hollow pit in her stomach, as though everything she had feared about the mafia world was suddenly coming true.

Victor's hand clenched into a fist, his knuckles white. He didn't speak for a moment, his gaze fixed on the papers in front of him. The silence was suffocating, and Elysia's heart pounded in her chest.

"I trusted him," Victor's voice was low, dangerous. "He was loyal."

Antonio's gaze dropped. "I'm sorry, boss. I didn't know who else to turn to."

The weight of the betrayal hung in the air, thick and suffocating. Elysia wanted to scream, to demand answers from Victor, but she remained silent. Her own fears gnawed at her, making her question everything she had come to believe about loyalty, trust, and the man who had so easily swept her into his dark world.

Victor's expression shifted, his eyes hardening as he turned to Antonio. "We handle this now. No more waiting. Get me Luca." His voice was ice-cold, every word laced with a deadly finality.

Antonio hesitated for a heartbeat, then nodded. He knew better than to question Victor when he was like this. "Of course, boss. It will be done."

The door shut behind Antonio with a soft click, and for a moment, the room was silent. Elysia's breath was shallow, her mind racing. She had always known that Victor's world was dangerous, that betrayal was an inevitability in a life governed by power and fear. But the reality of it was still a punch to the gut.

Victor's back was to her now, his hands pressed against the desk, his head bowed slightly as he processed the betrayal. His shoulders were tense, the muscles of his back shifting beneath his tailored suit. He was a man of power, a man who commanded the room with his mere presence. But in this moment, Elysia saw the cracks. The vulnerability in him, the weariness that came with being a man constantly on guard. A man who had lost so much.

Her pulse quickened, the need to speak overwhelming her. "Victor…"

His head snapped up at her voice, his expression unreadable. "What is it, Elysia?"

She wanted to ask him so many things. To demand answers for all the questions swirling in her mind, for the pieces of the puzzle that didn't quite fit. But what could she say? What was there left to say when the foundation beneath her feet had crumbled away?

Instead, she said the only thing that mattered. "What happens now?"

Victor's gaze softened for a moment, his lips parting slightly as if to say something—but he didn't. Instead, he straightened, his eyes hardening again with resolve. "We end this."

Elysia's heart raced. There was no turning back now.

The mansion's sprawling gardens lay quiet in the late afternoon, a stark contrast to the storm raging within the walls of Victor's fortress. Elysia stood at the edge of the terrace, her hands gripping the railing, the cool breeze brushing against her skin. The world outside felt distant—almost unreachable—compared to the chaos unfolding inside. The sun was dipping low, casting long shadows over the perfectly manicured lawns, but her mind was far from peaceful.

Victor's betrayal had shaken her to her core. She had always known that this world was dangerous, that loyalty and trust were fleeting, but the reality of it was a wound deeper than she'd anticipated. Her breath came in shallow gasps as she stared at the horizon, her thoughts tangled in a web of confusion, fear, and hurt.

Her body tensed as the door behind her creaked open, and Victor's presence filled the air like an electric charge. She didn't turn around immediately. Instead, she allowed the silence to stretch between them, feeling the weight of everything unsaid.

"You're avoiding me," Victor's voice was low, his tone tight with frustration. It was the kind of voice that commanded attention, but it held something more now—a trace of guilt, perhaps, though it was buried under layers of anger and control.

Elysia finally turned to face him, her expression unreadable. Her heart hammered in her chest, but she didn't let him see the vulnerability that had been gnawing at her for days. "Am I?" she asked, her voice calm, though the storm inside her continued to churn.

Victor took a step forward, his dark eyes never leaving hers. His usual confidence, the man who controlled entire empires with a word, now seemed slightly... off-balance. "You're pulling away," he said, his words almost a plea, though it was disguised in that same commanding tone.

"Why wouldn't I?" Elysia replied, her voice trembling only slightly. She hadn't planned to say those words—hadn't planned to expose the raw edge of her emotions—but the pain inside her demanded it. "You just told me that one of your most trusted lieutenants is working with the Verrinis. You're telling me that I've been living in a house of lies, where everyone around me is playing a game I don't understand. So why wouldn't I want to pull away?"

Victor flinched, a small crack in his otherwise impenetrable façade. But the moment was fleeting. "I didn't want you to be a part of this world," he said, stepping closer. "I didn't want you to see how ugly it truly is."

Elysia's heart thudded in her chest. The rawness of his words shook her more than she cared to admit. It wasn't the first time he'd tried to shield her from the truth, but this felt different—he wasn't just trying to protect her anymore. He was trying to keep her trapped in a cage of lies, hoping she wouldn't see the blood-stained bars.

"And yet you brought me into it," she replied, her voice growing sharper with every word. "You made me part of this world. You made me think I could trust you." Her hands balled into fists at her sides, nails biting into her palms as if she could somehow hold onto control by doing so. "How am I supposed to believe anything you say now, Victor?"

Victor's gaze darkened, and for a moment, Elysia saw something more in him—something that was at once dangerous and vulnerable. "You think I wanted this? You think I wanted to hurt you? This... this world, this empire... it's not something I chose. It's something that was thrust upon me, and I've done what I could to protect you. To protect us."

He reached out as if to touch her, but Elysia stepped back, the distance between them palpable. The space between them was no longer just physical; it was emotional, a chasm that was slowly widening with every word.

"You don't get to decide what's best for me," Elysia said, her voice a mixture of anger and fear. "You don't get to keep me in the dark and then expect me to just forgive you for it. I can't keep pretending that everything's fine when it's not."

Victor's jaw tightened, his hands curling into fists at his sides. For a moment, he seemed to lose his composure, his usual calculated demeanor slipping. "I didn't want you to be a part of this, Elysia," he repeated, but this time there was something more desperate in his voice. "I didn't want you to get caught up in all of this madness."

"Then why bring me into it?" Elysia demanded. "Why choose me if you wanted to protect me from it?"

The words hit like a slap, and Victor flinched as if she'd struck him physically. His voice dropped, becoming colder, more deliberate. "Because you're the one thing I can't let go of," he said, each word heavy with an unspoken truth. "You're the only thing I've ever wanted, the only thing that could have made all of this—" he gestured around him, indicating the life he had built— "worth something. But it's too late now. There's no turning back."

Elysia stood frozen, her mind struggling to grasp the weight of his confession. The truth of it shattered her more than she wanted to admit. She had always known that Victor was obsessed with her, but hearing him admit it so plainly—he wasn't just obsessed. He was consumed.

The silence between them stretched on, thick and suffocating, until Elysia finally broke it. "You're right," she said softly, her voice breaking slightly under the weight of the words. "There's no turning back." She looked at him, her eyes filled with a mixture of sadness and determination. "But that doesn't mean I have to stay."

Victor's expression faltered, the walls he had built so carefully around his emotions cracking for a fleeting moment. "Elysia…" His voice was almost pleading, a quiet desperation seeping through the cracks of his usually unyielding composure.

But Elysia had already turned away, her heart pounding in her chest, as she walked back toward the door of the terrace, the finality of her decision settling over her like a heavy cloak. There was no escaping Victor's world, not truly—not without consequences. But she couldn't keep living a lie. Not anymore.

And as she closed the door behind her, she knew that the storm had only just begun.

Victor's mansion felt colder than ever as Elysia walked through the marble halls, her footsteps echoing with every step. She hadn't expected the confrontation to be easy—nothing in Victor's world ever was—but the weight of it all was heavier than she had imagined. The guilt and confusion swirling inside her made her feel like a puppet, strings pulled in every direction by forces beyond her control.

Her mind replayed the argument on the terrace, Victor's words lingering in her ears: "You're the only thing I've ever wanted."

She didn't know if she should be angry or terrified by the raw emotion in his voice. The intensity of it was suffocating, and it unsettled her more than she cared to admit. He had always been a man of control, a mastermind behind every move, yet here she was, watching him unravel before her eyes. It was that vulnerability—his inability to hide the truth of his feelings—that made her question everything.

Elysia reached the doorway of the room she had been assigned in the mansion, the heavy oak door looming before her like an unyielding wall. She didn't even hesitate before she pushed it open and entered, seeking solace in the quiet isolation of the room. The plush velvet curtains were drawn, casting the room in a soft, dim light. The scent of roses—Victor's favorite flower—lingered in the air, but even that felt suffocating now.

She moved to the center of the room, her breath coming in shallow gasps as her mind raced. There was no escaping this life, no matter how far she tried to run. The mafia's grasp on her was too tight, and even if she walked away, Victor wouldn't let her go.

A soft knock on the door broke through her thoughts, and before she could respond, it creaked open. Victor stepped into the room, his presence filling the space like a storm on the horizon. His dark eyes met hers with a mixture of determination and something else—something more vulnerable.

"I know you're angry," he began, his voice quieter than before, but there was no mistaking the intensity of his words. "But you need to understand something. The Verrinis, they want to take everything from us. They want to take you. I won't let that happen."

Elysia turned away, her heart twisting at the words. "You don't get to control me, Victor," she said softly, but the sharpness in her voice betrayed the hurt beneath. "I've lived my entire life under someone else's thumb, first my father, then you. I can't do it anymore. I need space. I need freedom."

Victor's expression darkened, and he closed the door behind him with a quiet click, the soft sound echoing in the tense silence. He took a step forward, his gaze unwavering. "You think you can leave this behind? Leave me behind?" His voice was low, and the intensity of it made her stomach flip.

"I'm not leaving you behind," she replied, her voice faltering. "But I need to find myself. I need to understand what I'm doing here, what we are, before I can even begin to know what I want."

Victor didn't speak immediately, but the words hung in the air between them like a fragile thread waiting to snap. His gaze softened, though his jaw was clenched tight. "Elysia…" he said her name as if it was a prayer, a plea, his voice filled with something raw. "You're everything to me. I don't know how to let you go. I don't know how to fix this."

Her chest tightened at the vulnerability in his voice, the depth of his emotions, and for a fleeting moment, she saw the man beneath the mafia boss—the man who had lost so much, who was terrified of losing her too. But the truth was, she wasn't sure she could keep living in this world, this dangerous, suffocating world that had swallowed her up without her consent.

"I don't know if I can be everything you want me to be," she whispered, her voice cracking. "I don't know if I can be the person you think I am. I didn't choose this life, Victor. I didn't choose any of this."

Victor took another step toward her, his eyes softening as he reached out, his hand brushing against her cheek. His touch was gentle, almost hesitant, as if he was unsure of how she would react. "I don't want you to be anyone other than who you are," he murmured. "I just need you. I don't care about anything else."

The words echoed in her mind, and for the briefest of moments, the chaos of the world around them seemed to fade. She closed her eyes at the warmth of his touch, the truth of his words sinking in. But the warmth wasn't enough to erase the fear that clung to her—fear that she might lose herself in his obsession, in this world he had built around them.

The silence stretched on between them, thick and heavy, until she finally opened her eyes and took a small step back. "I need to think," she said softly. "I can't make decisions like this when everything is so tangled."

Victor's eyes flickered with something unreadable, but he didn't push her. He didn't move to stop her, and for a moment, Elysia thought he might understand. But then, his voice dropped to a whisper, a command disguised as a plea. "Please, don't walk away from me. Not now."

Elysia hesitated, feeling the pull of his words, the gravity of his presence. But in the pit of her stomach, a deeper truth began to stir. She could not live her life in the shadow of Victor's obsession. Not again. Not like before.

"I'm not walking away from you," she said, her voice firm, though it wavered with the uncertainty still clawing at her heart. "I'm just trying to find my own way. Please, give me that."

Victor looked at her for a long moment, the weight of everything between them settling over them like a suffocating fog. His eyes were unreadable, but something in his posture softened—just slightly.

"I'll wait," he said, his voice barely above a whisper. "But I need you to know, Elysia… I'll never let you go. Not now. Not ever."

Elysia stood frozen, the air between them thick with unsaid words, with promises and fears. And as Victor turned and left the room, she knew that nothing could ever be the same again.

Not now. Not ever.

13

Secrets Unveiled

Elysia stood at the edge of the terrace, her breath fogging in the cool evening air. The mansion loomed behind her, a fortress of secrets, its grand façade casting long shadows in the dimming light. The city below sparkled like a blanket of stars, but it felt distant, cold. Her pulse quickened, as if the entire world had sharpened into focus—the things she'd been denying, the truth she'd been running from, all coiling around her like an inescapable web. Victor's world was closing in, and there was nowhere left to hide.

From the moment her memories had returned, fragments of a life she didn't fully understand, the puzzle had been incomplete. She knew she had loved Victor once, in a life that felt more like a dream than reality. But now, every moment with him felt like she was drowning in a storm of unanswered questions and buried emotions. And still, she couldn't let go. She couldn't stop caring. It was maddening.

The wind whispered around her, as though urging her to leave, to break free from everything that bound her to this life—a life that had been forced upon her by the very man who claimed to love her.

But then there was the whisper, the voice that had begun to pierce the walls of her confusion: You were chosen for a reason. It's not fate. It's power. The words echoed from the letter she had found, hidden deep within Victor's library, a letter written by someone she didn't recognize, but whose words seemed to sear her soul.

She couldn't ignore it.

But she couldn't face him either. Not yet. Not with the guilt and the betrayal gnawing at her from every direction.

Victor had tried to explain the things she didn't understand—the visions, the feelings that stirred between them when their gazes met—but each explanation only left her feeling more lost. She had asked him about Isabella, had pressed him for answers, but all he had given her were vague reassurances and promises of protection. No real truths.

Was she just a replacement? A shadow of a woman who had died long ago, or was there something more? A strange, insistent fear began to settle in her chest.

The door behind her creaked open, and she didn't need to turn around to know who it was. The way the air shifted, the weight of his presence—Victor.

"You're still out here," he said, his voice low and rich, almost a whisper in the night. He came to stand beside her, not too close, but close enough that she could feel the heat radiating off him.

She swallowed hard, forcing herself to look at the city. "I needed some space."

Victor's gaze, sharp and calculating, flicked to the horizon before returning to her. "You've been asking questions. I know you have. And you don't like the answers you're finding."

Her heart twisted at his words, the truth of it cutting through her like a blade. "I'm not sure I want to know anymore." Her voice was tight, like a rope pulling her deeper into the pit of uncertainty.

Victor's jaw clenched, the muscles flexing in a way she had come to recognize as his sign of control slipping. He reached for her, gently but with that commanding force she couldn't escape, his fingers brushing against her wrist. "Elysia, you have to trust me. What you've learned is dangerous. It's too much for you to understand right now."

Elysia yanked her arm away, spinning to face him. "I don't need you to protect me. I need you to be honest with me." Her voice cracked with frustration, the raw emotion she'd been holding back threatening to break free. "I found a letter, Victor. A letter that says I was chosen. Not by fate, but for something else. You owe me the truth."

For a moment, Victor's face flickered with something unreadable—something darker than she had ever seen. His eyes, usually so focused, seemed distant, as if he was fighting something within himself. "That letter—"

"I know it's real." Her voice trembled, but she pressed on. "I know it was written by someone who knew what happened to me—what happened to Isabella. You've kept the truth from me, and I don't understand why."

Victor's expression hardened, a mask settling over his features as he took a slow step back. "You think you know what's going on, Elysia? You think this is some kind of game, some dark mystery to solve? You have no idea what it's like to live with the weight of the past I carry. Do you understand that?"

His words were sharp, slicing through the space between them. But even as the coldness of his anger wrapped around them like a shroud, Elysia felt the tiniest flicker of vulnerability behind his eyes, a crack in the wall he had so carefully constructed.

"I understand more than you think," she whispered, the words barely escaping her lips. The truth she'd been hiding for so long felt closer now, her heart racing with the desire to break free from the cage Victor had built around her. The moment stretched between them like a taut wire, ready to snap.

Victor's gaze flickered down, and for the first time in days, his voice softened. "Elysia, what we have… it's not just about you and me. It's about everything. The family, the power, the choices we've both made. There's more to your past than you realize. And there's a reason you came back. A reason that has nothing to do with fate, and everything to do with who you were—and who you are now."

His words sent a chill down her spine, and a flash of the letter she had found rushed through her mind. The cryptic message that had set everything into motion. But before she could say anything more, a sudden noise broke the fragile silence—a soft but unmistakable sound from behind them.

Elysia's heart stuttered in her chest as she turned, her instincts screaming. There, standing at the entrance to the terrace, was Dante Vero, his face impassive, his dark eyes watching them like a hawk. "I think we need to talk, Victor. There's something you need to know."

Victor's face tightened, and his hand instinctively moved to the gun at his hip. "Not now, Dante."

But Dante didn't flinch, didn't look away. "No. Now."

The tension in the air was palpable, thick with unspoken threats and promises. And as Elysia stood there, caught between two men—one who had claimed her heart, and one who was always lurking in the shadows—she felt the ground shifting beneath her. The world she thought she knew was crumbling, and there was no way out.

Not anymore.

The mansion felt colder now, as if the walls themselves had turned their backs on her. Elysia could hear the faint thud of her own heartbeat in her ears as she walked down the long corridor, her footsteps echoing against the polished marble floors. Each step felt like a decision she couldn't take back, each breath heavier than the last.

Victor's words still hung in the air like smoke, lingering in her mind long after he had left her on the terrace. *There's a reason you came back.* His words circled around her like a trap, and she couldn't escape them.

The door to Victor's study loomed ahead, the dark wood gleaming in the dim light. It was the one place in the mansion where she had always felt the weight of the secrets that Victor kept buried. Every inch of that room reeked of power and control, the kind of control that left no room for weakness. She had spent countless hours within these walls, always trying to decipher the enigma that was Victor. But tonight—tonight, the questions she had been too afraid to ask were finally demanding answers.

Elysia hesitated before pushing the door open, the quiet creak of the hinges breaking the stillness. Inside, the room was dim, only the faint glow of the desk lamp illuminating the stacks of paperwork and books that filled the shelves. Victor was seated behind the large mahogany desk, his posture rigid, his gaze fixed on a folder in front of him.

As she entered, Victor looked up, his expression unreadable. "What is it?"

he asked, his voice low, controlled. He had that air about him now—the kind that made her feel like a trespasser in his world, like a mere fragment of something much larger than herself.

"I need to know the truth, Victor." Her voice was steady, but the rawness beneath it cracked the surface of her composed exterior. "I need to know everything."

Victor leaned back in his chair, studying her for a long moment, his fingers tapping rhythmically on the desk. "You're asking questions you're not ready for."

Elysia's heart pounded, but she couldn't stop now. "I found a letter," she said, her voice barely above a whisper. "It spoke of a betrayal. My past life—it's not what you told me."

Victor's eyes narrowed, the tension in his jaw tightening. "What letter?"

"The one I found in the library." She stepped forward, her hands trembling slightly. "It said I was chosen. Chosen for a reason. Not by fate, but for something darker." The words felt like poison on her tongue, but she forced them out, her chest tight with the weight of what she had uncovered. "What does that mean, Victor? What are you hiding from me?"

For a brief moment, his gaze flickered with something—something she couldn't place. Then, like a mask slipping into place, his expression hardened. "You've gone too far, Elysia." His voice was calm, but there was an edge to it now, sharp enough to cut.

"No. I haven't gone far enough," she countered, her voice rising with an edge of desperation. "Tell me what happened to Isabella. Tell me why I'm here."

Victor rose from his desk, his movements deliberate and measured, like a predator circling its prey. He came around to the front of the desk, his eyes locking with hers. "I told you before—there are things you're not meant to know. Things that will change everything. If you want the truth, you'll have to accept the consequences."

Elysia felt the walls around her start to close in. This wasn't just about her past, her memories, her feelings for him—it was about something much bigger. The stakes were higher than she had ever realized, and now, with each passing second, the tension between them grew thicker.

"I deserve to know the truth," she insisted, her voice trembling with a mixture of fear and anger. "I was part of this. My past is tied to this family. I deserve to know why."

Victor's eyes softened, just for a moment, but the flicker of emotion was gone as quickly as it had appeared. He stepped closer, and she could feel the heat of his body against her own, his presence suffocating. "You think you're ready, but you're not. What you don't understand is that everything I've done, everything I've built, has been for you. You were the one who chose to come back. You're the one who opened that door. And now, you have to face what's on the other side."

Elysia shook her head, the words gnawing at her. You were the one who chose to come back. It was a revelation that twisted something deep inside her. She hadn't chosen this. She hadn't chosen him. She hadn't chosen any of this.

She stepped back, away from him, her mind spinning. "I don't know what to believe anymore." Her voice was shaky, but she refused to let the tears she felt rising in her throat escape. Not now. Not when she was so close to the truth. "You want me to trust you, Victor. But how can I when you've lied to me? When you've kept everything hidden?"

Victor's face hardened again, the soft vulnerability replaced by that familiar mask of control. "You think I'm lying to you? Everything I've done, every decision I've made, has been to protect you, to keep you safe. And yet, you doubt me."

"I don't trust you anymore," she whispered, the words slicing through the air between them. "You've turned my life into a prison. A cage I can't escape from."

The silence that followed was heavy, oppressive. Victor didn't speak, but the look in his eyes—the cold, unyielding gaze—told her everything she needed to know.

She had lost him.

And with that loss, something inside her broke. The web she had been caught in, spun by lies and half-truths, was unraveling, and she had no idea how to stop it.

With a final glance, she turned and left the room, the door closing behind her with a soft click that echoed in her mind. The darkness of the corridor seemed to swallow her whole, the weight of her decision pressing down on her chest. The truth was closer now than it had ever been, but it was not the salvation she had hoped for.

It was a trap. And she had walked right into it.

The mansion felt like a labyrinth now—each turn, each room, a place of shadows and echoes of the truth she was only beginning to understand. Elysia moved through the halls in a daze, her thoughts a jumble of anger, confusion, and disbelief. The mask that Victor wore, the perfect control he exuded, had cracked—only to reveal something darker and more complicated beneath. And she was caught right in the middle of it all.

Her hand brushed against the cold stone of the staircase as she descended, but she wasn't heading to her room. No, not anymore. The reality of what Victor had said—the implications of it—pressed against her chest like a weight she couldn't lift. He hadn't told her the truth. He had told her only what he thought she could handle, and even that was a lie. The feeling of being trapped—the feeling that she had always been a pawn in a game she didn't understand—was suffocating her.

But where could she go?

The question echoed in her mind as she reached the lower level, her feet carrying her aimlessly toward the back door. She couldn't leave the mansion—not yet, not when she didn't know the full extent of the dangers surrounding her. But she needed air. She needed space to think. And there was one person she needed to see.

Dante.

He had always been a silent observer, lurking in the background, but now, Elysia felt a sense of urgency to confront him. If anyone knew the secrets Victor wasn't telling her, it was Dante. And she had to know everything.

She made her way outside, the cool night air hitting her face with a sharpness that made her pause. The garden was still, the only sound the rustling of leaves in the breeze. The mansion loomed behind her, a dark monolith, but it no longer felt like home. Home had always been where the truth was, where love and trust intertwined. But now... the truth was a foreign thing, slipping through her fingers, just out of reach.

Elysia turned toward the shadows by the far end of the garden, where she had seen Dante disappear earlier that evening. His tall form emerged from the darkness like a ghost, his black suit blending into the night. His eyes—cold, calculating—met hers, and for a brief moment, she felt the weight of everything he knew pressing down on her.

"You're looking for answers," Dante said, his voice low, a trace of something almost sympathetic in his tone. "But you might not like the ones you find."

Elysia took a step forward, her heart pounding in her chest. "I need to know, Dante. I need to know what's going on. What happened to Isabella? What's Victor hiding from me?"

Dante's lips curled into a faint smile, but it didn't reach his eyes. "Victor isn't the only one with secrets," he replied cryptically. "You're asking the right questions, Elysia, but the answers you're looking for aren't so simple."

The air between them thickened, and Elysia felt an unsettling sense of dread creeping up her spine. There was something in the way Dante spoke, the hidden meaning beneath his words. He knew far more than he was letting on.

"Tell me what I need to know," she demanded, her voice growing more urgent. "I can't keep living in the dark. I can't keep trusting Victor when I don't know what's real anymore."

Dante tilted his head slightly, studying her. "You're right about one thing," he said, his tone cold and almost amused. "Victor has a way of keeping the truth buried. But not everything is as he makes it seem. Not all of us are loyal to him. Not everyone who appears to be on his side is truly… with him."

Elysia's pulse quickened. "What are you saying?"

Dante's smile deepened, though it lacked any warmth. "Victor's obsession with you—it goes beyond mere love or fate, Elysia. There's something much darker beneath it all. He's not the only one who's been playing games. You've been a pawn in a much bigger scheme."

Her breath hitched. "What do you mean?"

Before Dante could respond, there was a soft noise from behind her. A figure stepped into the garden from the shadows, and Elysia's heart skipped a beat when she saw who it was.

Victor.

His presence was like a storm breaking the silence, his eyes flashing with anger as they locked onto Dante. The tension in the air was thick enough to cut through, and Elysia could feel it—the volatile energy that was building between them, the storm that had been brewing ever since she stepped into this world.

"Dante," Victor's voice was a low growl, laced with warning. "What are you doing here?"

Dante, unbothered, turned his gaze toward Victor. "Just making sure she gets the answers she needs. Unlike you, I'm not in the business of lying to her."

Victor's jaw clenched. "Stay away from her."

Elysia's mind was reeling. The truth was slipping through her fingers, and now, more than ever, she felt like a puppet caught in the strings of two men—one who had manipulated her into this life, and the other who seemed to know far too much about everything that had happened. She didn't know who to trust. And the more she learned, the less she felt like she knew.

"I'm done, Victor," she said, her voice shaking with a mix of fear and defiance. "I can't keep living in this world of lies. I need the truth—the real truth. Or

I'm walking away."

Victor's expression faltered for just a moment, a flicker of something like regret crossing his face, before it hardened again. "You won't walk away, Elysia. You can't."

Her heart sank as she realized the weight of his words. He was right—she had nowhere to go. She was trapped in his world, and the more she fought against it, the more it pulled her back in.

But this time, the truth was a double-edged sword, and Elysia wasn't sure she was ready to face the consequences.

14

Betrayal in the Shadows

Elysia stood in the dimly lit hallway, the oppressive silence of the mansion wrapping around her like a shroud. The air was thick with tension, the weight of the revelation she had just unearthed pressing down on her chest, suffocating her. She felt as though the walls were closing in, their cold marble surfaces mocking her fragile state of mind. Her heart, once so sure, now beat erratically, like a drum warning her of an impending storm.

Dante's figure loomed in front of her, his sharp features cast in the shadows. He had always been an enigma—calm, calculated, with a smile that never quite reached his eyes. But tonight, there was something different about him. The smugness that usually defined him had slipped, replaced by a strange, almost regretful expression. His eyes flickered with something—guilt, perhaps, or fear—but whatever it was, it unsettled her.

"I never thought it would come to this," Dante's voice was low, almost a whisper, as though he were speaking more to himself than to her.

Elysia's breath caught in her throat. The words felt like a knife twisting into her already fragile heart. She knew it—she had always known that there was more to her death, to the betrayal that had shattered her life, than

Victor had let on. But hearing it confirmed by Dante, a man who had been so intricately woven into the web of deceit, made her blood run cold.

"You knew," Elysia's voice cracked, the accusation hanging between them like an electric charge. "You knew everything, didn't you?"

Dante didn't flinch. His gaze remained steady, though there was a flicker of something beneath the surface—regret, maybe, or the faintest trace of pity. "I knew," he admitted, his voice soft, his words more like a confession than a revelation. "But I never thought it would come to this. I never thought it would destroy you."

Elysia's mind whirled. How had she been so blind? How had she allowed herself to fall deeper into a world of lies, a world that had claimed her life once before? She had trusted Victor—trusted him with everything she had, her heart, her soul, her very being. But now, she realized that trust had been built on a foundation of sand.

"Victor…" Her voice faltered. She swallowed the bitter taste of betrayal. "You're telling me… he had a hand in it? In my death? Not directly, but indirectly? He… he allowed it to happen?"

Dante's silence spoke volumes. His eyes shifted, a shadow of discomfort flickering across his face. There was no need for words. She could see it now—the way Victor's family had woven the threads of her demise, each betrayal tied to another, all leading back to Victor. He had been the one to allow her to fall. He had been the one who had given her life away to the very people who had taken it from her.

Elysia's mind raced, her heart pounding in her chest. The world she had known, the love she had believed was real, was nothing more than a carefully constructed lie. The pieces of the puzzle clicked together, but the image they formed was one she could not reconcile with the man she had given her heart to. The man she had trusted with everything.

"You're wrong," she said, her voice shaking with the force of her words. "You're lying. Victor would never—"

Dante's cold laugh cut through her denial like a blade. "Oh, Elysia," he said, shaking his head. "You have no idea, do you? How deep this goes. How far back it reaches."

He took a step closer to her, his presence now overwhelming, suffocating. "Victor may not have pulled the trigger himself, but he was the one who enabled the betrayal. He was the one who let it happen. He was the one who stood by and watched as the woman he loved was destroyed."

Elysia recoiled as if he had struck her. The words, the truth they carried, felt like a brutal slap to the face. Victor had stood by. He had allowed it. He had allowed the woman he claimed to love to die, to fall victim to a betrayal so deep, so cruel, that it had been woven into the very fabric of their world.

Tears welled up in her eyes, but she refused to let them fall. She was done crying for the lies. She was done being the victim. She had been given a second chance at life, and now, the truth was all she had left.

"Why?" she asked, her voice a whisper of disbelief. "Why would he do that? Why would he let me die like that? Why would he—"

Dante's expression softened, but it was not kindness that filled his gaze. It was pity. "Victor has always been the same. He's ruled by his family, his loyalty, his thirst for power. He never thought twice about the price that would be paid. He didn't think it would cost him the woman he loved."

Elysia stepped back, her head spinning, the ground beneath her feet beginning to feel unsteady. "You're telling me he didn't love me?"

Dante's lips twisted into a bitter smile. "Oh, he loved you—he still does, in his own twisted way. But love doesn't make people blind to the world around them. Love doesn't stop the blood from spilling when the stakes are high. In his world, love is a commodity. A tool. A weapon."

The truth hit her like a freight train, smashing through the last of her defenses. Victor had never truly loved her. Not in the way she had believed. She had been a pawn—a prize to be claimed, a woman to be molded into a role that served the greater purpose of his family's empire. She had been nothing more than a tool in his hands.

Her vision blurred, but she forced herself to steady. "I can't do this," she said, her voice cold, detached, as if she were watching someone else speak. "I can't stay here. I can't stay in this world anymore."

Dante's eyes darkened, but there was a flicker of understanding in them. He had known this moment was coming. He had known she would eventually see the truth for what it was. And now, it was too late.

With a sharp intake of breath, Elysia turned away from him. Her heart shattered with each step she took, but there was no going back. Not now. Not after everything she had learned.

And as she fled, the weight of her decision settled on her like a stone, crushing her with the finality of it all. There was no escape from the world she had been born into. No escape from the shadows that would always follow her.

The wind howled through the cracked windows of the abandoned estate on the edge of Milan, stirring the dust and shadows like restless ghosts. The air was tinged with the metallic scent of old blood and betrayal—echoes of a past Elysia could no longer ignore. The room was barren save for a broken chandelier that dangled precariously from the ceiling, its crystals clinking like whispered warnings.

Elysia stood in the center, her arms folded across her chest, spine rigid, waiting.

Dante entered like a wraith cloaked in silence, the tail of his coat slicing through the air behind him. His expression was unreadable, carved from marble, yet his eyes—those pale, calculating eyes—were heavy with something deeper. Not remorse. Not grief. Something older. Regret aged into apathy.

"You ran," he said quietly, his voice echoing slightly in the vast, empty room.

"I walked away," Elysia replied. "There's a difference."

The distance between them was both physical and symbolic—a chasm of truth and silence neither had dared cross until now.

"You wanted answers," Dante said, his boots clicking over shattered tile. "But answers come with weight."

"I'm not afraid of weight anymore," she said, her voice brittle but unyielding. "Tell me everything."

Dante's jaw tensed, and for a moment, she thought he might lie again. Deflect. Retreat into silence like Victor always did. But then he stopped a few feet from her, and something shifted. The mask slipped.

"Isabella died because Victor allowed it," he said bluntly, the words slicing through the air like knives. "Not because he hated her. Not because he wanted her gone. But because he thought… he thought she would survive it."

Elysia's breath hitched.

"She was meant to be traded," Dante continued, stepping into the flickering light of the single, low-burning bulb. "Used as leverage in a deal with the Verrini family. She knew too much. She saw too much. Victor… he hesitated. He didn't sign the order—but he didn't stop it, either."

The room spun slightly. Elysia clutched the edge of a broken table to steady herself, her fingers ghosting over splinters like they were fragments of the life she used to have.

"So you all let her die," she whispered. "And now I'm her replacement."

"No," Dante said sharply. "You were never meant to replace her. You were… you were meant to silence the past."

Her eyes snapped to him. "What do you mean?"

He hesitated. Then: "Your reincarnation—it wasn't fate, Elysia. It was designed. Engineered. Victor's mother consulted the Mireille Circle—ancient blood magic. They found a way to bring back the soul of the one woman who could destabilize the Verrinis… and tie her to the very man who let her die."

Elysia staggered backward, bile rising in her throat. "You're saying I was made? That I'm just… part of some revenge plot?"

"No," Dante said, stepping forward quickly. "You're more than that. You are Isabella—but you're also more. You're Elysia. You're the only person left with the power to unravel everything. And that's why they fear you."

Elysia looked at him, her body shaking with the aftershock of too many truths at once. Her past had been a lie. Her love, manipulated. Her identity—

weaponized. Every kiss, every promise Victor had made was tainted now, soaked in blood and deceit.

"And you?" she asked coldly. "Where do you fit into all this?"

Dante looked away. A crack formed in his stoic mask. "I was tasked to watch over you. To make sure you didn't remember too quickly. To keep you in the dark until… until you were ready to be used."

"And now?" Her voice was a whisper of steel.

"Now," he said quietly, "I'm telling you because I owe you. Because even monsters get tired of the dark."

For a long moment, they stood in silence, broken only by the wind howling like a grieving widow through the broken windowpanes.

"You expect me to trust you now?" Elysia said, lifting her chin. "After everything?"

"No," Dante said with a dry laugh. "But I do expect you to survive. And for that, you'll need to run. Tonight."

Elysia narrowed her eyes. "Why?"

"Because the Verrinis know you're awake," he said. "And Victor's enemies will come for you now. They don't care who you are—they care what you are. You're the key to dismantling everything. And some would rather burn the world than let that happen."

Lightning forked outside the shattered windows, illuminating the anguish on her face.

"I have to leave," she murmured.

Dante nodded. "And you have to leave alone. If Victor finds you, he'll try to make you stay. And if the Verrinis find you first, they'll use you as a blade to slit his throat."

For a heartbeat, something ancient pulsed in Elysia's blood—a memory of fire and betrayal, of a knife in the dark, of drowning in her own blood. A flicker of Isabella whispered in her bones: *You've died once. Don't let them kill you again.*

She moved to the door, her mind whirling. "What if I never come back?"

Dante's expression darkened. "Then maybe the world stands a chance."

But as Elysia stepped into the night, she felt the invisible hands of fate close around her throat again. She wasn't escaping.

She was walking into the eye of a greater storm.

Night in the countryside carried a chilling stillness, like the world itself was holding its breath. The trees stood tall and silent, their gnarled branches clawing at the dark sky as if to scratch out the stars. The road ahead was slick with rain, reflecting moonlight in broken shards, and Elysia's boots splashed through the puddles as she ran.

Every heartbeat echoed like thunder in her chest.

She didn't know how long she'd been running—only that she had to get away. From Victor. From Dante. From the ghosts of Isabella that haunted her now more than ever. Her chest heaved, each breath laced with the cold burn of fear and betrayal.

Her phone had no signal. Her coat, barely warm enough against the wind, clung to her soaked body. But still, she didn't stop.

Not until headlights flared behind her.

She turned, blinded, as a black SUV barreled down the narrow road. Tires screeched. Doors slammed. Voices barked orders in a language she hadn't yet learned to fear—but would soon come to loathe.

Before she could run again, hands seized her from the shadows.

She screamed, thrashing violently, nails clawing at skin and fabric. Her training—what little Victor had given her—kicked in, but she was outnumbered. Two masked men held her down, another covered her mouth with a cloth that stank of chemicals. Her limbs turned to lead. Her vision swam.

And then—darkness.

When she woke, it was to the slow drip of water and the hum of electricity.

Concrete walls surrounded her, damp with mildew. A single, exposed bulb hung from the ceiling, casting her prison in a sickly yellow glow. The cot beneath her creaked as she sat up, head pounding.

A door groaned open.

In stepped a tall, silver-haired man with a cruel smile and colder eyes. His tailored suit was immaculate, the stark opposite of the rot that surrounded him.

"Elysia," he said, his accent smooth, dripping with old-world venom. "Welcome to our little sanctuary."

She swallowed. "You're... Verrini."

"Luciano Verrini," he said with a mock bow. "Head of the family, architect of many... unfortunate events, and now your gracious host."

"I won't be your pawn," she snapped, the fire in her voice belying the fear twisting in her gut.

He chuckled. "Oh, my dear, you already are. But unlike Victor, I won't lie to you about it."

She stood slowly, fists clenched. "What do you want?"

Luciano approached her, slow and deliberate, like a serpent. "I want balance. And you, bella, are the perfect scale weight. You've already begun to remember, haven't you? The betrayal. The blood. The fire."

Her lips parted slightly. "You knew Isabella."

"I killed her," he said softly, tilting his head. "Well, not by my hand. That pleasure went to one of Victor's own. But I made the call. She threatened everything."

Elysia reeled. Her knees nearly buckled.

"Now you've returned," he continued, "and what a delightful twist. Fate always did have a flair for the dramatic. We don't need to kill you this time, Elysia. We only need you to do what Isabella never would—bring Victor to his knees."

"I'll never help you," she spat.

Luciano's smile never faltered. "Oh, you will. Everyone has a price. Or a pressure point."

He nodded, and one of the guards dragged a chair to the center of the room. Another man brought in a tablet, displaying live security feeds—Victor's compound.

"Imagine what he'll do when he sees you in our custody," Luciano murmured. "Imagine what *you'll* do when we show you what he's done in your name."

The tablet flickered to a paused frame: Victor in his office, hands bloody, standing over a corpse.

"Lies," she whispered.

"Truth," he corrected, his voice like poisoned silk. "Your beloved has always been a butcher. You just chose not to see the blood."

Tears prickled at the corners of her eyes, but she refused to let them fall. She couldn't afford fragility—not here, not now.

Luciano stepped back. "Rest, bella. Tomorrow, we begin the real work."

He left, the door slamming shut with finality.

Elysia collapsed back onto the cot, trembling. Her world was in ruins—past, present, and future reduced to ash. She didn't know who to trust. She didn't know if she'd ever see the sun again. But one thing she did know: if she survived this, she'd never be anyone's pawn again.

As the lightbulb above her flickered like a dying star, she whispered the promise into the silence:

"I'll burn this world down before I let it cage me."

15

The Verrini's Grip

The Verrini estate sat like a brooding monarch on the cliffs above Lake Como—its windows glinting in the morning light like watching eyes, its stone façade weathered and silent as if it had witnessed centuries of betrayal and bled none of it. From afar, it might have been mistaken for a Renaissance masterpiece, but up close, its grandeur was merely a veil—a cage forged not of bars but of marble, silence, and secrets.

Elysia stood at the center of a high-ceilinged chamber, sunlight pouring through stained-glass panels that painted her skin in fractured reds and golds. The irony wasn't lost on her: a room built like a sanctuary, dressed in cathedral opulence, and yet it throbbed with the quiet menace of a trap. Every inch of this place whispered curated civility, but beneath the surface, something darker breathed.

She'd been given silk robes, pearl earrings, and an ivory comb for her hair—but no freedom. No phone, no windows that opened. Even the mirrors seemed to reflect not just her face, but a question that haunted her now more than ever: **Who am I really, and why do they want me so badly?**

In the hallway outside, footsteps echoed—measured and deliberate, like the tick of a grandfather clock counting down her time. The door creaked open with reverent slowness.

"Buongiorno, Signora Lupo," said a voice as smooth as poisoned honey.

Enter **Giovanni Verrini**, the youngest of the three Verrini brothers and the most dangerous for his charm. He carried a tray with breakfast—figs, espresso, and warm croissants—as if this were a romantic vacation instead of a hostage situation.

"You're not my husband," Elysia said coolly, not even glancing his way.

"Not yet," he said, placing the tray on the table with exaggerated care. "But wouldn't it be something? The widow reborn… and claimed by her rightful side."

Elysia's hands tightened around the arms of her chair. "Why am I here?"

Giovanni offered a theatrical sigh. "So many reasons. You're a symbol. A legacy. A key." He turned, his smile sharpening. "Victor sees you as salvation. We see you for what you truly are—a thread that unravels everything."

She met his eyes then, green steel against black ice. "I'm not a pawn."

"Oh no, my dear," Giovanni said, chuckling. "You're the queen. And queens are either worshipped—or sacrificed."

The line chilled the air.

After he left, she paced the room, her bare feet cold on the marble. The Verrinis were not keeping her alive out of mercy. They had a plan—she just didn't know if it ended with Victor's destruction, or her own. Her thoughts twisted in spirals, every memory of Victor now cast in a different light. Was his love truly devotion—or obsession? Did he rescue her… or remake her into what he wanted to remember?

On the desk lay a red leather-bound journal. She hadn't noticed it before. Curious, cautious, she flipped it open. It wasn't a diary. It was a ledger.

Code names. Dated correspondences. Payments.

A name leapt from the page—**Isabella D'Amico.**

Her heart stuttered.

The journal didn't say much—only that Isabella had been under surveillance, considered a "critical liability," and marked with a symbol she didn't understand: Δ . Beside it, her death was recorded like a business expense.

And then, more chillingly, in ink darker than the rest, a name was scribbled beside Isabella's file:

Elysia Vale.

Reborn.

The breath caught in her throat.

It wasn't fate that brought her back. It was design.

Meanwhile, beyond the estate walls, the lake shimmered under a sky too bright for the darkness that churned beneath it.

High above on the estate's tower balcony, **Adriana Verrini**, matriarch of the bloodline, watched Elysia from a telescope hidden behind antique curtains. Her fingers curled around a crucifix worn thin from decades of whispered sins.

"She's beginning to remember," Adriana murmured to no one.

From the shadows, her eldest son, Matteo, stepped forward. "Should we accelerate the plan?"

"No. Let her unravel it slowly," Adriana said. "If she breaks too quickly, she may run back to him. But if she sees the truth piece by piece… she will burn him herself."

A gust of wind swept across the terrace, fluttering the crimson drapes like spilled blood.

Back inside the chamber, Elysia sat with the journal cradled in her lap like a newborn secret. Her reflection in the gilded mirror stared back, haunted, questioning. The woman she once was—whoever she had been—wasn't dead. She had been buried. Forgotten. Twisted into a story told by someone else.

Now, piece by piece, the truth was clawing its way back to the surface.

And when it did, she knew—nothing would ever be the same again.

Not for her.

Not for Victor.

Not for any of them.

As Elysia hides the journal under a floorboard, a shadow passes under the door. A voice, faint and male, whispers through the keyhole:

"Be careful what you find, bella. Some ghosts don't want to be remembered."

The Lupo estate had never known silence like this.

Once a palace of order and command, it now breathed with unease, as if the walls themselves had absorbed Victor's fury and were afraid to echo it. In the war room, once a place of calculated strategy, maps were torn, glass shattered, and a single photo of Elysia lay cracked beneath Victor's boot.

Victor's eyes, normally cold and sharp as obsidian, now glowed with a dangerous edge—a man tethered to the edge of reason by a fraying thread. His tailored jacket hung open, his tie discarded. He paced like a caged predator, jaw clenched, every muscle taut with the hunger for vengeance and the ghost of fear he refused to name.

"She's not just missing," he growled, turning on his second-in-command. "She was taken. And I let them."

Domenico Varo, loyal to the bone and quiet by nature, stood like a statue near the doorway. "The Verrinis are ghosts, Victor. You know this. We move, we bleed."

"Then let them bleed," Victor snapped. "I want every satellite tracking their movements. I want their associates interrogated. If it breathes and smells like Verrini blood, bring it to me."

He turned back to the smashed monitor. The last footage he had of Elysia was at the gala—her figure in red, spun like a ruby in a whirlpool of shadows. Then... gone. Swallowed by the night.

Victor slammed his fist on the table, veins bulging under his skin like snakes. "She trusted me. I swore I'd protect her. And now she's in the hands of the same bastards who took Isabella."

There it was. **Isabella.**

The name bloomed like a bruise in the silence. The woman he couldn't save. The memory he buried. The chain around his soul that Elysia had unknowingly yanked free.

Domenico's voice was low. "You think this is about Isabella?"

Victor didn't answer. He couldn't.

Because in his heart—beneath the layers of rage and control—he feared it was.

He stepped away from the wreckage, shoulders stiff. "They're not just trying to hurt me. They want her to find something. They want her to remember."

Domenico hesitated, then dared the question. "What if she does?"

Victor turned slowly, his gaze burning. "Then I lose her. Not to death. To the truth."

Outside, storm clouds rolled in from the coast, a tempest building in tandem with the one inside him.

Victor walked into the chapel that his mother once used—now abandoned, filled with dust and the scent of old prayers. He dropped to one knee before the altar, not out of faith, but fury. His hands curled into fists as he stared at the cracked crucifix above.

"I let her in," he murmured. "I let her inside me. And now she's paying the price."

His thoughts twisted.

Could he have stopped this?

Was it his obsession with keeping Elysia close that made her a target?

Or worse… was she always meant to be one?

His mind spiraled, dragging up whispers from the past—Isabella's screams, Dante's betrayal, and a single promise spoken in a fever dream: *"If you ever lose me, look for me in the fire."*

Elysia had walked into his world like that—like flame. Burning down the walls he'd built. Lighting up the truth he'd tried to forget.

Now she was gone. And Victor was no longer a man. He was a wolf without a pack, a king without his queen. And kings—when cornered—**burn kingdoms to the ground.**

Elsewhere in the estate, deep in the old records vault, a technician rushed forward, holding a single frame from surveillance footage taken an hour before the blackout. He placed it on the screen in front of Domenico, who immediately called Victor.

Victor arrived in seconds.

On the screen, blurry but unmistakable, was **Giovanni Verrini**. Behind him, wrapped in a silk scarf and drugged into stillness—**Elysia**.

Victor's breath vanished.

"They took her straight from under our eyes," Domenico said bitterly. "They knew our blind spots."

Victor's fingers slid down the edge of the monitor, blood seeping from where his nails dug into his palm. "Then we give them no shadows to hide in."

He turned to his men—every capo, soldier, tech analyst, and enforcer summoned into the hall. His voice rang like a war drum.

"Listen to me. She is not a bargaining chip. She is not collateral. She is the one thing I've ever loved that I didn't break. I will get her back, or I will burn every last one of them alive trying."

No one moved. No one breathed.

And then, almost in reverence, Domenico placed a handgun in Victor's palm. "We ride at nightfall."

As Victor loaded his weapon, a whisper came through the encrypted radio line—a Verrini informant embedded in Milan's south district.

"She's alive," the voice hissed. "But she's not the same anymore. She's... remembering."

Victor froze.

And for the first time in years, **fear** slithered through his veins.

Because he knew—if she remembered everything...

She might never choose him again.

The Verrini estate was a cathedral of shadows—high-arched ceilings, walls lacquered in secrets, and a silence that rang louder than screams. It sat like a vulture on a cliff's edge, overlooking the churning Ligurian Sea. The waves below crashed like distant gunfire, relentless and wild, much like Elysia's thoughts.

Her wrists were raw beneath the silk restraints. Not tight enough to wound, but snug enough to remind her of her place: not a guest, not quite a prisoner—something between a bargaining chip and a revelation.

She stood at the edge of the room, eyes scanning her surroundings. Gilded mirrors lined the corridor, all reflecting versions of herself that looked... wrong. As though she was walking through the memory of someone else's life. A ghost in flesh.

"You look like her," came the voice that had the weight of a monarch and the chill of a grave.

Elysia turned.

Adriana Verrini stood in the doorway, dressed in all black—a silk robe trailing like spilled ink behind her. Her silver-streaked hair was pulled into a crown-like braid, and her eyes... her eyes were wolves wrapped in diamonds. Cold, ancient, and sharp.

"I'm not her," Elysia replied, though the words caught like glass in her throat.

"No," Adriana murmured, walking in slow circles around her. "But you carry her soul, her sins... and her secrets. Reincarnation doesn't erase blood debt. If anything, it collects interest."

Elysia bristled. "What do you want from me?"

Adriana stopped in front of her and reached out, brushing a strand of hair from her face with a grandmother's tenderness—before gripping her chin with icy fingers. "I want you to wake up."

"To what?"

"To who you are."

Adriana released her, walking toward the grand fireplace where a low flame licked at logs carved with old Italian script. She tossed in a piece of parchment. It flared bright blue.

"Your death was never an accident, Elysia. And Victor—he's not your savior. He's your consequence."

The words landed like thunder.

"I don't believe you."

Adriana gave a slow, pitying smile. "You will. It's already started, hasn't it? The dreams. The whispers. The faces you don't remember until they start screaming."

Elysia faltered. The air felt heavier now, tinged with the scent of burning lilac—a memory she couldn't place but which made her heart thud like a war drum.

"You were Isabella. You betrayed this family once before. You loved the wrong man and died for it. And now… fate brought you back, but not out of mercy. You were brought back to finish what was started."

Elysia shook her head, though doubt was creeping through her like poison in her veins. "Why would I trust anything you say?"

Adriana stepped closer, sliding a folder across the table. "Because truth doesn't need your belief. Just your eyes."

Elysia opened the file. Photos. A young woman—her face nearly identical to Elysia's—laughing with Victor. Then others… ones of her screaming, bleeding, held back by men with Verrini rings. A final photo: Victor standing over her body, drenched in guilt, and something darker—acceptance.

"You lie," Elysia whispered, the paper trembling in her hand. "Victor said he tried to save her."

Adriana leaned in. "And do you believe him?"

Silence.

"No," Elysia said at last, the word cracking through her like an earthquake.

Adriana turned away. "Good. Then you are almost ready."

"For what?" Elysia asked.

"To become what Isabella never could. The Queen."

That night, sleep eluded Elysia. Shadows played tricks on her in the Verrini guest room, whispering lullabies in a language she didn't remember knowing. Her hands shook as she splashed water on her face, staring at her reflection in the gold-framed mirror.

She looked the same. But she wasn't.

The woman who had kissed Victor under moonlight, who had laughed over espresso in the garden, who had once believed love could be enough—was slipping away. In her place, something else was rising. Something colder. Wiser. And furious.

She opened the window. Far in the distance, through the fog, she saw the edge of the Lupo territory. The moon hung above it, stark and silver like a blade waiting to fall.

Would he come for her?

Would he kill for her?

Or… had he already?

The door creaked behind her.

She turned sharply—but it wasn't Adriana.

It was **Luca Verrini**, Adriana's youngest son. With a knife at his side and a strange look in his eyes.

"Time to go, bella," he said with a grin. "Victor's coming. And mother wants you somewhere… dramatic."

Elysia didn't flinch.

Let him come, she thought. Let the devil walk through fire.

Because this time, she wasn't the girl who needed saving.

She was the storm he should've never loved.

16

Under Siege

The night was heavy with smoke, thick enough to choke the stars and blacken the moon. The air, pungent with the bitter scent of gunpowder and burning flesh, hung over the Verrini estate like a shroud. Victor stood at the edge of the sprawling compound, his eyes narrow slits of fury beneath the brim of his dark cap. The world around him was chaos—shouts echoed from the blackened trees, the crack of gunfire splintered the silence, and the screams of the dying were muffled by the rise and fall of distant explosions.

His breath was steady, each inhale sharp, each exhale controlled. This was the moment. The moment when the Lupo family would burn their enemies to the ground. The moment when he would burn it all, for her.

For Elysia.

The marble columns of the Verrini mansion loomed in front of him, towering over the bloody scene. They were statuesque, unyielding, the pillars of a family that had once thought itself invincible. Now, they were nothing more than witnesses to the beginning of their destruction. Flames licked at the base of the columns, sending jagged shadows dancing across the courtyard. The fire seemed almost alive, as though it, too, was angry.

Victor moved forward, his steps sure and purposeful, his boots grinding into the gravel like the sound of fate itself. His men moved with him, a silent army forged in blood and loyalty. Each one of them knew the stakes, knew the price of failure. But Victor didn't fear failure—not now, not when everything was on the line. Not when Elysia was still in the hands of the Verrini family.

His heart, once a fortress of ice, thudded painfully in his chest. The familiar weight of his gun—cold steel, a symbol of his power—was a comfort now, a reminder of how far he'd come and how much he was willing to sacrifice. But there was something heavier now. Something that clung to him like a chain he could never escape.

Her.

Elysia. Her face, her laughter, the softness of her touch—it was all there in the back of his mind. A beacon in the storm of violence and betrayal that consumed him. His heart clenched. He hadn't known what she was to him when she first walked into his life. But now, she was the reason for everything. She was the fire that ignited his purpose. She was the flame, and he was the moth. He would burn for her, if necessary.

But first, he had to destroy everything that stood between them.

The sound of glass shattering echoed from the mansion's eastern wing. Victor's gaze snapped toward it, his instincts on high alert. His men were already moving, shadows in the dark. But it wasn't just the sound of destruction that made his skin crawl—it was the memory of her face, so close, so real. She was still alive. He could feel it in his bones, in the blood that ran through him. She was out there, and the Verrinis were going to pay.

With a flick of his wrist, he signaled his men to advance. They moved with lethal precision, sweeping through the estate, taking out anyone who stood in their way. The Verrinis had been expecting an attack—Victor had made sure of that—but no one could prepare for the fury of the Lupo family once it was unleashed. No one could stop it.

Victor's thoughts were a blur, each moment threading into the next, as he pushed forward, driven by the singular thought of reaching her. He had to find her. He had to. There was nothing more important than that.

A gunshot rang out—close enough to rattle the ground beneath his feet. One of his men fell, clutching his side, his eyes wide with shock. But Victor didn't flinch. He didn't slow down. His men had their orders: protect the boss. And they would.

They swept through the mansion's darkened halls, moving like shadows, their footsteps a whisper against the marble floors. The air inside the mansion was thick, heavy with the scent of old money and the weight of centuries of power. This was the Verrini family's kingdom, but it was crumbling, piece by piece.

Victor's fingers tightened around the handle of his gun as they approached the inner chambers. His breath was shallow, his pulse a drumbeat in his ears. Every step felt like an eternity, each moment pulling him closer to the heart of the estate. To her.

And then, through the broken door, he saw it.

A figure, draped in shadows, slumped against the wall. It wasn't her. The man's silhouette was too broad, too muscular. But the way he held himself, the way his eyes glinted beneath his mask, told Victor everything he needed to know. It was Luca Verrini. His rival. His enemy.

"You're too late," Luca's voice rang out, low and mocking, cutting through the smoke like a blade. He coughed, blood speckling the floor beneath him. "She's gone. She chose."

Victor's heart skipped a beat. A cold knot formed in his stomach. He stepped closer, his gaze never leaving Luca's eyes.

"Where is she?" Victor demanded, his voice a controlled growl.

Luca smirked, blood trailing from the corner of his lips. "You think you're the only one who can control her, Victor? You think she's just some prize to be won?"

Victor's gun was raised before Luca could finish his sentence. The muzzle glinted in the dim light, the weapon a silent promise of death. But Victor hesitated. He couldn't afford to waste time with this. His thoughts were consumed by one thing, and one thing only.

Elysia.

Luca's grin widened, his lips curling in defiance. "You'll never find her. She's already made her choice."

Victor's world tilted on its axis, but he forced himself to breathe. Find her. You have to find her.

But Luca's smirk told him everything. The Verrinis had won.

The mansion was nothing but a maze of darkness now, the grandeur of its halls drowned in the weight of violence. Elysia's breath came in shallow gasps as she pressed herself against the cold stone wall, trying to still the frantic pounding of her heart. The sounds of battle—gunfire, shouting, the cracking of wood—echoed from all sides. She could feel the vibrations through the ground, like a distant warning tremor, telling her that time was running out.

But it wasn't the chaos outside that filled her with fear. It was the silence in the room.

The room where she stood alone. Where her thoughts were louder than the explosion outside. Her thoughts, her doubts, her heart—a tangled mess of confusion.

She hadn't seen him—Victor—in hours. He was out there, somewhere, engaged in a war to retrieve her, and yet… she didn't know if she wanted to be found. She didn't know if she wanted to be part of this anymore.

This—the bloodshed, the constant tension, the endless games. It was a world she had never asked for, yet one that had embraced her in its cruel, unforgiving grip. The Verrini family's cold touch had already marked her, and now the Lupo family had claimed her as its own.

But she was no one's possession. She couldn't be.

A sharp sound broke through her thoughts. The scrape of boots on marble. Her body tensed, her eyes flicking to the door. Her pulse thundered in her ears, and she didn't have to guess who it was. She could already feel him—the weight of him, the presence of him. Victor.

He wasn't alone. Dante, his most trusted advisor, was with him. The two of them made their way through the darkness, their figures casting long shadows that seemed to stretch out before them, as if trying to escape their owners.

Victor's expression was unreadable, his face hidden in the darkness of his cap, but Elysia could feel the anger radiating off him. It was a physical thing, like a storm pushing against her skin, threatening to tear her apart. His gaze found her, his eyes locking onto hers, and in that moment, nothing else existed. The chaos, the world—they all faded away.

But then, just as quickly, it all rushed back.

She took a step back, her body jerking involuntarily. It wasn't fear. It was something else—a mix of anger, confusion, and betrayal. She hadn't forgotten the words he'd said to her before, the harshness in his voice, the coldness that had replaced the passion he once felt for her.

Find her. You have to find her. His words echoed in her mind, but they felt empty now. His mission to protect her had always seemed like a burden to him. Was she just a pawn in this violent game? A distraction? A way to maintain his power?

"I don't need you to save me anymore," she said quietly, the words barely above a whisper, but they felt like an explosion inside her chest. "I can take care of myself."

Victor's eyes softened, his jaw tightening as he fought against the storm of emotion that surged within him. His hands clenched into fists at his sides, but he made no move toward her. He didn't want to push her further away.

He couldn't. He wouldn't.

Dante, ever the cynic, glanced between them, a smirk playing at the corners of his lips. "You're playing a dangerous game, Elysia. You think you can escape from this life?" His voice was mocking, as if daring her to challenge him. "You're already too deep. No one walks away from the mafia."

Elysia met Dante's gaze, defiance flashing in her eyes. "I'm not afraid of you. And I'm certainly not afraid of him." She gestured toward Victor, her gaze never leaving his face.

Victor flinched at the coldness in her tone, his throat tightening as if he had swallowed glass. The words stung more than he cared to admit, but he couldn't blame her. Not now. Not after everything.

Her heart was breaking too, and he could feel it—feel the fracture between them widening with each passing second.

"I didn't want this for you," he said quietly, his voice rough. "But you're part of this world now, Elysia. You've always been part of it. You think you can run away from me? From us?"

Her gaze flicked from Dante to Victor, her body trembling with the weight of his words. From us. He made it sound so simple, as though there was no choice for her, as though she belonged to him.

Elysia turned away from both of them, a sudden, sharp pain twisting in her chest. She didn't belong to anyone—not him, not the Lupos, not the Verrinis. But as much as she wanted to fight, to reclaim her life, she couldn't shake the feeling that she was caught in a trap—a trap of her own making, perhaps, but still one she couldn't escape.

"Please," Victor's voice was lower now, strained. "Don't do this. Don't leave."

But Elysia had already made her choice. She had already begun to walk away from everything that had defined her.

"I'm not leaving you," she said, her voice thick with emotion, "I'm leaving the life you've made for me. I won't be a pawn anymore, Victor."

She didn't know where she would go. Didn't know what she would do. But she knew one thing—she couldn't stay here. Not like this.

The silence between them was suffocating. And then, Dante's voice cut through it once again, taunting, almost gleeful.

"Go ahead, Elysia," he said, his grin widening. "Try to escape. But remember—you're not as free as you think. None of us are."

Victor said nothing. He stood there, rooted to the spot, watching as she turned her back on him for the second time.

The night had fallen thick with smoke and blood, the stench of destruction hanging heavy in the air as Victor Lupo stood in the heart of the chaos. His empire, the family he'd fought to protect, was crumbling before him. His own bloodline, torn apart by betrayal and greed, was now fighting a war on multiple fronts. Yet none of it mattered, not in this moment, not while Elysia was still out there, in the hands of the Verrini family.

Victor's fists clenched as he looked at the once-pristine courtyard of his mansion, now riddled with bullet holes and the aftermath of a brutal siege. The Lupo family had been under attack for hours—his men were dead, his allies scattered—but it was not the loss of his empire that gnawed at him. It was the cold realization that Elysia might be lost to him forever.

Every step he took felt heavier than the last, his heart a leaden weight in his chest. He had promised to protect her. He had sworn it.

And now, the Verrinis had her.

Dante Vero, his trusted advisor, stood beside him, surveying the wreckage, his gaze sharp, calculating. Dante's expression was unreadable, as always, but Victor could see the glimmer of something in his eyes. Satisfaction? Guilt?

"Victor," Dante said quietly, breaking the silence. His voice, though calm, was tinged with something else, something dark. "You've failed. You know that, don't you?"

Victor's gaze snapped to him, his jaw tight, but he said nothing. There was no need for words. The truth hung between them, unspoken but clear.

"I didn't fail," Victor growled, his voice low and dangerous. "I'll never fail her."

Dante studied him for a moment, then sighed, his shoulders slumping as if the weight of the world had just been placed on him. "You're blind, Victor. Blinded by your obsession with her. You've ignored the bigger picture—the Verrinis are using her against you. You're fighting a losing battle, and you're dragging everyone down with you."

Victor's eyes darkened. "If you think I'll stand down and let them have her, then you don't know me at all."

For a moment, there was only silence, the crackle of flames in the distance the only sound between them. Then, Dante spoke again, his voice softer, but no less cold.

"You're right. You won't stand down. But what are you willing to sacrifice to save her? Your family? Your empire? The lives of everyone who trusts you?"

Victor's pulse quickened, but his mind was clear. His gaze shifted toward the shadows that clung to the edges of the courtyard, where the shadows of his men—those who had survived—waited for orders.

"If it comes to that," he said, his voice low and steady, "I will sacrifice everything."

Dante chuckled darkly, a humorless sound that echoed in the stillness of the night. "And yet, there's one thing you haven't considered, Victor. What if saving her means destroying yourself? What if your choices, your actions, have already doomed her?"

Victor's heart skipped a beat. The thought had crossed his mind more than once, but he refused to entertain it. He would not let Elysia slip from his grasp—not after everything they had been through, not after everything she had meant to him.

Without another word, he spun on his heel and stalked toward the gates, where the black cars of the Verrini family awaited. His mind raced, but his steps were deliberate. He was done talking. He was done being passive.

As he neared the car, his heart tightened. The thought of Elysia in the Verrini's hands—helpless, broken—was more than he could bear. But worse still was the knowledge that he was the one who had led her into this mess. He had pushed her into the world of crime, of bloodshed, and it had cost them both more than he had ever imagined.

A sharp pain pierced his chest. If it took everything to undo the damage, he would do it. His family. His empire. His name. None of it mattered anymore. Not when she was at stake.

But then the decision came—an impossible one. He reached into his coat pocket, pulling out the small, velvet-lined box that had been weighing him down for days. It was a family heirloom, passed down for generations, a symbol of Lupo bloodline. The diamond inside it glittered coldly under the moonlight, its sharp edges catching the light like a cruel reminder of what he was about to do.

He handed the box to Dante, his voice hard. "Take it. Use it. Do what must be done."

Dante didn't even flinch as he took the box, his face impassive. "You really are prepared to burn everything for her, aren't you?" he murmured, almost as though the question were rhetorical.

Victor nodded, his gaze unwavering. "Everything."

Dante tucked the box inside his jacket and gave a curt nod. "Then let's make sure she's still worth it."

As the two men entered the car, Victor's mind was already on the Verrinis—on the coming confrontation, the cost of his decision. His eyes were locked on the road ahead, but his thoughts were elsewhere, consumed by the single, painful truth he had to live with: He had already lost more than he could ever gain.

And now, there was no turning back.

17

A Fragile Peace

The wind whispered through the trees as Victor and Elysia stood on the balcony of the secluded villa, the sun beginning its slow descent toward the horizon. The picturesque view of the sprawling countryside stretched endlessly before them, but the serenity of the moment felt like a lie. The tension between them, palpable and unspoken, weighed heavier than the air itself.

Elysia's gaze lingered on the distant hills, but her mind was elsewhere. She wasn't looking at the horizon. She was looking inward, reflecting on the tumultuous journey that had brought her to this point. How had they gotten here? How had she become so intertwined with a world that was as dangerous as it was intoxicating?

She wanted to believe that this was a moment of peace, a moment of respite. But there was no peace in the chaos of their hearts.

Victor stood beside her, his posture rigid, his expression unreadable. He had insisted on bringing her here, far from the violence and intrigue of the mafia world. But even in the quiet of the villa, with the sound of the wind and the occasional bird call, the storm inside him raged.

He had done the unthinkable to protect her, but now, with the walls of their chaotic lives temporarily down, he couldn't escape the shadow of his own guilt. His empire was fractured, and no matter how many battles he had won, the war with his own demons felt endless. The very woman who had once been the focal point of his darkest obsessions was now the center of his quiet, unsettling thoughts.

His fingers itched for control, for something solid to hold on to. But the only thing that seemed real, that made sense, was her. She had become his anchor, his salvation—and his prison.

"You're quiet," he said, his voice breaking the silence that had stretched too long.

Elysia glanced at him, her eyes briefly meeting his. She didn't reply at first, unsure of what to say. The truth felt too raw, too dangerous to voice. She had spent so long protecting herself from the world he had brought her into, but in the quiet moments like these, the walls she had built around herself felt like a prison.

"You're thinking about everything that's happened, aren't you?" Victor's voice softened, a rare vulnerability slipping through. "We've both made choices, Elysia. And they've brought us here."

Her chest tightened at the weight of his words. She turned fully toward him, her face flushed with the conflicting emotions swirling within her. "I don't know if I can keep doing this, Victor," she whispered, her voice trembling. "This... this life we're living. The lies, the betrayals... I feel like I'm losing myself."

Victor's jaw clenched. His eyes darkened, and the air around them seemed to crackle with tension. "You think I don't feel the same way?" He stepped closer to her, closing the gap that had grown between them. "I've given everything for this empire, for my family. But now... now it's all falling apart. And the only thing that matters is you."

Elysia flinched, her heart hammering in her chest. His words were both comforting and suffocating. She couldn't deny that she cared for him—her heart had betrayed her in that way—but the weight of his obsession, the possessiveness in his gaze, was suffocating.

"I don't want to be your obsession, Victor," she said softly, her voice steady despite the emotions swirling within her. "I want to be free. I want to be able to choose who I am... without the shadow of this world hanging over me."

Victor's expression faltered, a flicker of something unreadable passing through his eyes. He reached out to touch her, but stopped himself, his hand hovering in the air as if unsure whether to cross the line she had drawn. "I never wanted to trap you, Elysia. But I've seen what happens to those who try to escape this life. I couldn't let that happen to you."

She stepped back, the movement instinctive. "But I don't need you to save me, Victor. I need you to let me go."

The silence between them deepened, an abyss that neither of them seemed able to bridge. Victor's eyes searched her face, looking for something—some sign that she still wanted him, still needed him. But all he saw was a woman who had grown weary of the games he played, the promises he made, and the cage he had built around her heart.

Elysia's pulse quickened as she glanced at the horizon again, but this time, it wasn't the view that caught her attention. It was the realization that she couldn't stay here, not in this fragile peace that felt like it could crumble at any moment. She had been torn between him and her own desires for too long.

"I can't do this anymore, Victor," she said, her voice barely above a whisper, but the words cut through the silence like a knife. "I need to find out who I am without you."

Victor recoiled as if she had slapped him. The raw emotion on his face was almost more than she could bear, but it was nothing compared to the ache in her chest. The connection they shared—strong, undeniable—was also a chain. And for once, she needed to break free of it.

"You think I can just let you go?" His voice was low, a growl of desperation. "You belong with me, Elysia. I will do anything to protect you. Don't you understand that?"

Elysia took another step back, her mind swirling with a hundred conflicting emotions. The part of her that had fallen for him—the part that still longed for his touch—fought against the growing realization that she couldn't live in this world anymore. Not with him, not with the mafia, not with the lies.

"I don't belong to anyone, Victor. Least of all you."

Her words hung in the air, thick with finality. She had no idea where this path would lead, but she knew one thing for certain: she couldn't stay here any longer, suffocated by the shadow of his empire, and even more so, by the shadow of his love.

Victor's eyes darkened, but this time it wasn't with anger. It was with something darker—something that might have been fear.

Elysia turned away, her heart racing as she walked toward the door of the villa, leaving Victor standing in the fading light, his world unraveling in silence.

The fragile peace had shattered. And with it, everything they had built.

The night was heavy with the weight of unspoken words, and the villa, once a place of fleeting tranquility, now felt suffocating. Elysia paced the length of the spacious living room, her thoughts tangled in knots that no amount of deep breathing could unravel. Her fingers brushed over the cool surface of the stone fireplace as she moved, her restless energy bouncing off the walls, reverberating in her chest.

Victor had stayed outside, his presence a lingering shadow in the background, as if he were waiting for something—a moment to change, to fix, to undo the rift between them. She didn't know if such a moment existed.

Elysia stopped by the large windows that framed the darkened world outside, the flickering lights from the distant city below reminding her of the life she had almost left behind. She knew she had to make a choice, but the lines had blurred. It was no longer just about her and Victor—it was about everything they represented, everything they had sacrificed.

Her fingers tightened around the edge of the curtain, her knuckles white. She could feel him, even from this distance, the pull of his presence a constant tug at her soul. She couldn't deny it—she still wanted him, still craved the touch of his hands, the fire in his eyes when he looked at her. But she had to be stronger than that, had to remind herself that the chains they had built were suffocating, no matter how sweet the poison.

The sound of footsteps behind her made her tense, and she knew, without looking, that it was Victor. She felt him before she saw him—his weight in the air, the intensity of his gaze. She didn't turn to face him.

"Elysia," he said her name like a prayer, his voice rough, like he hadn't spoken in days. "I didn't mean to push you away. But I'm not going to let you walk away from me. Not now. Not when we're so close."

She closed her eyes, her back still to him. "You don't get it, do you?" Her voice cracked under the strain of the emotion she was holding in. "You've never let me breathe, Victor. And now you want to hold on even tighter? That's not love. That's control."

Victor was silent for a moment, and Elysia almost wondered if he understood, if he truly saw the cracks that were beginning to show in the foundation of everything they had built. The room seemed to grow colder as she waited for his response, each second stretching longer than the last.

Finally, he spoke, his voice softer, more hesitant than she'd ever heard it. "I'm trying, Elysia. I'm trying to be the man you need me to be. But I can't do that if you keep running from me. From us."

Her heart fluttered painfully in her chest, the echo of his words a deep reminder of how much he still held onto her—how much he was willing to sacrifice. But it was too much, too intense. She couldn't live in the shadow of his need anymore. She couldn't disappear into his world, a world where she had no control, no voice.

Turning slowly, Elysia met his gaze for the first time since their conversation had started. His eyes were darker than she remembered, more intense, as if he had been lost in the same storm of confusion that she was trapped in. She searched his face, looking for the man she had once known—looking for something she could hold on to. But all she saw was a man consumed by his empire, by his obsession with keeping her safe, by his desire to possess everything she was.

"I'm not a prisoner, Victor," she said quietly, the weight of her own words heavy in the air between them. "And I don't want to be one."

Victor took a step toward her, his movements deliberate but filled with a tension that made her want to retreat. "I never meant to make you feel trapped. But Elysia… you are my world. I can't lose you. Not after everything."

Her breath caught, the raw vulnerability in his voice striking her deeply. She wanted to reach out, to tell him that she understood, that she knew the sacrifices he had made, the things he had done to protect her. But the part of her that longed for freedom—the part of her that had been smothered by his love, by the weight of his world—screamed against it.

"I'm not your world, Victor," she said, her voice quieter now but no less firm. "And you can't make me your world just because you want to protect me. I have to protect myself, too."

The words hung between them like a fragile thread, barely holding the weight of everything they had built. The silence stretched on, thick and heavy, before Victor finally broke it, his voice rough with something she couldn't quite place.

"I don't know how to let you go," he admitted, his eyes searching hers, vulnerable in a way that she had never seen before. "But I'll try. If that's what you really want."

Elysia's heart ached as she watched him, her chest tightening with the knowledge that no matter what she said, the damage had already been done. There was no going back from this moment. No more pretending.

"I don't know what I want anymore, Victor," she said, her voice breaking just slightly. "I just know that I can't live in this world anymore. Not like this. Not for you. Not for anyone."

Victor stood there, his face frozen, the weight of her words settling over him like a slow, suffocating tide. She saw the flicker of pain in his eyes before he turned and walked away, his back straight and his shoulders tense.

Elysia stood there, watching him go, feeling the emptiness spread inside her, but also the flicker of something else—a spark of freedom, a glimmer of the life she could have outside of this cage.

She couldn't help but wonder, as the darkness outside seemed to swallow the last of the light, whether she had made the right choice. Or if she had just let go of everything she had ever wanted.

But it was too late for doubt now. There was no turning back.

The fragile peace they had once shared was now broken beyond repair. The silence of the room lingered long after Victor's departure, settling over Elysia like a heavy blanket she had no desire to shake off. The echoes of their conversation clung to her, but so did the weight of her decision.

She didn't know what tomorrow would bring, or where this path would lead, but she was certain of one thing—there was no going back to the life she had known.

The moon hung low in the sky, casting its pale light over the villa, now eerily quiet. Elysia sat by the window, her fingers brushing the cool glass, her eyes searching the horizon. The night felt endless, like the void that had opened up between her and Victor. Even now, after everything, she couldn't escape the nagging pull of him—the weight of his absence pressed down on her chest.

Her thoughts were chaotic, a storm she couldn't outrun. She had made a decision—she had told him the truth, at least the truth she thought she knew. She had told him she couldn't live in his world, and yet, part of her still longed for the safety of it. Part of her still needed him, needed to believe that the connection they had was something she couldn't easily sever.

But could she live in a cage made of love, of promises she wasn't sure she wanted anymore?

The thought left a bitter taste in her mouth, and she stood abruptly, pacing the length of the room once again. Her footsteps were the only sound in the silence, the soft click of her shoes against the polished floors a stark reminder that she was alone in this decision. Alone, in the choices she had to make. She couldn't run to Victor anymore—not after the weight of his world had been laid at her feet. She couldn't hide behind the illusion of love when it had started to suffocate her.

A sharp knock on the door jolted her from her thoughts. She froze, her pulse quickening in her throat. No one had come to check on her since Victor left, and her first instinct was to retreat further into the shadows, to hide from whatever awaited her beyond the door.

But she knew. Deep down, she knew who it was.

"Elysia," a voice called from the other side, low and urgent. "Open the door. We need to talk."

It was Dante. Of course it was. He had been a constant presence, always watching from the periphery, like some silent guardian—or perhaps something more sinister. She hesitated for a moment, her hand hovering over the handle, then slowly turned it.

The door creaked open, revealing Dante standing in the hallway. His sharp gaze immediately found hers, his face a study of intensity, his jaw clenched tight. His eyes flickered over her, as if assessing the damage, reading the emotion that hung in the air like a thick fog.

"Victor's gone, isn't he?" Dante's voice was quiet, but it cut through the air, like the first warning of an approaching storm.

Elysia didn't answer. She couldn't. The words were trapped in her throat, the knot of confusion and guilt too thick to let anything else pass through. She simply nodded, her gaze dropping to the floor, unable to meet his.

Dante stepped into the room, the door closing softly behind him. He didn't ask for permission. He never did.

"He's gone," he said again, more firmly this time, as if trying to make sense of it. "But you need to understand something, Elysia. There's more at play here than you realize. This isn't just about you and Victor. It's about the Lupo family—and the Verrini. You can't just walk away from this. You can't erase what's been done."

Her eyes snapped up to meet his, her chest tightening with every word he spoke. "What are you talking about?" she demanded, her voice sharp, the first hint of anger slipping through her carefully constructed walls.

Dante stepped closer, his presence overwhelming, his shadow falling across her. "You think you're free, that you can simply choose to walk away from everything?" His gaze softened for a brief moment, but it quickly hardened again. "Victor made sacrifices. He's been fighting for this family, for you, even when you weren't looking."

Her breath caught in her throat, and her mind swirled with the force of his words. She knew that. Knew it all too well. But still… still it wasn't enough to quiet the ache inside her—the ache that had been there long before he'd come into her life, before his love had woven its way into every corner of her soul.

"Maybe it's time I start fighting for myself," she said quietly, her voice trembling with the weight of her resolve. "I can't keep fighting for a world that's not mine, Dante. I can't keep running in circles, hoping it will all make sense one day. I've given enough."

Dante's eyes darkened, his jaw tightening. "You don't get it, do you?" he said, a hint of frustration lacing his tone. "You think you can escape the mafia world like it's a bad dream, but it's real. All of it. You're already too deep, Elysia. You can't just leave. You can't just walk away from Victor and the family without consequences."

She shook her head, feeling a deep, hollow feeling in her gut. "I never asked for any of this. I didn't ask for any of it, Dante."

His voice softened, and he reached out, placing a hand on her shoulder. "I know. But you're here now. And you're part of it. Whether you want to be or not." His eyes met hers, and there was something in them—a glimmer of pity, or perhaps understanding—that made her heart lurch painfully in her chest.

There was no easy way out. Not for her, not for Victor, not for any of them. The world they lived in wasn't one that allowed for peace, not real peace. Only fragile moments between battles, only half-hearted attempts at control.

"I don't want this, Dante," she whispered, her voice barely audible. "I don't want to be a pawn anymore."

The silence between them was deafening. Dante took a step back, his expression unreadable. "No one wants to be a pawn. But sometimes, we don't get to choose."

Elysia looked away, her gaze falling once again to the window. The moonlight illuminated the landscape outside, casting long shadows over the villa. It was beautiful. But it was also a prison. A gilded cage.

And she had no idea how to escape it.

Victor was out there, somewhere. She had pushed him away, and now the weight of that choice sat heavily on her shoulders. Yet, in the stillness of the night, the realization hit her with full force: she couldn't escape her own heart. No matter how much she wanted to flee, she was still tethered to him, still caught in the web of his love and his world.

18

Old Enemies Resurface

The air was thick with tension, the kind that clawed at the chest and sank into the soul, pressing heavy against the very fabric of the Lupo family's carefully constructed empire. Victor sat at the head of the long, polished oak table, his sharp eyes narrowed as he stared at the map laid before him. The mansion's grand dining room, usually bathed in golden light, now felt cold, its grandeur a stark contrast to the dark thoughts swirling in his mind.

Elysia stood by the window, her fingers trailing absently across the glass. The soft rain outside mirrored the disquiet in her heart, each drop a tiny echo of the growing uncertainty that threatened to engulf them all. She had seen Victor in many moods—raging, calculating, triumphant—but never like this. His silence was a weapon, honed and deadly. It was the silence of a man on the verge of losing everything.

Elysia's thoughts were a tangle of confusion. She could feel the shift between them, the delicate balance of trust and fear that had once been their tether. That bond, once so strong, was now fraying, like the edges of an old, worn rope. She had known him to be ruthless, but now, something darker was taking hold of him. And it terrified her.

"Victor," she said, her voice a quiet plea that barely rose above the hum of the storm outside. Her gaze locked with his across the room, her heart skipping a beat at the flicker of something dangerous in his eyes. "What's happening? What aren't you telling me?"

His fingers flexed against the table, and for a moment, she could have sworn the world itself held its breath. "Luca Vellini is alive."

The name struck Elysia like a physical blow. Her pulse quickened, and the words hung in the air, thick and acrid. It had been years since Victor had spoken of Luca, the former associate whose betrayal had once almost shattered the empire. The man was thought to be dead—his body had been burned beyond recognition. But now, to hear his name again, it was as if the shadows of the past had crawled back to life.

"You're sure?" Elysia's voice was barely a whisper, her disbelief etched across her face. She turned to look at Victor, searching for any sign of the calm, calculating leader she had come to rely on. But there was nothing there now but raw fury.

Victor's lips thinned into a tight line. "He's been orchestrating the attacks on the family. Everything that's happened in the past few months—this is his doing." He slammed his fist against the table, and the glass of water beside him trembled. "He's using my mistakes, twisting them, and he's playing a game that's about to cost us everything."

Elysia's heart pounded in her chest, the weight of his words pressing down on her. The room seemed to close in around them, the walls no longer offering the sanctuary they once had. She had never seen him this unhinged, and a deep, gnawing fear crept up her spine. There was no telling what lengths Luca would go to now. He was as dangerous as he was cunning.

And yet, amidst the swirling chaos in her mind, a question bubbled to the surface. "Why now? Why would he resurface after all these years?"

Victor's eyes darkened, his hand clenching into a fist. "Because of you."

The words hit her like a gust of wind, knocking the breath from her lungs. "Me?" she repeated, her voice shaking. "What do you mean?"

Victor's gaze never wavered. "He knows what you are. What you were. And he wants you back." The quiet menace in his tone sent a chill crawling up Elysia's spine.

It wasn't the first time she had heard whispers about her past life, about the shadowy ties between her and the Lupo family. Victor had always been cagey about the details, but now, as the pieces of the puzzle began to shift, the truth seemed to be slipping through the cracks like sand through her fingers.

"He knows everything about you, Elysia," Victor continued, his voice low, barely above a growl. "He knows you were—are—linked to Isabella's death. And he will stop at nothing to use that against us."

The name of Isabella was like a razor's edge. The woman Victor had loved, the one who had been killed years ago, sending him spiraling into the abyss of revenge and power. Elysia's heart twisted at the mention of her, knowing the weight that name carried. She was not the first woman to be entwined in the Lupo family's brutal history. But she had no idea that her past had been so deeply woven into this web of lies and death.

"I never asked for this," Elysia said, her voice thick with the weight of her words. "I never asked to be a part of your world, Victor. I never asked for any of this."

Victor stood abruptly, his chair scraping against the floor, the sharp sound cutting through the tension. His eyes, full of an emotion Elysia couldn't quite place, locked onto hers. "I know. But you are. And now, we fight. For everything."

The tension between them crackled like electricity in the air, a palpable force that neither could ignore. Elysia's mind raced, her thoughts a blur. What was Victor asking of her? To stand by him? To fight against an enemy who had been lurking in the shadows all this time? She had never wanted this life, but now, the darkness was all she knew.

Her gaze shifted to the map before them, the intricate lines marking the family's territory and the growing threat of Luca's forces. She had seen this kind of planning before—ruthless, unforgiving, a battle for control. But as she looked at the map, at the paths that would lead them into battle, she saw more than just strategy. She saw the faces of the people she had come to care for, the ones who would be caught in the crossfire of this war.

Victor turned toward the door, his back rigid with determination. "I'm going to end this, Elysia. One way or another."

And as he stepped into the hall, the weight of his words hung heavily in the air. The world outside may have been soaked in rain, but inside, the storm had only just begun.

The night had fallen, draping the mansion in a shroud of darkness that seemed to suffocate the air. Victor stood in the hallway, his hands clenched at his sides, his jaw tight with barely contained rage. The weight of his words from earlier still lingered in the air, an oppressive force he couldn't shake off. Luca Vellini—the name echoed like a curse in his mind, and he could almost hear it bouncing off the walls.

Elysia was still in the study, staring at the same map, trying to make sense of the chaos that had come crashing down on them. The mansion, which had once been their sanctuary, now felt like a prison. Every room felt like it was closing in on them. Every shadow seemed to whisper the threat of Luca's return.

Victor had no time for distractions, no space for weakness. He could almost feel Luca's presence in every crevice, every corner of the house. He was here, somewhere—out there—pulling the strings. And Victor would be damned if he let him get away with it.

His mind was racing through the possibilities—betrayal, vengeance, power plays, alliances torn apart—all of it. Luca had always been the more calculating one, the type to lurk in the background, waiting for the perfect moment to strike. But now, the game had changed. Victor wasn't about to play by Luca's rules.

The sound of footsteps echoed through the hallway, bringing him out of his thoughts. Elysia emerged from the study, her face pale, her eyes wide with a mixture of fear and confusion. She had never seen Victor like this before. The man who had always been a force to be reckoned with, the man who could command the world with a single glance, was now unrecognizable.

"I need you to understand, Elysia," he said, his voice gruff, his eyes unwavering as he turned to face her. "Luca doesn't just want control of the family. He wants you. And he won't stop until he has you. This—" He gestured to the mansion, to the world they had built, "—this is nothing to him. It's just leverage."

Elysia swallowed hard, the words sinking into her chest like a stone. "Why? What is it about me that matters to him?" Her voice trembled despite her best efforts to keep it steady. She had never asked for any of this—never asked for the danger, the violence, or the ties that bound her to this mafia world.

Victor's eyes hardened. "It's not just you, Elysia. It's who you were. Who you are."

The air between them grew thick, the weight of his words settling on her like a fog. She could feel the chill creeping into her bones, the way the past she had tried so desperately to escape was now pulling her back into its grasp. She was part of a story she hadn't written, and Victor had just unveiled the first few chapters.

Victor's gaze flickered momentarily to the window, where the first light of dawn was beginning to edge into the dark sky. The world outside seemed eerily calm, as if the universe itself were holding its breath in anticipation of what was to come.

"Elysia," Victor's voice dropped lower, and for the first time since their conversation began, there was a trace of vulnerability in his tone. "I can't lose you. Not like this. Not after everything we've been through."

She met his gaze, the battle inside her intensifying. She had seen the world he lived in—the darkness, the bloodshed, the ruthlessness—but it wasn't supposed to touch her. Not like this. Her heart ached as she watched him struggle to hold onto the fragments of control he had left. He had already sacrificed so much for this family, for this empire, but now he was asking her to be the thing that tethered him to it. And what did that mean for her?

Victor's footsteps were measured as he closed the distance between them. His presence enveloped her, the familiar scent of his cologne mingling with the cold tension that had settled in the room. He reached out, his hand brushing against hers in a moment of rare tenderness, a touch that belied the dangerous man he was.

"I'll protect you," he murmured, his words dark with the promise of vengeance. "But I need you to trust me. Trust that everything I'm doing is for us."

For a moment, Elysia's heart beat against her ribcage, as if trying to break free from the walls she had built around herself. She wanted to pull away, to scream, to demand her freedom, but she knew the truth. She wasn't free. She never had been.

"I don't know if I can trust you anymore," she whispered, her voice trembling with the weight of the confession. "You've kept so much from me, Victor. All these secrets, all these lies."

Victor flinched, his jaw tightening. "I did it to protect you. To protect us."

"But it doesn't feel like protection," she retorted, the pain in her voice unmistakable. "It feels like a cage."

The silence between them stretched taut, like the calm before a storm. Elysia took a step back, her gaze never leaving his, her heart caught between the man she had come to love and the world she had never asked for. She wanted to run, to escape—to find the freedom she had lost. But something deep within her hesitated, pulling her back to him.

Victor's hand reached for her again, this time more insistent, his grip firm. "You can't run from this, Elysia," he said, his voice low and dangerous. "This is who we are. This is our fight now."

Elysia's eyes searched his, seeking the man she had once known—seeking the man who had promised her safety, warmth, and loyalty. But now, all she saw was the embodiment of the world that had trapped them both in its unrelenting grip. The mafia world, with its promises and its betrayals, was a force far stronger than either of them could escape.

"I'm not running," she said quietly, her voice steadying with the weight of her resolve. "But I'm not sure I can follow you into this darkness anymore."

Victor's expression softened, but only for a moment. He knew the fight ahead would not be won with words. It would be won with blood, with strategy, with sheer force. But for the first time in their shared journey, Victor felt the sharp sting of doubt. Could he truly protect her? Or was he dragging her down into the abyss with him?

With a final, reluctant glance, he turned toward the hallway, his figure swallowed by the shadows. Elysia stood motionless, the storm inside her far fiercer than the one outside.

She wasn't sure if she was ready to fight, but she knew one thing—Victor wasn't going to let her go. Not without a fight.

And that thought made her fear the future more than she had ever feared anything before.

The mansion felt colder than it ever had. Even with the heavy curtains drawn shut, the sense of foreboding lingered like a tangible weight in the air. Victor's footsteps echoed through the marble hallways, each step growing heavier, more deliberate, as though he was walking toward his own fate.

He had tried to prepare for Luca's return, but how could anyone truly be ready for this kind of war? His past with Luca was one of mutual ambition, respect, and, ultimately, betrayal. But the memories—though sharp and cutting—were nothing compared to the man who had once been his ally now resurfacing from the shadows.

Luca's return was more than just a threat to Victor's empire—it was a direct challenge to everything Victor had fought for. He had built the Lupo family into something unshakable, and Luca, with his devious manipulations and ruthless schemes, was intent on bringing it all down.

Victor's thoughts were interrupted by the sharp ringing of his phone. He didn't even need to check the screen to know who it was.

"Talk to me," Victor answered, his voice low, barely above a whisper, as if speaking too loudly might provoke the inevitable storm.

"It's done. He's here," came the terse voice of his closest lieutenant, Matteo. "Luca Vellini's men are moving into position."

Victor gritted his teeth. "Where?"

"Close," Matteo's voice crackled through the line. "Too close. He's already sent a message."

Victor's pulse quickened. He knew this was coming, but it felt too sudden, too abrupt. There had been no time for preparation, no time for strategy. The game had shifted, and Luca had made his first move.

Victor's fingers clenched around the phone, his knuckles white. "What's the message?"

There was a pause, a thick silence that seemed to stretch forever. Matteo's voice returned, quiet but edged with unease. "He knows about Elysia."

Victor froze. The words hit him like a physical blow. Elysia. His mind reeled. How much did Luca know? How had he gotten so close?

Victor's thoughts raced, torn between the immediate need to protect Elysia and the overwhelming fury that simmered just beneath the surface. He couldn't lose her—not like this.

"I'll handle it," Victor said, his voice hardening. "Get the men ready. I want every exit covered. No one leaves without my say-so."

A low chuckle echoed from behind him, shattering his concentration. A voice Victor knew all too well. A voice that had once been a whisper in the dark, and now, it was the harbinger of all the nightmares he had buried.

"Well, well. It's been a long time, hasn't it, Victor?"

Victor's heart stopped for a split second as he slowly turned around. There, standing in the doorway, with the faintest smirk tugging at his lips, was Luca Vellini.

The same dangerous presence. The same cold eyes that had once been his equal, now twisted with malice. The man was no longer the ally Victor had once trusted. He was the enemy—the kind of enemy that came back from the dead, clawing its way into the present with no remorse.

Luca's suit was dark and impeccably tailored, the silver of his cufflinks gleaming in the low light. He hadn't changed. But Victor? Victor had changed—he had to. He had built something from the ground up, something Luca would never understand.

"You," Victor said, his voice barely a rasp, an edge of disbelief running through it. "You should've stayed dead."

Luca's laugh was a dry, bitter sound. "If only that were the case, Victor. But you see, I have unfinished business." He stepped further into the room, his gaze sweeping over Victor with a mixture of nostalgia and disdain. "And you... You've made a mess of things."

Victor's hands twitched, his mind calculating the best way to neutralize the threat before it consumed him. But Luca's presence was suffocating, as though the air itself had thickened around him.

"What do you want?" Victor demanded, his voice dark with the venom he had worked so hard to suppress. "You had your chance, Luca. You threw it all away."

Luca's smirk deepened, his eyes narrowing with dangerous intent. "What do I want?" He paused, considering, before continuing. "I want what's mine. What you took from me." His gaze flickered, then sharpened as it landed on a figure standing in the corner of the room—Elysia.

She stood motionless, her eyes wide, her breath shallow as she watched the confrontation unfold. A part of her, deep within, had feared this moment. The moment Luca would come for her.

Victor immediately moved to her side, positioning himself between her and Luca, his stance protective, defensive. "You stay away from her," he growled.

Luca's lips curled into a cruel smile. "Protective, aren't we?" He took a step forward, his gaze never leaving Elysia. "She doesn't even know what she is, does she? What she's meant to be."

Victor's pulse thundered in his ears. Elysia's confusion mirrored his own, the weight of Luca's words bearing down on them both. But before he could respond, Luca spoke again, his voice deceptively soft, like a serpent weaving through the underbrush.

"She's more than just a pawn in this game, Victor. She's the key. The key to everything you've worked for, and everything you'll lose."

Victor's heart skipped a beat. "What are you talking about?" he demanded, his voice rising despite his best efforts to remain in control.

Luca's smirk widened, satisfaction gleaming in his eyes. "The game is only just beginning, my friend. And you'll find out soon enough. It's a shame you won't have the time to prepare."

Without another word, Luca turned on his heel, his footsteps echoing ominously as he disappeared into the shadows.

Victor's hand clenched into a fist, the muscles in his jaw tight with rage. He could feel the walls closing in around them, the danger of Luca's return now fully realized.

But there was something more pressing, something that sent a chill through his spine. The warning in Luca's words, the certainty in his tone—Victor wasn't just fighting for his empire anymore. He was fighting for Elysia's life. And no matter what it cost him, he would not let her fall into Luca's hands.

19

The Final Stand

The cold wind howled through the trees, carrying with it the promise of something far worse than just the biting chill. Victor stood at the edge of the cliff, his eyes fixed on the dark horizon, where the clouds had gathered like a storm cloud ready to break. His fists were clenched at his sides, the weight of responsibility pulling at him more than any physical force could. Elysia was behind him, her breath shallow as she tried to steady herself, the danger closing in on them like a vise.

Victor could feel her unease—she was no longer the confident woman he had once known. The events of the past weeks, the betrayals, the secrets, had fractured her in ways that he couldn't begin to repair. And yet, he had no choice but to keep her close. He needed her. His empire was crumbling around him, and she was the only thing that had kept him grounded, even if she was pulling away.

"Victor," Elysia's voice trembled, breaking through his thoughts like a shard of glass. He didn't turn to face her but instead clenched his jaw tighter, staring into the distance.

"What?" His voice was low, a growl that barely escaped his lips. He knew what she wanted to say, the questions that had been festering in her mind ever since the first revelation about their past lives. She had learned more than she should have—about him, about herself, and now they were standing on the precipice of a truth neither of them were ready to face.

"You're not telling me everything," she continued, her words hesitant but sharp. "I can feel it, Victor. You're hiding something, something more than just your past. What are you planning? What aren't you telling me?"

Victor exhaled slowly, his breath forming small clouds in the cold air. His mind was spinning, trying to figure out how to protect her, how to protect everything they had worked for, even as everything threatened to unravel. He had no answers. No easy solutions.

"It's not the time," he muttered, his gaze unwavering from the horizon. "Not yet. You need to trust me."

Elysia's lips pressed into a tight line, her resolve growing. She had trusted him once, blindly, but now, every word he spoke felt like a riddle wrapped in lies. The truth of their shared past haunted her, and she had to know more.

"I'm not trusting you blindly anymore, Victor," she said, stepping closer. Her voice, usually soft and gentle, now held an edge of determination that had been buried for far too long. She was no longer the frightened woman who had been swept into this world by his charms. She was a woman who had fought for answers, and now she demanded them.

Victor's body stiffened, his jaw tightening with the weight of the revelation. He wanted to turn to her, to face her, but he couldn't. There was too much at stake. His empire. His blood. His past. And now, her future was tethered to his.

"The truth?" He finally spoke, his voice thick with reluctance. "You want the truth, Elysia? You're not ready for it."

Elysia recoiled, her heart hammering in her chest. The truth—what truth? He had told her so much already, about their past lives, their connection, but there was always more, always something just beyond her grasp. What was he hiding? What was he afraid of?

"Then tell me now, Victor," she demanded, the words slipping past her lips before she could stop them. "What is it? What are you planning? What's so terrible that you can't even look at me?"

Victor turned then, his eyes darkened with conflict. His gaze pierced her, and for a moment, Elysia felt the full weight of his emotions—rage, regret, fear—pulsing through him. She had never seen him so vulnerable, and it unsettled her.

"I can't protect you from this," he said quietly. "From the truth. From everything that's coming. Vellini is coming. And you're caught in the middle of it all."

Elysia's stomach dropped. Vellini. The name still made her blood run cold, despite all the time that had passed. He had been the architect of their suffering, the shadow lurking behind every betrayal. She had always suspected there was more to his return than just power. But now, hearing Victor's words, the truth seemed to settle like a heavy fog around her.

"I don't care about the empire, Victor," she said, her voice rising. "I don't care about your world. I care about us. I care about the truth. I—"

She stopped herself, her breath catching in her throat. She could feel it—the bond between them, ancient and unbreakable, like an invisible thread tying her heart to his. It was suffocating. She didn't know whether to embrace it or tear it away. The choices before her were too much, and yet she couldn't escape the pull of their connection.

Victor reached for her, his hand brushing against hers, a fleeting touch that spoke more than any words could. "I know you don't care about my world, Elysia. But you're already in it. And I won't let you go."

The words echoed in her mind, each one a reminder of the love they had shared, the bond they had forged, and the inevitable darkness that surrounded them both. It was a world of power, of bloodshed, and she was no longer naive enough to believe that love could overcome it all.

Suddenly, the ground beneath their feet trembled. A distant rumble grew louder, followed by the sound of engines—a convoy of vehicles, dark figures approaching. The storm was here.

"Victor," she whispered, her voice breaking. "What's happening?"

His expression hardened. "It's time."

With a swift motion, he grabbed her wrist, pulling her toward the waiting helicopter that would take them to the heart of the battle. The final stand. The truth, the pain, and everything they had fought for would be tested here.

The helicopter soared through the sky, a silent predator cutting through the cold wind, its rotors slicing the air with a rhythmic hum that seemed to mirror the pounding in Elysia's chest. She sat across from Victor, her eyes fixed on the horizon, where the jagged silhouette of the city was slowly fading into the distance. The landscape below was blurred by the motion, as if her life itself was slipping out of focus, far away from the chaos she knew was coming.

Victor remained silent, his eyes scanning the landscape below, his posture stiff, as if he were bracing for impact. He had always been the master of control, of maintaining the calm facade that he had perfected over the years. But Elysia could feel it—his nerves, the tension in his shoulders, the faint tremor in his hands when he reached for his phone. His empire, his entire world, was crumbling beneath him, and he was caught in the storm of it all.

She wanted to reach out to him, to ease his mind with a single touch, but the distance between them was greater than the miles of air separating the helicopter from the ground below. The truth that hung between them—unspoken, unresolved—was too large to bridge with words. She could feel the weight of it pressing down on her chest, suffocating her.

"Victor," she said softly, the word falling like a whisper into the cold air between them. Her voice was raw, unsteady, as if speaking his name could unravel the last of her resolve. She had fought so hard to maintain her composure, but now, in this empty space between them, she found herself faltering.

He turned to her, his gaze intense and unreadable. "What?"

The bluntness of his response made her flinch, but she held her ground, forcing herself to meet his eyes. "What are we really fighting for? This empire, this life you've built—does it mean more than us? More than what we have?" Her voice wavered slightly, the vulnerability she had kept hidden for so long spilling out despite her best efforts.

Victor's jaw tightened, and for a moment, the air between them crackled with the weight of unspoken words. He looked away, his gaze hardening once more as he faced the horizon. "You know what we're fighting for. You know what's at stake."

Elysia's chest tightened. She had heard these words too many times, and yet they never seemed to answer the questions that haunted her. She wasn't asking about the empire. She was asking about them. About the future. About the choices they had made and the ones still waiting to be made.

"I'm not talking about the empire, Victor," she said, her voice growing more insistent. "I'm talking about us. This thing between us. The connection we have. The love… Is that enough to overcome everything else? Or am I just another piece in your world—a pawn to be moved around as needed?"

Victor's expression softened, his eyes momentarily betraying the harshness he had tried to maintain. His voice, when he spoke, was quieter, more raw than she had ever heard it before. "Elysia…" He trailed off, as if searching for the right words, but none seemed to come. He opened his mouth again, then closed it, as if the weight of her question was too much to answer.

The helicopter lurched slightly, its altitude adjusting as it began to descend. Elysia's stomach twisted with unease, but it wasn't just the motion that unsettled her. It was the feeling of being trapped—not just in the confined space of the helicopter, but in a life she hadn't chosen, a life that had been forced upon her by fate, by Victor, and by the blood-soaked world of the mafia.

She had come to terms with some of it. She had accepted that her life, her soul, was forever entwined with Victor's. But there were moments, like this one, when she couldn't help but wonder if she had made the right choice. If love was enough to sacrifice her freedom for.

The helicopter began to circle over the compound—the place where the final battle would take place. Elysia's breath caught in her throat as she saw the sprawling estate below, the army of men waiting in the shadows, the very same men who had been hunting them for weeks.

"We're here," Victor said, his tone clipped, professional. The man she had known, the man who had always been in control, was back—cold, detached.

The cracks in his armor had been sealed once more, but Elysia could still sense the turmoil underneath. It was a mask, one that couldn't hide the reality of what was about to happen.

Elysia's fingers tightened around the armrest as the helicopter touched down, its engines powering down in a low growl. She glanced at Victor, her heart heavy. There was no turning back now. The war was here. And no matter what happened, they would have to fight—not just for their lives, but for everything they had built together.

Victor reached across the space between them, his hand settling over hers with a surprising gentleness. It was a small gesture, but it felt like a lifeline, something that tethered her to him in this storm of chaos. His eyes met hers, and for a brief moment, the walls between them seemed to crumble.

"I'll protect you, Elysia," he said, his voice soft, yet filled with the weight of his promise. "Whatever happens, I'll keep you safe."

Her pulse quickened at the sincerity in his voice, but she knew, deep down, that there were no guarantees in this world of violence. Safety was a fleeting illusion. But as she stared into his eyes, she realized that she would fight by his side—not because she had to, but because she wanted to. The connection between them was too deep, too powerful to ignore.

With a final breath, Elysia nodded, her resolve hardening. "Let's end this."

The helicopter's doors slid open, and the cold night air rushed in, filling the cabin with the scent of rain and blood. The final stand had begun.

The night air was thick with tension as Victor and Elysia moved through the estate's shadowed halls, their footsteps eerily quiet on the polished floors. The silence was deceptive, as the storm of violence was just moments away from breaking loose. The walls seemed to press in on them, the weight of their choices, the weight of their enemies, all bearing down on their shoulders.

Victor's hand was firm on the small of her back, guiding her through the labyrinthine corridors. His eyes never strayed from the darkness ahead, his body tense, ready for whatever threat lay hidden in the shadows. He had been in countless battles before, but tonight, this felt different. Every move, every decision, carried the weight of more than just his empire. It carried the weight of Elysia's life, their future, and the fragile bond between them that had survived so much.

Elysia could feel the coldness of the marble beneath her feet, each step echoing the fear she had buried deep inside. Her heart raced, her thoughts a whirl of confusion and doubt. She had never wanted this world—Victor's world—yet here she was, standing beside him as the enemy closed in. Her hands clenched into fists at her sides, the need to fight, to protect, clashing with the desire for freedom, for escape. But there was no running now. There was only survival.

They reached the heart of the estate, the grand atrium where the final confrontation would unfold. The large windows framed the chaos outside, where a fleet of black SUVs surrounded the perimeter, their headlights cutting through the darkness like searchlights. The sound of distant gunfire, muffled by the thick stone walls, sent a shiver through her spine.

Victor stopped, turning to face her. His face was hard, his expression unreadable. But in his eyes, Elysia saw something she hadn't seen before—a flicker of uncertainty. For the first time since she had met him, she saw him as vulnerable as she felt.

"I need you to stay close," he said, his voice low but urgent. "No matter what happens, don't move without me. Do you understand?"

Elysia nodded, swallowing the lump in her throat. She didn't trust her voice—not when her chest felt like it was being crushed under the weight of everything that was happening. But she didn't need to speak. The bond between them, the connection forged in fire and blood, said everything.

The first shot rang out, loud and clear, shattering the fragile calm. The air seemed to explode with the sound of gunfire, the screams of men, and the violence that had always been lurking just beneath the surface of their lives. Elysia flinched, instinctively stepping closer to Victor as he reached for his weapon, a sleek black pistol that gleamed under the dim light.

"You stay with me," he growled, his voice barely a whisper as he pulled her behind him, shielding her with his body. His every movement was precise, calculated. A man who had been bred for war.

Elysia's pulse thundered in her ears as she followed him, her heart in her throat. She didn't know how to fight like Victor did—didn't have the ruthless efficiency that he wielded like a weapon. But she had something he couldn't take from her: determination. She would not let him fall. Not again. Not after everything they had been through.

Another volley of gunfire cracked through the night, but Victor was already moving, his body fluid and swift, a shadow among shadows. Elysia's breath caught in her throat as she followed, the distant hum of helicopters overhead filling the air, drowning out all other sound. The estate was under siege, and the enemy was closing in on all sides.

They moved through the chaos, dodging bullets, weaving between pillars, the tension mounting with each passing second. Elysia's mind was numb, a blur of movements and flashes of light, but one thing stood clear—she would not leave Victor's side.

But just as they neared the exit, the doors to the atrium were flung open, and a figure stepped into the doorway, silhouetted against the dim light.

Luca Vellini.

Elysia's breath hitched in her throat. The man she thought was dead, the man who had orchestrated so much of the chaos in their lives, stood before them. His dark eyes glinted with malice, a grin curling on his lips as he surveyed the two of them.

"Victor," he said, his voice smooth and mocking, like a serpent coiling its way around them. "You're late to the party. I thought you'd be the first to arrive. But then, you've always been predictable, haven't you?"

Victor's jaw tightened, his hand steady on the grip of his gun. "You should've stayed dead, Luca."

The grin on Vellini's face widened, and his eyes flicked to Elysia. "Oh, but you see, Victor, it's not just you I've come for. I've always had a… special interest in your little wife. She's more than she appears, isn't she?" His words dripped with venom, the insinuation clear.

Elysia's heart stopped. The secret she had buried, the truth about her past life, the connection to Victor, was exposed, and she felt the ground beneath her shift. She was no longer just a pawn in this game—she was the prize.

Vellini's gaze locked onto hers, and the twisted amusement in his eyes sent a chill through her. "It's time for you to face the truth, Elysia. You've always known there was something more to you, something deeper. I'm here to remind you of it."

Victor stepped forward, his gun raised, but before he could pull the trigger, Luca moved with lightning speed, knocking the weapon from his hand. The force of it sent Victor stumbling back, but he didn't falter. His fists clenched as he prepared for the fight ahead, but the weight of Luca's words lingered in the air, an insidious poison.

"You should've stayed dead," Victor repeated, his voice now a low growl, full of rage and desperation.

The battle for their lives, their future, had only just begun.

20

The Choice

The moon hung low over the horizon, casting a pale glow over the secluded estate where Elysia had sought refuge. The silence of the night was a rare luxury, the kind that only came after chaos had wreaked its havoc. She sat at the edge of the garden, her fingers curled around the rim of a glass of wine, though her attention was far from it. Her gaze wandered over the darkened landscape, the towering trees and quiet shadows, as if they might hold answers to the turmoil within her.

Elysia's mind was a storm—an overwhelming surge of confusion and longing that she could not escape. The weight of the choice she had to make pressed down on her like a suffocating blanket.

Stay or leave? That was the question that lingered, hanging in the air like a blade ready to drop. And with every breath she took, it became clearer that neither path would bring her peace.

In her heart, she loved Victor. He was her anchor, her protector, the man who had saved her time and time again from the dangers of the world they both inhabited. But he was also the reason she was trapped in a cycle of violence, betrayal, and death. Her mind flashed back to all the times he had ordered men to kill without hesitation, all the lives that had been destroyed because of his thirst for power. The brutality that ran through his veins was not something she could ignore.

Yet, there was still that undeniable pull—an invisible thread that kept her bound to him, even as she tried to break free.

The wind rustled the leaves of the trees, carrying with it the faintest scent of jasmine. Elysia closed her eyes, inhaling deeply, as if the air itself could offer her the clarity she so desperately sought. Her memories were tangled, fragments of a past life that had begun to seep into her present like ink spreading across a blank page.

She remembered her former self—Elysia, not the woman who had been reborn, but the one who had lived before. Her connection to Victor stretched beyond this lifetime, beyond the walls of this cruel world. She had loved him before, in another life, in another time. That love had been twisted by the very forces that now threatened to tear them apart.

The sound of footsteps broke through her reverie. Victor's presence was unmistakable, even before he spoke. His shadow fell over her, large and imposing, and Elysia stiffened, though she did not turn to face him.

"You're still out here," he said, his voice low and rough, as though he had been through a battle of his own. He knelt beside her, his fingers brushing hers. She flinched slightly but did not pull away.

"Thinking," she replied softly, her voice carrying more weight than she intended.

He studied her for a long moment, his gaze intense. "About what?"

Elysia's eyes met his then, her heart heavy with words she wasn't sure she could say. She had always known that their love was doomed from the start, that it was bound to collapse under the pressure of the world they lived in. But now, with the future unfolding before her like a path full of obstacles, she wondered if it was even possible to escape.

"About you," she said, her voice barely a whisper. "About us."

Victor's lips parted as if to say something, but he hesitated. The tension between them was palpable, the distance they had been unable to bridge growing wider with every passing day. He reached out to touch her cheek, his thumb tracing the curve of her jaw. His touch was tender, but there was a hardness behind it that she couldn't ignore—the weight of the mafia world that constantly loomed over them.

"I'll do whatever it takes to keep you safe," he murmured, his breath warm against her skin. "You know that, right?"

Elysia wanted to believe him, wanted to surrender to the comfort of his words, but the truth was more complicated. "Victor… I don't know if you can. Keep me safe, I mean."

The silence that followed felt like an eternity. Victor drew back slightly, his brow furrowing as he studied her. "What are you saying?"

She turned away from him, her gaze once again drifting to the darkened landscape. "I'm saying that I don't know if I can live in this world anymore. Your world, Victor. The violence, the betrayals… it's too much. I don't want to be part of it."

His hand dropped from her cheek, and for a moment, she thought she heard the faintest sound of his heart breaking. She didn't look at him, couldn't bring herself to. The conflict within her was too raw, too real.

"I'm not asking you to live in it," he said, his voice strained. "I'm asking you to be with me. To stay with me. We'll leave this place, Elysia. We'll go somewhere far away, where we can live in peace. We don't have to be part of this anymore."

Her heart twisted painfully in her chest. The idea of running away with him sounded like a dream—one she had longed for. But there was always a shadow that followed them, one that would never let them escape. The world would always come knocking, dragging them back into its darkness.

"I don't know if that's enough," she said, her voice barely above a whisper. "I don't know if we can outrun it. Not when everything we've done is tied to this world. To the mafia. To your family."

Victor's eyes hardened. "I'm not asking you to outrun it. I'm asking you to choose me. Choose us."

Elysia's breath caught in her throat as his words settled over her like a shroud. Choose us. The weight of that decision threatened to crush her, the implications of what it meant reverberating through her entire being. She wanted to choose him, wanted to believe in the possibility of a future free of the mafia's grasp, but how could she? How could she leave behind everything she had known, every piece of herself, just to live a lie?

And then there was the question of her past life, the memories that had begun to surface. Her connection to Victor had not just been born in this lifetime. No. It had been forged long ago, in another time, in another world. She had once loved him—perhaps still did. But was it enough to carry them through this? Was it enough to overcome the darkness that defined them both?

Tears pricked at the corners of her eyes, but she refused to let them fall. This was a decision she had to make on her own. No one else could make it for her—not Victor, not anyone.

"I need time," she whispered, her voice trembling.

Victor nodded, his jaw clenched. He didn't say another word, but his presence lingered as he stood and stepped back into the shadows. Elysia remained where she was, staring into the night, feeling the weight of the world pressing in on her.

The choice lay before her—stay and embrace the life she had with Victor, or walk away and forge her own path.

And no matter what she chose, there would be no going back.

The mansion felt colder than it had in days, the grand halls echoing with the silence that had descended after their conversation. Elysia walked through the marble corridors, her footsteps sharp and deliberate, though her mind was far from the present moment. She passed by the rooms, each one a silent witness to the life they had built together—the whispered confessions, the stolen glances, the passion that had once burned so brightly between them.

Victor was nowhere to be seen. She didn't expect him to be. The space between them had grown far too wide for words to bridge. And yet, here she was, trapped in a labyrinth of her own making, unable to escape the truth that clawed at her insides.

Her fingers brushed the cool surface of a nearby table, but she did not stop to touch or examine anything. Her thoughts were consumed by the man she had once believed to be her salvation, the one who had broken her down and built her up again, only to now stand at a crossroads.

A knock on the door interrupted her reverie.

She turned sharply. It was not Victor. His presence was unmistakable, like a storm on the horizon. Instead, standing in the doorway was Luca Vellini, the very last person she expected to see in this house, and yet his presence felt like the inevitable consequence of her choices.

His sharp features were set in a mask of amusement, as if he found this moment of turmoil both predictable and amusing. "We need to talk," he said, his voice cutting through the quiet like a blade.

Elysia's chest tightened. "About what?"

His eyes glinted in the dim light. "You and Victor. It's time for you to face the truth about everything you've been running from."

She took a step back, heart hammering against her ribs. The last time she had seen Luca, he had been a distant figure—someone she had only heard whispers of. Yet there was no mistaking the shadow he cast. Luca Vellini was not just another enemy. He was a reminder of the world she had tried so hard to escape.

"What are you doing here?" she demanded, her voice firmer than she felt.

He took a slow, deliberate step into the room, his gaze never leaving hers. "I'm here because you can't keep running from what you are. And you certainly can't run from Victor, no matter how hard you try. His past is tangled with yours in ways you don't even understand."

Elysia's breath caught in her throat. "You're lying."

Luca's lips curved into a cruel smile. "I'm not lying, Elysia. You can keep pretending all you want, but the past is catching up with you, and it's bringing you back to the very heart of this world—the world of the Lupo family."

Her mind spun as she took a step back, trying to steady herself. "No. I don't believe you."

"Oh, but you will," Luca said, his voice lowering, as if savoring the moment. "You will believe me when you realize that the life you want—the peace you dream of—is a lie. You've always been part of this world, whether you accept it or not. And now, Victor's world is your world, no matter how much you fight it."

Her pulse raced. She could feel the pull of his words, the undeniable truth hidden beneath his venomous tone. It was inescapable, like a spider's web slowly drawing her in. She wanted to deny him, to push him away, but a part of her was already listening. Was everything she had known really a lie?

Luca stepped closer, and the room seemed to close in around her, the air thick with the tension between them. "Victor will never change, Elysia. He's too far gone. He's a monster—just like the rest of us."

Elysia shook her head. "No. You're wrong."

But doubt lingered in the back of her mind, gnawing at her like a constant ache. Could she really trust him? Could she trust Victor? Her love for him was the only thing that had kept her grounded, but now, in the face of Luca's dark insinuations, she wasn't so sure.

Luca was waiting for her to respond, for her to crumble, and he knew exactly how to push her buttons. "I'm not here to deceive you, Elysia. I'm here to show you the truth. Victor cannot protect you from this. He cannot protect you from your own blood, the blood that binds you to this cursed family."

Elysia's knees felt weak, and she fought to stay upright. "Stop." Her voice cracked, but the words came out more forcefully. "I don't want to hear it."

Luca's eyes gleamed, and for a moment, there was something almost sympathetic in his gaze—an understanding of her pain, her inner conflict. "I'll let you decide, Elysia. But remember this—Victor will never let you go. Not until you've paid the price for your past."

She could barely breathe, the weight of his words pressing against her chest. He was right about one thing: there was no escape. She was bound to this world, no matter how hard she tried to resist. But that didn't mean she had to accept it.

As Luca turned to leave, a cold shiver ran down her spine. "Think carefully, Elysia. The choice you make now will determine everything."

The door clicked shut behind him, leaving her alone with her thoughts. She stood in the silence, the tension in the air thick and suffocating, as the reality of what Luca had said settled over her.

Victor's world. Her world. Their world. It was all one in the same, inextricably linked by fate, blood, and choice.

Her heart raced in her chest. Was this the moment she had been dreading? The moment when the past she had been running from caught up to her?

Elysia closed her eyes, trying to steady her breathing, but she knew—deep down—that the choice was no longer hers to make. The world had already made it for her.

And now, the only thing left was the final reckoning.

Elysia stood at the edge of the terrace, her back to the dimming sky. The fading light bled through the clouds in soft hues of orange and purple, casting long shadows over the sprawling gardens below. The mansion seemed a world away, its grandeur a silent reminder of everything she could never truly escape.

Her thoughts were a whirlpool of chaos—Victor's face, Luca's words, the remnants of her own identity, all swirling together in a storm she couldn't control. She didn't know how long she had been standing there, only that the weight of the decision pressed down on her like a suffocating force.

Behind her, she heard the faint sound of footsteps. She didn't need to turn around to know it was him—Victor. His presence was an undeniable force, one that had haunted every corner of her heart from the moment they had met. And yet, standing here now, it felt as if the space between them had never been wider.

He was silent at first, as if waiting for her to speak, to offer the words that would break the stillness. The world around them seemed to hold its breath.

"I never wanted this for you," Victor finally said, his voice rough, as though the words had been ripped from him. "This life. This world."

His words hung in the air like the scent of rain before a storm. She didn't turn to face him, but she felt his presence, the magnetic pull of his power, the faint warmth of his body so close to hers.

"I don't know who I am anymore," she whispered, barely audible, her voice trembling with the weight of the truth. The truth that had been creeping in, slowly unraveling everything she thought she knew. "I thought I was free. But all I've done is run from the past. And now it's here, catching up to me."

Victor stepped closer, his hand brushing lightly against her shoulder, as if testing whether she would pull away. "Elysia, you are not your past. You're not the person Luca says you are. You're stronger than that."

A bitter laugh escaped her lips. "Am I? Because right now, it feels like I'm just one more pawn in a game that's already been decided for me."

He was silent for a moment, the tension thick between them. "You're not a pawn. You're my equal," he said, his voice softer, more vulnerable than she had ever heard it. "I know I've dragged you into this world. I know I've made mistakes, but I would never let you become a victim of it."

She wanted to believe him. She wanted to reach out to him, to accept the comfort his words offered, but something held her back. A part of her was still clinging to the version of herself that had stepped into this world with nothing but hope. But that hope was slipping through her fingers, disappearing like mist in the morning sun.

"I love you," Victor said quietly, almost as if the words themselves were a plea. "I love you more than I've ever loved anyone, and I've destroyed everything for that love. But I can't make this decision for you. I can't make it easier for you."

Elysia closed her eyes, swallowing against the lump in her throat. The choice was excruciating—stay with him, this dangerous, beautiful man who had become her everything, or leave, carving out a future of her own, free from the violence, free from the lies, but at the cost of the only love she had ever truly known.

"I don't want to leave," she admitted, her voice raw. "But I can't stay, not if it means being trapped in this world forever."

Victor moved behind her, his breath warm against her ear as he spoke. "Then don't leave. Not yet. Stay with me, and let's end this, together. We can fight them, Elysia. We can make this right. We can take back control."

Her pulse quickened, but doubt crept in, dark and suffocating. The shadows of the past loomed over them both, their consequences waiting to be paid.

The bloodshed, the betrayals, the tangled web of lies that had kept them tethered to each other—it all came rushing back, drowning her in the weight of what she had to accept if she stayed.

"I don't know if I can be with you in this world," she whispered, almost as if she were speaking to herself. "I don't know if I can live with the choices we've made."

Victor's voice cracked with desperation. "You can. You've already made it this far, Elysia. We're stronger than this. You and me."

But Elysia's heart ached as she thought about her own soul, the part of her that had always longed for peace, for freedom. She could feel the suffocating weight of the past—of her reincarnation, of the legacy of the mafia world, and the chains that bound her to it. How could she run from it, when it was her own blood that had kept her tied?

"Victor..." Her voice faltered as the finality of it all began to settle in. "I don't think I can stay."

His breath hitched, and she felt the sharp sting of his rejection before he spoke. "Then leave."

His words cut through the silence like a knife, and for a moment, Elysia's heart shattered. But then, as the seconds stretched on, she realized something—she had already made her decision.

"I have to go," she whispered, more to herself than to him.

Victor stood there, the weight of her decision settling between them, the distance between them growing wider than ever before. He said nothing more, just stood in silence, his presence a ghost she would carry with her always.

With one last look at the man she had loved, the world she had once wanted, she turned away, her footsteps echoing as she walked away from everything.

21

Unmasking the Truth

The heavy air in the room seemed to vibrate with tension, thick enough to be sliced with a knife. Shadows clung to the edges of the dimly lit mansion, the walls bearing the weight of secrets that had festered far too long. Victor stood at the center of the room, his eyes sharp and calculating, his jaw clenched as if he were about to deliver a death sentence. Elysia, standing slightly behind him, felt the chill in her spine, a shiver not from the cold but from the heaviness of the moment—the moment when everything they thought they knew would unravel before them.

Victor had always been a man who lived in the shadows, but now, as he faced the truth of his family's betrayal, the darkness seemed to press in from all sides. The weight of responsibility crushed his shoulders, and yet, he did not waver. For once, the stakes were not just about survival—this time, it was about exposing the lies that had been buried beneath layers of power, deception, and blood.

His gaze flicked over to Elysia, and for a brief moment, something softer passed between them—a silent understanding, perhaps even a shared dread. She had grown too accustomed to these moments of tension, moments where the air seemed thick with the expectation of violence. But today, it was different. Today, the enemy wasn't just the Verrini family. Today, the enemy was closer than she could have ever imagined.

"Victor…" Elysia's voice was barely a whisper, as if speaking louder would shatter the fragile silence that had enveloped them. "What if we're too late?"

Victor's lips tightened, but he did not respond immediately. Instead, he stepped forward, his boots echoing on the marble floors, a sound that seemed to reverberate off the walls like the beat of a drum, signaling a march toward war. He paused, hand hovering over a leather-bound folder—the one that contained the evidence they needed to expose the conspiracy that had been brewing within the Lupo family for years.

For a brief moment, Elysia's mind wandered back to the events that had brought them here. She remembered the first time she'd crossed paths with Victor—a powerful, dangerous man who had seemed so sure of everything. And yet now, with everything unraveling, she saw the cracks beneath the surface. The way his hand trembled as it reached for the folder. The way his eyes darted between her and the evidence, as if looking for answers he couldn't find.

"You won't believe it." His voice, though low, carried the weight of a man on the edge of losing everything. "It's worse than I thought. Someone inside the family has been playing both sides."

Elysia's heart skipped a beat. She had feared it—feared the betrayal that had been hovering like a shadow just out of reach, waiting to pounce. But hearing it spoken aloud brought a chilling sense of finality. "Who?" she asked, her voice trembling.

Victor's eyes flicked to the folder, then back to her, the sharpness in his gaze growing more intense. "My brother."

The words hung in the air like poison, thick and bitter. Elysia felt the world tilt, her breath catching in her throat. The brother she had heard about in hushed whispers—Dominic Lupo—had always been a ghost to her, a figure shrouded in mystery and rumors. But to hear Victor speak his name with such disdain sent a chill crawling up her spine.

Victor continued, his voice low but tinged with fury. "He's the one who's been feeding information to the Verrinis. The one who's been orchestrating the power play behind my back, trying to take control of the family."

Elysia's mind raced, the revelation sinking in like a stone in water, rippling outward, spreading a cold panic through her veins. "But why? Why would he do this?"

Victor's jaw tightened, his hand gripping the folder with white-knuckled force. "Greed. Power. He's always wanted to rule. But now... Now, it's personal."

A bitter laugh escaped him, the sound hollow and empty. Elysia's heart ached at the sight of him, so broken in his anger and disillusionment. He was a man who had built his life on trust—on the idea that family meant something—and now, that very foundation was crumbling beneath him.

Elysia took a tentative step forward, reaching out to him, but he pulled away before she could touch him. The distance between them felt like a canyon, one that neither of them could bridge, even though they both desperately wanted to.

"Victor," she said softly, her voice full of concern, "we can't do this alone. We need a plan."

His eyes met hers, and for a moment, there was something vulnerable in his gaze. Something raw and unguarded. But just as quickly, it was gone, replaced by the steely resolve that had carried him through countless battles before.

"I know," he replied, his voice cold and controlled now. "We'll go after him. Expose him for the traitor he is."

He turned away from her, walking toward the window, his silhouette framed against the darkening sky. The city sprawled beneath them, a glittering sea of lights that seemed so distant, so out of reach. It was a reminder of what was at stake. Victor was not just fighting for his life or the Lupo family. He was fighting for the very soul of everything he had built.

But as Elysia watched him, she couldn't help but feel a growing sense of dread. The man standing before her—strong, ruthless, and determined—was a man who had already lost so much. And now, with Dominic's betrayal laid bare, she feared that even if they exposed the truth, it might not be enough to save them.

She swallowed hard, her thoughts a whirl of uncertainty. "And after that?" she asked, the question hanging in the air between them, fragile and delicate.

Victor's gaze didn't leave the window. "After that, we end this. Once and for all."

Elysia's heart skipped a beat. There was no turning back now. The truth was out, and nothing would ever be the same again.

The Lupo mansion felt like a fortress, cold and impenetrable, its walls steeped in a legacy of power and secrets. As Elysia made her way down the grand hallway, the echoes of her footsteps seemed to reverberate through the silence that had settled over the house. The weight of the truth Victor had revealed earlier still clung to her, its impact lingering like a bruise on her soul. She had seen Victor's cold anger, his willingness to confront the very heart of his family's treachery—but now, she wondered if he could handle the consequences.

Her own heart raced with a mixture of dread and resolve. The betrayal of Dominic, a man she had only heard rumors about, had shattered the fragile peace they'd managed to carve out of their violent world. It was a betrayal that threatened to engulf them both. Yet, amid the uncertainty, something else gnawed at Elysia—a deepening understanding of the gravity of their situation. There was more at stake now than just their lives. The future of the Lupo family was on the line. And with it, perhaps the future of the empire Victor had built—and the one she had reluctantly become a part of.

Her thoughts were interrupted by the sound of footsteps behind her, deliberate and unhurried. She turned, her breath catching in her throat. Standing at the end of the hallway was none other than the man she had come to fear and love all at once—Victor. His figure was silhouetted against the muted light streaming in from the windows, his expression unreadable. The tension between them was palpable, a thread pulled taut, ready to snap at any moment.

"Victor," Elysia breathed, her voice barely above a whisper, the weight of her emotions threatening to choke her.

Victor took a step forward, his face illuminated by the low light. His eyes—cold, but filled with a flicker of something unspoken—locked onto hers. "Are you ready for what's coming?" he asked, his voice hoarse, as though he, too, was struggling to contain the storm brewing within him.

Elysia nodded, her throat tight. "I don't know. But I have no choice, do I?"

Victor's lips curled into something resembling a smirk, but it lacked the usual confidence. "No," he said simply. "There's no going back."

The truth of that statement hung in the air, heavy and suffocating. In a world built on loyalty and blood, there was no room for hesitation, no time for second-guessing. The stakes were too high. Yet, as Elysia gazed into Victor's eyes, she couldn't help but wonder how much of her own soul she was willing to lose in the process.

"Dominic is a traitor," Victor continued, his words a grim declaration. "He's played both sides for years, feeding information to the Verrinis, undermining everything I've worked for. But now, we end it."

Elysia stepped closer to him, her heart pounding in her chest. She could see the fire in his eyes, but she could also sense the exhaustion beneath it, the toll that betrayal had taken on him. She had always known Victor to be a man of strength—untouchable, unwavering—but now she saw the cracks in his armor, the vulnerability that only she had glimpsed in fleeting moments.

"I'll stand by you," Elysia said, her voice steady despite the chaos brewing inside her. "Whatever comes next, we face it together."

Victor's gaze softened for a fraction of a second. But it was gone as quickly as it appeared, replaced by the unrelenting determination that had kept him alive through countless battles. He reached for her, his hand clasping hers with an intensity that sent a jolt of warmth through her. For all the darkness that surrounded them, this small gesture grounded her, reminding her of what they had—what they could still have, if they made it through this.

But then, just as quickly, Victor released her hand, his focus returning to the task at hand. "We need to move fast. Dominic is expecting us to come for him. We can't give him the upper hand."

Elysia swallowed hard, her mind racing. She could feel the fear coursing through her veins, but it was tempered by a strange sense of purpose. There was no room for fear now. Not if they wanted to survive.

The two of them moved quickly through the mansion, the cold stone floors clicking beneath their shoes as they made their way to the study—Victor's war room. It was there that all the final pieces of the puzzle would be put together.

As they entered, the atmosphere in the room was different. The usual cold, calculating presence of Victor seemed to have morphed into something darker, more foreboding. The desk in the center of the room was cluttered with maps, files, and photographs—a chaotic reflection of the battle they were about to face.

Victor went straight to the desk, his fingers moving swiftly over the papers, his mind already racing through the strategies they would need to implement. Elysia stood by the door, watching him. She wanted to say something—anything—that would ease the tension between them, but words seemed insufficient. She had seen the man who had once been so sure of everything—so untouchable—become a shadow of himself, fighting to reclaim what was his. She couldn't help but wonder if he could pull himself out of the abyss that Dominic's betrayal had pushed him into.

Victor finally turned to face her, his face hard, but his eyes softer than before. "We need to make sure we have all the information," he said, his voice a little more controlled now. "Dominic has allies. He's not just going to sit back and let us take him down."

"I know," Elysia replied, her mind already working through their options. "We'll have to be smart about it. No mistakes."

Victor studied her for a moment, as though weighing her words. "I won't let him destroy everything I've built," he said finally, his voice low and dangerous.

Elysia nodded, her own resolve hardening. She had no choice but to trust him—to trust in their shared strength. But as she met his gaze, she realized that she, too, had become entangled in this web of power, deception, and blood. The truth about Dominic was only the beginning.

They had no idea what lay ahead. But whatever it was, they would face it together.

The clock on the wall ticked away, each passing second a drumbeat in the tense silence that had settled over the Lupo mansion. The weight of the moment hung heavy in the air, and Elysia could feel it in her chest, a suffocating pressure that threatened to break her. She stood beside Victor, who was still going over the documents sprawled across the desk, the flickering candlelight casting shadows over his sharp features. His focus was intense, but she could sense the turmoil beneath it. He had been betrayed by his own flesh and blood—Dominic, the man who had been his closest ally, had sold him out to the Verrini family. And now, that same man was a traitor they had to confront head-on.

Victor's hands trembled ever so slightly as he sifted through the papers, his jaw clenched, teeth grinding with the effort of maintaining his control. The cold, ruthless killer that he had been known as—the one who had built his empire on blood and betrayal—seemed so far removed from the man she saw before her now. Elysia could see the cracks, the vulnerability, but she also saw the man who was still capable of great strength, despite the betrayal that had cut him to the core.

"We need to move," Victor's voice broke through her thoughts, low and urgent, a command that made her heart stutter. "Dominic knows we're coming. If we wait too long, he'll have a plan in place to turn the tables."

Elysia nodded, her pulse quickening with the realization that they were entering the final stretch. There was no going back now. They had exposed Dominic for the traitor he was, but that didn't mean victory was assured.

This fight wasn't just about power—it was about survival.

As they gathered their weapons, Elysia felt a cold rush of adrenaline surge through her. She had been in this world long enough to know that nothing was guaranteed. But there was something different about this fight. The stakes weren't just about the Lupo family's future, or the empire Victor had built. This was personal. This was about her, about them, and about what they had—or what they could have—if they made it through this.

The mansion's corridors felt darker now, the shadows stretching long and ominous as they moved toward the main hall. The air seemed to thicken with anticipation, the sound of their footsteps the only noise that broke the stillness. It was as if the mansion itself had become a mausoleum, a tomb of secrets, waiting to swallow them whole.

Victor's hand brushed against hers as they walked, his touch brief but electrifying. It was the smallest of gestures, but it spoke volumes. Despite everything, despite the danger, they were still in this together.

When they reached the front door, the sharp crack of gunfire echoed in the distance, shattering the silence and sending a jolt of panic through Elysia. The air was thick with the scent of gunpowder, the sharp tang of danger drawing nearer. Victor's eyes narrowed, his lips pressed into a thin line as he surveyed the landscape beyond the mansion. The Verrini forces were already closing in.

"We move now," Victor said, his voice sharp and commanding, a man who had long since abandoned hesitation. He turned to Elysia, his gaze piercing. "Stay close. I won't let them get to you."

Elysia nodded, her heart pounding in her chest. She knew the danger was real. She had seen it before, but this time, it felt different. This wasn't just a battle for power; it was a fight for their lives. The odds were stacked against them, and yet, she couldn't shake the feeling that something—someone—was waiting in the wings, ready to tip the balance in their favor. Or against them.

As they stepped outside, the chaos of the battlefield unfolded before them. The Verrini forces had arrived, their black SUVs lined up at the gates, their men already taking positions, their weapons glinting in the dim light. It was an ambush, a planned assault that they had prepared for—but it didn't make it any less terrifying.

Elysia's breath hitched in her throat as the first round of gunfire rang out. She ducked instinctively, her heart racing as she followed Victor's lead, darting between the shadows, moving fast but carefully. The sound of the bullets whizzing past her, the crack of glass shattering, the shouts of men yelling orders—all of it felt like a nightmare, surreal and disorienting.

Victor was beside her, moving with deadly precision, his every step calculated, every movement purposeful. She had never seen him so focused, so relentless. This was his world—the world of violence, of power struggles, and of betrayal. She had known that from the moment she met him, but now, as she fought beside him, she felt the weight of it press down on her.

They were moving toward the trees, where the next phase of the battle awaited. Elysia's senses were on high alert, every nerve firing as they closed in on their destination. But as they reached the cover of the trees, a sudden noise caught her attention. She turned, her heart leaping into her throat.

Dominic.

He stood at the edge of the woods, a sinister smile playing on his lips as he looked at them, his figure framed by the flickering lights from the mansion. He had been waiting for them—just as Victor had feared.

"I knew you'd come for me, brother," Dominic said, his voice dripping with mockery. "But I didn't think you'd bring your little girlfriend along for the ride."

Victor's eyes blazed with fury, but he didn't take the bait. Instead, he stepped forward, his voice cold and dangerous. "You've betrayed everything, Dominic. This ends tonight."

Dominic's smile widened, but there was something in his eyes—something that told Elysia he wasn't done yet. "This isn't just about betrayal, Victor. It's about power. And you're too weak to see that."

Before Victor could respond, a sharp crack split the air. The bullet that whizzed past them sent Elysia's heart racing, and she realized, with a sickening jolt, that Dominic had no intention of making this quick. This was a game to him, one he intended to play until the very end.

Victor grabbed Elysia's arm, pulling her down as another volley of gunfire erupted around them. The battle for survival had begun in earnest—and there was no turning back.

22

Crossing the Line

The weight of the air in the war room pressed on Victor's chest, a crushing reminder that the final hour had arrived. His empire, his bloodied legacy, was on the line—his family's power teetering at the edge of an abyss. The Verrini family had pushed them into a corner, but Victor had never been one to back down. He would make them regret ever challenging the Lupo name.

Standing at the center of the room, Victor's gaze flickered over the map sprawled out on the table. His fingers traced the perimeter of his territory, his mind calculating, calculating, and calculating once more. But there was no room for hesitation now. Not when the risk was this high. His empire had been built on loyalty and ruthlessness; there would be no mercy now. No more second chances. The Verrini would burn.

But then there was Elysia.

Her presence was a reminder of everything that had changed—the tenderness that had begun to pierce the cold steel of his heart. Her eyes, haunted by fear yet filled with a fierce defiance, had become his anchor. She was the reason he fought, the reason he hadn't completely fallen into the abyss of his own making.

Victor lifted his gaze to meet hers, standing at the edge of the table. Her expression was unreadable, her features still bruised from the fight they'd barely survived just days earlier. The sight of her—so broken, yet still standing—tore through him in ways he couldn't name.

"You're sure about this, Elysia?" he asked, his voice low, hoarse. The question wasn't just about the war, it was about them. About her place in this world he had forced her into.

Her lips parted for a moment, the words coming slowly, carefully. "I'm not sure of anything anymore. But I'm with you. We've come this far."

A flash of uncertainty flickered behind her eyes, but she masked it quickly. She was the only thing in this world that grounded him. Still, he couldn't shake the nagging worry that she would break under the weight of the choices they had made. Choices he had forced her into.

Victor exhaled sharply, brushing his hand through his dark, disheveled hair. "I won't let them hurt you again. Do you understand me? I will burn this world to the ground if it means protecting you."

Her gaze softened as she took a step closer, her hand brushing against his. The subtle touch was a comfort, but it also served as a painful reminder of everything at stake.

"I know," she said, her voice trembling ever so slightly. "But we both know this war... it's more than just us now."

The truth of her words gnawed at him, making his stomach tighten. She wasn't wrong. The stakes were higher than they had ever been before, and no matter how many enemies he destroyed, it wouldn't bring back the innocent lives lost. He couldn't escape the blood on his hands, nor could he shield Elysia from the consequences of his past.

"I've made mistakes," he admitted, his voice rough. "So many mistakes. But I'm not going to let this destroy us, Elysia. I won't let them take you from me."

Elysia's eyes shone, but there was no mistaking the sadness that flickered within them. She hadn't just been thrust into his violent world—she had willingly chosen to stay. But at what cost? The very question made her heart ache, torn between the love she felt for Victor and the part of her that longed for something beyond the shadows of the mafia.

Her mind churned with memories of the past. Her heart, conflicted, pulled her in two directions. She had long been a prisoner of circumstances—first in her past life, and now, in this twisted reality. Could she walk away from it all? Could she truly leave him, when every part of her was tethered to him in ways she still couldn't fully understand?

"Victor…" Her voice cracked, a sign of the vulnerability she rarely showed. "You're not just fighting for me. You're fighting for everything you've ever known. But I'm not sure I can keep living in this world. This… this war isn't just about survival anymore. It's about destroying people. You're becoming someone I don't recognize."

Victor's heart clenched. He knew. He knew that every moment they spent in this battle pulled them further apart. But if he allowed himself to stop, even for a moment, everything they had fought for would crumble. The empire, their lives—everything.

"I know who I am, Elysia. And I know what I'm capable of." His words were hard, like steel being forged in fire. "But I won't let this consume me. Not completely."

Elysia's eyes searched his face, as if looking for a crack in the facade, something that might show him as more than the monster he had become.

For a moment, she almost found it. A flicker of doubt. But then it was gone, replaced by the cold, unrelenting edge that had always been a part of him.

She wanted to believe him. She wanted to see the man beneath the empire, beneath the violence. But how could she when every time he pulled her closer, he was pulling her deeper into the chaos?

"I don't know if I can live with the things you've done," she whispered, her voice barely audible. "But I can't live without you either."

Victor's heart skipped a beat, the weight of her words settling in. His hand, trembling ever so slightly, reached for her cheek, his thumb brushing the tear that had silently escaped her eye. She had always been so strong, so fierce in her resolve. But in that moment, she was as fragile as glass—shattered and whole at once.

"I won't make you stay," he said, the words raw and aching. "You can leave if that's what you want. But if you do, know that you're leaving behind everything that we are. Everything that I am. I won't survive without you."

The silence between them stretched, heavy and suffocating. Elysia's heart drummed against her ribs, a pulsing reminder of the war within her. Her eyes searched his, trying to find the man she once saw beneath the ruthless, cold killer. But all she saw now was the weight of his choices—the empire, the bloodshed, and the sacrifices that had led them to this moment.

Victor's gaze never wavered. "Make your choice."

The night had fallen heavy around them, a blanket of shadows that seemed to close in from every angle. The war was no longer just a fight for power; it had become personal. The Verrini family's forces were on their way, closing in from all sides. In the distance, gunfire echoed through the streets, a grim reminder of what was coming.

Victor stood in the courtyard, his gaze fixed on the horizon. The chill of the night air cut through the fabric of his jacket, but it was the coldness in his chest that truly numbed him. His fingers flexed involuntarily at his sides, itching for the familiar grip of a weapon, but for now, he remained still. There was too much to lose.

Elysia stepped out beside him, the faint click of her boots on the stone barely audible over the distant sounds of warfare. She didn't need to say anything. The silence between them was comfortable, yet charged with an undercurrent of tension. They both knew what was coming, but neither was willing to say it aloud. The unspoken words hung between them like a weight neither could escape.

"Are you ready for this?" Victor asked, his voice barely above a whisper. The question seemed absurd, even to him, as if readiness could truly prepare them for what was to come. But it had to be asked. This war had already cost them so much, and the cost was only rising with every passing moment.

Elysia didn't hesitate. "I've already made my choice," she said, her voice firm. "I'm not backing down now."

Victor turned his head, his dark eyes meeting hers. For a brief moment, he saw the woman he had fought to protect—the woman who had stood by his side even when the world had turned against them. But there was something else in her gaze now. A hardness. A resolve.

Victor couldn't help but feel a pang of guilt, one that tightened in his chest. "I never wanted you to be a part of this, Elysia. This life… it's not for you."

"I don't get to choose, do I?" she replied, the edge in her voice betraying the calm exterior she had perfected. "This isn't just your war, Victor. It's mine now, too."

Victor's heart ached at the truth of her words. She had become intertwined with his world in ways he hadn't anticipated, and now, no matter how much he tried to shield her, she was as much a part of this as he was. And with that, the realization hit him with the force of a sledgehammer: he wasn't just fighting for his empire anymore. He was fighting for her life. For their future. A future that had become a fragile thread between them, fraying with every battle, every betrayal.

He reached out, his hand brushing against hers. The contact was brief, but it was enough to send a jolt of warmth through him. The connection they shared was more than just physical—it was the anchor they both needed in this storm. It had to be enough.

"Stay close to me," he said, his voice thick with emotion he refused to acknowledge. "If we're going to get through this, we do it together."

Elysia nodded, her expression softening for a split second before it hardened once more. She was prepared. She had to be. But even as the words left her lips, doubt gnawed at her from the inside. The choice between survival and love was never an easy one. Not when both were pushing her in opposite directions.

The sound of footsteps behind them broke the silence, and they both turned to see Luca, Victor's trusted lieutenant, approaching. His face was grim, the usual confidence replaced by something darker. The war had taken its toll on everyone. Even Luca, who had always worn his stoic demeanor like armor, seemed more vulnerable than usual.

"They've moved in closer," Luca said, his voice low. "They're ready for a fight."

Victor's jaw tightened. "Then we give them one they'll never forget."

Luca nodded, his eyes briefly flicking to Elysia. The unspoken understanding between them was clear: she was not just Victor's weakness, but his strength. And protecting her was as much a priority as taking down their enemies.

As Luca turned to walk back toward the inner chambers of the estate, Victor and Elysia lingered for a moment longer, each lost in their own thoughts.

"Victor," Elysia said, breaking the silence once more, her voice softer now, as if she were searching for something she wasn't sure she'd find.

"Yeah?" His gaze didn't leave the horizon.

"I've seen what you're willing to do for your family," she continued. "But I need to know if you'll do it for me, too. When the line is crossed, when there's no turning back… will you be able to come back from it?"

The question hung in the air like smoke, curling around them, wrapping itself around their hearts. Victor turned to face her, his eyes searching hers for something that would tell him he wasn't lost. That there was still a way out. A way to keep her safe.

But the truth was, he wasn't sure anymore. The lines had blurred. The man who had once fought for honor and loyalty had long since been consumed by a world of bloodshed and betrayal. And as much as he wanted to protect Elysia from it, he couldn't promise her that he could stop. Not now. Not when the world was coming for them.

"I don't know," he said finally, the honesty in his voice a rare thing. "I don't know if I can come back from it. But I'll fight to make sure you don't have to."

Elysia studied him, her eyes searching for some trace of the man she loved beneath the cold, calculating warrior. And in that moment, she realized that they were both lost in the same war—fighting not just for survival, but for each other. And as much as she feared what the future held, she knew she would stand by his side. No matter the cost.

"I'll be with you," she said, her voice resolute.

As the two of them turned and walked toward the war room, the weight of their decisions pressed down on them. There was no going back now. The final battle was upon them, and there was only one thing left to do: fight.

The battlefield was a place of nightmares—gunshots rang in the distance like thunderclaps, the acrid scent of smoke curling through the air, heavy and suffocating. Victor and Elysia had long since passed the point of no return. The Verrini family's soldiers were closing in, their numbers overwhelming, their tactics brutal. And yet, as they stood side by side, there was a strange kind of clarity in the chaos.

The walls of the Lupo estate had been breached hours ago, and now, they stood in the heart of the compound, waiting for the storm to break.

Victor's eyes never left the horizon, his face a mask of determination and cold calculation. His thoughts were as sharp as the knives he had learned to wield, but tonight, he was no longer just a man of power. He was a man who had chosen to protect the woman beside him—no matter the cost. His chest tightened, and the gnawing dread that had been festering for days now clawed at him with a ferocity he couldn't ignore.

The war had always been about control, about domination, but now, it was about survival. And Elysia… she was his anchor. The thought that he might lose her was unbearable, something that shook him more than any weapon or enemy ever could.

"You're not going to like this," Luca said, his voice gravelly as he emerged from the shadows, eyes scanning the battlefield with the same grim focus. "We've got less than an hour before the Verrinis are inside the main house. We need to move."

Victor turned, his gaze piercing. "And what's the plan?"

Luca hesitated, a brief flicker of uncertainty crossing his face. It was a momentary crack in his otherwise unflappable demeanor. "We fight to the death if we have to. But I don't know if we'll survive this one, Victor. Not all of us."

Victor's jaw clenched, a dark promise flickering in his eyes. "Then we die fighting."

Elysia, ever the silent observer, felt the tension shift in the air. The words they spoke weren't just for the battle they faced—they were the unspoken truths of a world that had always been corrupt, always been soaked in blood. They were the consequences of a life she had chosen to be a part of. But now, standing at the edge of their doom, the reality of that choice cut deeper than any wound could.

"Victor," she said softly, her hand reaching out to grasp his arm. "We don't have to do this. We don't have to be part of this violence anymore."

Victor's eyes softened, but only for a moment. He knew the weight of her words. Knew the depth of the choice she was offering him. But this life—this world they had fought to build together—was too far gone to walk away from. Even if they wanted to. Even if he wanted to.

"Elysia," he said, his voice low and steady, "there is no going back now. We're in this together. Whatever happens next, we fight for each other. And for the family we've built."

The look she gave him was a mixture of love, regret, and understanding. The kind of look only a woman who had seen the man she loved struggle with his morality could give. And in that brief exchange, something unspoken passed between them—an acknowledgment that no matter the outcome, they were bound by a shared fate. A fate neither of them could escape, no matter how much they wanted to.

The sound of footsteps echoed from the hallway beyond. Luca's men were moving into position, and the final battle was at hand. Victor straightened, his posture shifting into the cold, commanding presence he had always embodied. He reached for the weapon at his side, his hand steady as he checked the ammunition, the cold metal a reminder of the violence that would soon unfold.

Elysia stepped forward, standing tall at his side. The woman who had been thrust into a world she never asked for, now a warrior in her own right. Her eyes sparkled with something fierce—a determination that matched Victor's. It wasn't just love that had brought her this far. It was survival, the fight for their lives, and the desire to protect the man she had come to love despite the cost.

"We go in, we finish this," Victor said, his voice a low growl. "No mercy."

"No mercy," Elysia echoed, her voice unwavering.

They walked together toward the gates of the estate, the echoes of their footsteps heavy on the stones beneath them. As they reached the outer perimeter, the distant rumble of approaching enemy soldiers grew louder. They didn't have much time.

The sight that awaited them was more grim than any had imagined. The Verrini's forces were massed in the distance, their silhouettes cutting through the smoke, their weapons drawn. The tension was so thick, it could have been cut with a knife.

Luca nodded, signaling to his men to take their positions, their faces set in grim determination. They all knew this would be the fight of their lives—the final stand. There would be no second chances.

Victor's eyes scanned the field, mentally calculating the best course of action. But all thoughts of strategy were cut short when a lone figure stepped forward from the enemy's ranks—a man Victor recognized with a sickening twist in his stomach.

Nico Verrini. The brother of the man Victor had killed. The brother who had sworn revenge and now, stood before him like an executioner awaiting the final blow.

"You're going to regret this, Victor," Nico called out, his voice carrying through the smoke, mocking and confident. "This ends tonight."

Victor's grip on his weapon tightened, and for a moment, everything else fell away. The world, the chaos, the bloodshed—it all disappeared. There was only Nico. And there was only one thing left to do.

"Not tonight," Victor said, his voice cold as ice. "This ends with you."

The battle was about to begin, and there was no turning back.

As the first shots rang out, Elysia moved beside Victor, her heart pounding in her chest. This was their moment—the moment when everything would change. For better or for worse, they were crossing the line together.

And as the first wave of enemies charged, she knew they would either survive together, or fall together.

23

Rebirth

The smell of antiseptic hung in the sterile air, mingling with the faint scent of roses from the vase beside the bed. The soft hum of medical equipment was the only sound that accompanied the stillness in the room. Elysia lay motionless, the white sheets pulled tightly over her, her face pale against the darkened backdrop of the night. The cool light filtering through the curtains cast long shadows on the walls, drawing out the lines of the room that felt too confining, too silent.

Victor stood at the foot of the bed, his broad shoulders hunched as if the weight of the world was resting on them. He watched her—his gaze unwavering, yet distant. His hands were clasped in front of him, the dark rings under his eyes more pronounced than ever before. The battle, the bloodshed, the sacrifices—it was all etched in the lines of his face. He had always been a man who wore the burden of his decisions with silent grace, but now, as he stood there, watching Elysia fight for breath with each shallow rise of her chest, he was unraveling. The pieces of the empire he had built, the empire he had tried to protect, lay shattered in front of him. And yet, his most important battle was here, in this quiet room, where the woman he loved clung to life.

The rhythmic beep of the heart monitor was the only thing keeping him tethered to reality. Every beat of her heart was a reminder of the fragility of this moment—the fragility of her life. He didn't know how to fix this. He didn't know if he even could.

He couldn't bring himself to leave her. Every part of him screamed to stay, to be here, to fix what had broken between them. But what if it was too late?

Elysia's eyelids fluttered, her long lashes brushing against her pale skin as she slowly came to. The fog of pain, the remnants of the battle still clouded her mind, but she knew one thing for certain—she was alive. Her body screamed in protest, every inch of her sore and bruised, but she could still feel him. Even with the distance between them, she could feel the gravity of his presence. It pulled at her, anchored her to this fragile reality.

Her voice was hoarse, barely a whisper, but it was enough to break the silence that had stretched between them.

"Victor?"

His heart clenched at the sound of her voice, fragile and raw. He moved to her side, taking her hand with the tenderness of someone afraid to break something delicate. His thumb brushed across her knuckles, and for a moment, he couldn't find the words. It wasn't that he didn't want to speak—it was that he didn't know where to start.

"You're awake," he managed, his voice low, filled with unspoken emotions. He wanted to say more, to tell her that everything would be okay, but he couldn't bring himself to lie to her. Not now. Not after everything they had been through.

Elysia's gaze locked with his, and in the quiet that followed, she searched his eyes for answers. She saw the guilt, the fear, the weariness etched into his expression, and it made something inside her twist painfully. She had always known Victor was haunted by his choices, but now she saw just how deeply those choices had cut into him.

"I..." Her voice faltered. "I thought... I thought I had lost you."

Victor's grip tightened on her hand, as if he could somehow hold the weight of the world in the simple contact. "I'm still here," he whispered, the words carrying more weight than either of them could comprehend.

A fragile silence settled between them. Elysia closed her eyes, taking in a shaky breath. Her body ached, but it wasn't just her body that was bruised. It was her soul. She had been through hell, and she was still standing—barely. The world they had tried to escape from had found its way back into their lives, and now they were left to pick up the pieces. The choices they had made, the bloodshed they had left in their wake—it was all too much to bear.

"I'm sorry," she whispered, her voice barely audible. "For everything."

Victor's heart stuttered at the words, and a sharp pang of guilt twisted inside him. He had failed her in so many ways. He had pulled her into his world, his battles, and now, here she was—broken, hurting, and afraid.

"You don't have to apologize," he said softly. "This... this is my fault. I brought this all upon us." His voice cracked slightly, and for the first time in what felt like an eternity, he let his guard fall. The mask he had worn for so long, the cold, unyielding mafia boss who never showed weakness, shattered in that moment.

Elysia's eyes softened as she reached up, her fingers grazing the side of his face. The roughness of his stubble against her fingertips reminded her of the man she had come to love—a man who had never known peace, a man who had been forged in a world of violence. Yet, beneath that exterior, she knew there was more. There was a tenderness, a vulnerability, that he rarely allowed others to see.

"We can't change the past," she said softly, her hand falling back to the bed. "But we can rebuild. Together."

Victor's breath caught in his throat at her words. Rebuild. Could they really do that? Could they rebuild a life from the ashes of the one they had destroyed?

"I'll do whatever it takes," he said, his voice thick with emotion. "I'll fix this. I swear."

The sincerity in his voice was unmistakable, and Elysia felt something shift inside her. There was hope. Despite the blood that had been spilled, the lies that had been told, there was still a chance.

But that hope was fragile—just like her.

As the night stretched on, the weight of their shared pain hung heavy between them, but in that moment, they had found something worth fighting for. The road ahead would not be easy. There would be more battles to face, more sacrifices to make. But as long as they had each other, maybe—just maybe—they could rebuild the life they had lost.

The sun had risen, casting a soft golden light into the room, but for Victor, the warmth of the morning was an unwelcome reminder of the battle that had left its mark on everything he had ever known. His empire—the one he had spent years building, shaping with cold precision, was no longer the fortress it had once been. The walls he had carefully constructed, the power he had wielded so effortlessly, had crumbled in an instant. Now, all he was left with was a fragile, fractured reality.

Victor stood by the window, staring out at the sprawling city below. The world felt far away, as though it existed in another lifetime. His empire, the Lupo family, the underworld that he had commanded, had never seemed so distant, so irrelevant. In that moment, all he could focus on was the woman who had somehow found a way to break through the walls he had spent so many years erecting.

Elysia's voice broke through the haze of his thoughts. He turned to see her sitting up in the bed, propped against the pillows, her expression tired but resolute. She was still pale, her body a map of the violence that had been inflicted upon her. But her eyes—those fierce, unyielding eyes—were as sharp as ever. They reminded him of the woman who had walked into his life, ready to face the chaos of his world. And yet, here she was, a shadow of the person she had been, struggling to find herself again.

"How long have I been out?" Her voice was rough, but there was a quiet strength in it. Elysia wasn't one to remain a passive observer, and Victor knew that in her silence, she was already analyzing everything, processing the weight of the world.

"Long enough," he replied, his tone flat, betraying none of the anguish he felt. His eyes lingered on her for a moment before he turned back to the window. "The battle… it was worse than I thought. The Verrinis are relentless. They've torn apart everything."

Elysia's gaze softened, her brows knitting together in concern. She could see the shadows under his eyes, the strain in his shoulders. He was carrying the weight of the world, just as he always had. But now, it felt heavier, darker. She had seen him face impossible odds before, but this—this was different.

"The Verrinis will pay for this," she said, her voice stronger now, more certain. "We'll rebuild. But we need to find a way to regain control, Victor.

You can't keep carrying the entire weight of this empire on your own."

Victor turned back toward her, his eyes narrowing. "I'm not carrying it alone. I have you."

Elysia held his gaze. There was something unsaid between them, something that neither of them had fully addressed, not yet. She could feel the depth of his words, but she also knew that he was holding back. There was a distance between them, a tension that neither of them had been able to bridge since she had woken up. The air between them crackled, filled with things they hadn't said and things they didn't yet understand.

Her lips parted, but before she could speak, the door opened without a sound. The familiar figure of Luca stepped into the room, his presence like a storm cloud, heavy and ominous. He had been a constant in Victor's world, a trusted ally, but his arrival brought a new sense of uncertainty.

"You're both awake," Luca said, his voice low and clipped. His gaze flickered briefly to Victor before resting on Elysia. "We need to talk. There's no time to waste."

Victor's expression hardened at the interruption, but he gestured for Luca to continue. Elysia, too, shifted slightly, feeling the tension in the room tighten. Luca was the last person she wanted to face right now, but she knew that what he had to say was likely more urgent than any of the quiet conversations she'd wanted to have with Victor.

"What's happened?" Victor asked, his voice sharp, every inch of him on edge.

Luca's eyes met his, and for a moment, the two men shared an unspoken understanding. The weight of their world was about to come crashing down on them both.

"The Verrinis have made their move," Luca said, his voice cold with the kind of certainty that came only from years in the underworld. "We've lost more ground than we thought. There's talk of another alliance forming—something bigger, something more dangerous than anything we've dealt with before. And if we don't act fast, the Lupo family will be wiped off the map."

The news landed heavily, like a fist to the gut. Elysia's stomach churned as she processed the gravity of what Luca was saying. She had known that the war between the families had been escalating, but this—this felt like the point of no return. The Lupo family's future was hanging by a thread, and they were standing at the precipice of complete annihilation.

"Who's behind it?" Victor's voice was tight, his jaw set in a hard line as he turned to face Luca fully.

Luca hesitated for a moment before answering, his gaze shifting toward Elysia. "There's a traitor in our midst. Someone close to you, Victor. Someone inside the family."

Victor's eyes darkened, a flicker of rage flashing across his face. He had always known that betrayal was an inevitable part of the life they led, but this was different. The betrayal had come from within, from someone who had been trusted.

"Who?" Victor demanded, his voice low and dangerous.

Luca's eyes shifted again, the tension in the room palpable. "We don't know yet. But I suspect it's someone who's been playing both sides for a long time. We need to act fast, or we'll lose everything."

Elysia watched the exchange, her mind racing. This was no longer about fighting for survival—it was about fighting for the soul of the Lupo family.

And in that moment, she realized something. No matter how hard she tried to escape the world Victor had pulled her into, it would always find a way to pull her back.

"We'll find who did this," Elysia said, her voice steady, even as her heart hammered in her chest. She would stand by Victor, no matter the cost. She had to. This was her battle, too.

Victor glanced at her, his expression softening just a fraction, but there was no time for sentiment. The clock was ticking, and the enemy was closing in.

"Then let's go," Victor said, his voice hard as steel.

And as they left the room, the weight of their choices pressing down on them, Elysia couldn't shake the feeling that this was only the beginning of a storm that would test them all in ways they could never imagine.

The quiet of the mansion felt suffocating in the aftermath of the storm. The battle was over, but the damage lingered in the walls, the floors, and in the minds of everyone who had been caught in the chaos. Victor stood in the dimly lit corridor, the flickering lights casting shadows over his face as he stared at the ground beneath his feet. The silence in the house was deafening, a stark contrast to the violence they had just survived.

Elysia's soft footsteps echoed down the hall, drawing his attention. He didn't look up as she approached, but he could feel the weight of her presence. She was healing, physically. But more than that, he sensed she was beginning to heal emotionally, too. There was something about her now—something different. Something more grounded, more certain. It was as though the chaos of the last few days had stripped away the remnants of her fears, leaving behind the woman he had always known was inside her.

Victor finally turned his gaze to her, his expression unreadable, his eyes dark pools of thought. His mind still raced, calculating what had to be done to secure what little was left of the empire. The Verrinis had taken too much. Their allies, the ones who had pledged loyalty to him, were now divided, unsure whether to side with the fallen leader or to break away and forge their own path. But through it all, one thing remained clear to him.

Her.

Elysia had been his anchor, his constant in the storm. Through every betrayal, every moment of uncertainty, she had remained steadfast by his side. But now, as the dust settled, the reality of their relationship—of everything they had built together—felt fragile. The love between them, so fierce and undeniable, was tested as never before. And it scared him.

"Victor," she said, her voice breaking the silence like a whisper of a storm. "We can't keep doing this."

He frowned, her words cutting through him like shards of glass. She was right, of course. They couldn't keep living in this cycle of violence, of constant battles, of destruction. They had both suffered enough.

"I know," he replied, his voice hoarse. The words tasted foreign to him, but he couldn't deny the truth in them. "But what other choice do we have? The Verrinis won't stop until they've destroyed everything we've built. And there's no escaping this world, Elysia."

She stepped closer to him, her expression filled with a mixture of sadness and resolve. Her eyes met his, and in that moment, Victor saw the vulnerability in her—something he had never allowed himself to acknowledge before.

"You're wrong," she said softly. "There's always a choice. And maybe, for once, we need to stop asking ourselves what's best for the family, what's best for the empire, and start asking ourselves what's best for us."

Victor's chest tightened as the weight of her words settled on him. He wanted to believe her. He wanted to believe there was a future where they could leave all of this behind, escape the world of power and bloodshed that had shaped their lives. But could they? Could he?

"I want to believe that," he said, his voice thick with emotion. "I do. But leaving this life—leaving everything behind—it's not that simple."

Elysia's hand reached out, her fingers brushing against his, the touch gentle but firm. Her eyes never wavered as she spoke, her voice steady despite the storm swirling around them.

"We don't have to leave it all behind, Victor. But we need to stop running from the truth. We need to stop pretending that we can fix everything with power and violence." Her eyes softened as she spoke again, the intensity of her gaze unwavering. "We've been through hell, both of us. And we're still here, still standing. But I'm not the same person I was when I first walked into your world. I've changed. And so have you."

Victor's heart hammered in his chest. He wanted to pull away, to shut her out, to retreat into the familiar, hard shell of the man he had been before. But her words—the truth in them—compelled him to stay, to listen.

"I've always been driven by fear, Elysia," he said, his voice barely above a whisper. "Fear of losing control, fear of being weak, of being vulnerable. But every time I try to protect us with power, I end up losing something—someone. I've lost so much already."

Elysia's gaze softened, her fingers tightening around his as she stepped closer, closing the distance between them. "But we don't have to fight alone anymore. We have each other. And that's enough, Victor. We've faced our demons. We've bled together, fought together. I'm not asking you to give up everything. I'm asking you to choose me. Choose us. Choose love."

Victor swallowed hard, his throat tight. It was the first time he had truly heard her—heard the woman beneath the walls he had built, the woman who had loved him through every wound, every scar. And for the first time, he realized something that made his chest ache with the enormity of it all.

He wasn't afraid anymore.

Victor reached for her then, his hand finding her cheek, the touch gentle, reverent. His thumb brushed across her skin as he gazed into her eyes, the depths of their shared pain reflected in them.

"I'm scared," he admitted, the words feeling like a confession. "But I want to try. For us."

A smile tugged at the corner of Elysia's lips, a fleeting, bittersweet thing, but it was enough.

"We'll rebuild," she said, her voice low but unwavering. "Together."

As their lips met, the kiss was slow, measured, as though they were both savoring the moment, tasting the promise of something new. In that kiss, there was a new understanding between them—a recognition that their love had been tested in ways neither of them could have ever imagined, and yet, here they were, standing on the precipice of something more.

But even as they embraced the possibility of a future together, a shadow loomed on the horizon. The war was far from over. The enemies they had vanquished would not stay down forever. And as the kiss deepened, Victor's mind already began to race, preparing for the next battle, the next threat.

But for now, for this fleeting moment, they had peace.

24

Moving On

The soft hum of the ocean waves crashing against the rocky shoreline echoed in the distance, mingling with the scent of salt and the cool breeze that swept across the secluded beach. Elysia stood at the water's edge, her toes barely touching the wet sand, the retreating tide leaving a trail of foam behind her. The morning sun was breaking through a blanket of clouds, casting the beach in a gentle, golden hue. It was a scene that felt almost too perfect—too serene to be real.

She inhaled deeply, the air filling her lungs, pushing away the remnants of anxiety and fear that had once ruled her life. The past had left scars, invisible to the world but deep within her. Yet, in this moment, there was no trace of the darkness that had clung to her, no echo of the violence and manipulation that had once been her reality. For the first time, she felt… free.

Victor, a few paces behind her, leaned against a nearby rock, watching her with a mixture of admiration and cautious longing. His eyes, dark and unreadable, followed her movements, but his mind was a battlefield of its own. He wanted to reach out, to touch her, to pull her close, but something inside him held him back. The weight of everything they had been through, the blood spilled, the lives torn apart, still hung between them like an invisible thread. Was this peace? Or merely the calm before the storm?

"Are you coming?" Elysia's voice broke through his thoughts, soft and steady, but carrying a subtle note of uncertainty.

Victor straightened, his gaze shifting from her to the horizon. "I'm not sure. It feels like we're waiting for something."

Her lips quirked in a faint smile, the first one he'd seen in days. "We're not waiting for anything. We're moving forward."

Victor's gaze softened, though he remained silent. He'd been with her through the darkness, but this... this felt different. Was he ready to leave the chaos of the mafia world behind? Could he truly step away from the life that had defined him for so long? The answer, he knew, was both simple and complicated. He was willing to try for her. For them. But the road ahead was not as clear as the horizon before them.

Elysia turned her back to the sea, her silhouette framed by the shifting light of the sun. "I've been thinking," she said, her voice barely above a whisper. "About what comes next for us."

Victor tensed, his body instinctively shifting closer, but his feet stayed rooted in place. "What do you mean?"

She hesitated, chewing on the inside of her lip, her eyes looking out to the vast expanse of the ocean. "For years, I was defined by the choices other people made for me. I didn't have control over my life. But now, I do. And I think... I think I want to create something new. Something that's mine. Not built on lies, or blood, or fear."

Her words hung in the air, a declaration that felt both empowering and terrifying. For the first time since their lives had collided in the whirlwind of danger and betrayal, Elysia was starting to carve out a life for herself. And yet, there was still a shadow of doubt that clouded her heart. Could she ever fully escape the life she had known? The scars, the connections, the people who would never let her go?

Victor's gaze softened as he watched her, his heart clenching with a mix of pride and sorrow. "And where does that leave me?" he asked, his voice quiet but tinged with a vulnerability that startled him.

Her eyes flicked to him, searching for an answer that would set her own heart at ease. But the truth was, she didn't know. She loved him, more than she had ever loved anyone. But love alone couldn't erase the chaos they'd lived through, couldn't make up for the things they had done. She couldn't continue to live in the shadows of the past. She wanted to live—for herself, not for anyone else.

"It leaves you with the same choice," Elysia said, her voice steady, though her heart was a whirlwind of emotion. "We both have to choose. We can't keep looking over our shoulders, wondering if someone's going to come for us. We can't keep living in the wreckage of what was. We have to build something new."

Victor's breath caught in his throat. The words were a challenge, a reckoning. She wasn't just talking about a future together—she was talking about an entirely different life. A life without the weight of the mafia, without the constant threat that had defined them for so long.

He took a step closer, his gaze locked on hers. "I'm ready to do whatever it takes," he said, his voice low, a promise. "For you. For us."

But even as he spoke the words, doubt lingered in the back of his mind. Could they truly escape their pasts? Could they leave behind everything that had shaped them? Or were they doomed to be dragged back into the violence and deceit that had always been part of their world?

Elysia reached out, her hand brushing against his, a spark of warmth that reverberated through his entire being. "I don't want this life anymore, Victor. I want freedom. I want peace. I want us to be something different."

His hand closed around hers, the touch grounding him in the moment, in her words. "Then we'll have it. Together. We'll make it happen."

For the first time in what felt like forever, there was a flicker of hope. It was small, fragile even, but it was there. A possibility that they could rebuild their lives, carve out something more than the darkness that had once consumed them.

But as the sea whispered behind them, the world felt infinitely larger, the stakes higher, and the road ahead uncertain. There would be no easy answers, no guarantees. They could try to outrun the shadows, but the shadows had a way of following.

As Elysia squeezed his hand, she looked back toward the horizon, the sun rising higher in the sky. There was a new day ahead. And for the first time, it was theirs to claim.

But just as they began to feel the weight of the future lift, a sound broke through the silence—the distant hum of a car engine, drawing closer, the tires crunching against the gravel. The world was about to remind them that some things could never be outrun.

The soft clink of glass against wood echoed in the quiet room as Victor poured himself another drink. The amber liquid swirled in his glass, catching the light from the chandelier above. He wasn't thirsty, not really, but the act of pouring—of creating some semblance of normalcy—was the only thing that seemed to keep the storm brewing inside him at bay.

He'd spent the better part of the morning reflecting, analyzing, and questioning everything that had led him to this point. Elysia's words kept replaying in his mind, each one a quiet challenge, a call for something he wasn't sure he could give. Freedom. Peace. A future without the chains of their past lives.

But could he do it? Could he truly let go of everything he had been—everything he had fought for? The Lupo family had defined him, had shaped him, for so long. The mafia world wasn't just his business; it was his identity. And yet, he knew it was suffocating him. The weight of bloodshed, betrayal, and the lives destroyed under his rule was something he could no longer ignore. Elysia had been right. They couldn't keep looking over their shoulders forever.

But letting go meant severing ties with everything he had known. It meant abandoning the empire he had built from nothing, and worse, it meant walking away from a legacy that had been passed down through generations. The thought was enough to send a chill through his veins, but as he glanced across the room at Elysia, who was sitting by the window, staring out into the vast expanse of their new life, the chill in his bones seemed to melt away.

She was everything he had ever wanted—and everything he had ever feared. She embodied the possibility of a life outside the mafia, a life filled with hope, love, and redemption. But she also represented a future that he had to fight for, a future that required him to let go of the one thing he had clung to for so long.

Victor exhaled slowly, swirling the drink in his hand, watching the liquid spin in the glass as if it could offer him answers. But there were no easy answers, only the weight of his decisions and the consequences they carried.

Elysia's voice interrupted his thoughts. "What are you thinking about?"

He looked over at her, finding her eyes already on him. Her gaze was soft, but there was an edge to it—an understanding that she was waiting for him to make a decision. He could see the way her hands fidgeted in her lap, the subtle tension in her posture, as if she were holding herself back, afraid of pushing too hard.

Victor set the glass down, the sound a sharp contrast to the quiet stillness of the room. "I'm thinking about how hard this is," he admitted, his voice uncharacteristically raw. "About how much I want to walk away from it all… but how much harder it is to let go."

Elysia's eyes softened, and she stood, crossing the room with a grace that made him pause. When she reached him, she didn't speak immediately. Instead, she simply sat next to him, her hand brushing against his. The contact was small, simple, but it grounded him in a way nothing else had.

"You don't have to do it alone," she said, her voice steady, though there was a vulnerability in it that he hadn't expected. "You've never had to do this alone. And you don't have to now."

Victor's gaze lingered on their hands, intertwined as if they were two halves of the same whole. The warmth of her touch spread through him, and for a fleeting moment, he could almost believe they were living in a world that was untouched by violence and betrayal. A world where they could walk away from the past and build something better.

But then the harsh reality of their lives returned to him. The mafia world didn't let go easily. They couldn't simply walk away and expect everything to be okay. There were enemies to face, debts to be settled, and a legacy that wouldn't disappear overnight. And Victor knew, deep down, that his role in the mafia wasn't something that could be erased.

"I don't know how to leave it behind," he confessed, his voice rougher now, as if the words were cutting through him. "I don't know if I can."

Elysia turned her head to look at him, her gaze soft but unyielding. "Then let me help you," she whispered. "Let me be the reason you do it. Let me be the reason you walk away and never look back."

Victor felt a lump form in his throat, a mix of gratitude and fear. Fear that what she was asking was impossible, that the life he had built was too deeply ingrained in him to ever truly escape. But as he looked into her eyes—into the deep well of understanding, of love, and perhaps even of hope—he realized something.

He didn't want to be the man he was anymore. Not for her. Not for himself. Not for anyone.

"I want to," he said, his voice a bare whisper. "More than anything. But it's not just about us. It's about everything we've built and everything we've lost."

Her hand tightened around his, a silent promise that, whatever came next, they would face it together. "Then we rebuild. We rebuild from the ground up, together. And we don't let the past control us."

Victor's eyes locked onto hers, and in that moment, something inside him shifted. It wasn't easy, and it wouldn't be simple, but for the first time, he truly believed it was possible.

The weight of the past still clung to him, still lurked in the shadows, but with Elysia by his side, he felt a spark of hope. It wouldn't be quick. It wouldn't be painless. But they could build something new, something worth fighting for. And this time, it would be theirs—not the mafia's.

Elysia smiled, the warmth of it filling the space between them. It wasn't perfect, but it was a beginning. A new chapter. A chance for them both to move forward, to leave the past behind and embrace a future that, for the first time in a long while, seemed within reach.

The night had settled in, thick and heavy like a blanket smothering the city below. Elysia stood by the window, her fingers tracing the cool surface of the glass as she looked out into the darkness. The view from their new home, perched high above the bustling streets of the city, was both serene and alien. No longer bound by the constant threat of violence, they had sought solace in a place that offered peace—a peace that felt both fragile and essential.

Victor stood behind her, his presence looming like a shadow even in the quiet of the room. She didn't need to turn around to feel the weight of his gaze. His fingers brushed the small of her back, his touch gentle but insistent, a silent reassurance that he was there, that they were in this together.

"Elysia," his voice rumbled softly, thick with unspoken words. She didn't need to look at him to sense the turmoil swirling inside him—the same unease, the same restlessness that had gripped her for weeks.

She didn't answer immediately, instead taking in the view before her. The city lights twinkled like stars below, but it felt distant, foreign to her now. The life they had known, the life of constant tension, fear, and bloodshed, seemed impossibly far away. And yet, she knew that it was never as easy as simply walking away.

"I've been thinking about what we talked about," she said finally, her voice steady but tinged with something like regret. "About leaving everything behind."

Victor moved closer, his warmth pressing against her back. He didn't speak, but his proximity was enough to let her know he was listening.

"I know we've said we're going to build something new," she continued, her voice barely above a whisper. "And I want to. But I keep thinking about how easy it is to say those words and how hard it's going to be to make them real. We can't just pretend that the past doesn't matter."

Her words hung in the air between them, heavy with truth. There was no denying the power of their past lives, no escaping the fact that they had both been shaped by the world they had left behind.

Victor's breath was warm against her neck as he spoke, his voice a low murmur that sent a shiver down her spine. "I know, Elysia. But I'm tired. I'm tired of the games, the lies, the blood. I'm tired of living in a world where everything is just… a transaction."

Elysia turned in his arms, her face searching his, trying to read the depths of his feelings, the layers of guilt and longing he so often kept hidden. "Then what do we do? How do we start over when the world won't let us?"

Victor's hands cupped her face, his thumbs gently brushing the lines of tension from her brow. "We do it together. We fight for the life we want, not the life we've been handed. We rebuild, slowly. It won't be easy. But as long as we're standing here, together, we can make it."

Her breath hitched at the sincerity in his voice, and for the first time in what felt like forever, she believed him. She believed in them, in their future. She had spent so much time running, hiding from the past, but maybe it was time to stop. Maybe it was time to face what lay ahead with him, not as a shadow of the past, but as a promise for the future.

"I'm scared," she whispered, the admission raw and vulnerable. "Scared that we'll fall back into it, that it'll be too hard to escape what we were. I don't want to lose us, Victor."

His lips found hers then, slow and tender, grounding her in the moment. When he pulled away, his eyes were fierce with determination. "You won't lose me. We won't lose each other."

Elysia nodded, her heart thudding in her chest. She had always feared that the past would come back to haunt them, that they would be unable to outrun the ghosts of the mafia world. But with Victor, with their shared resolve, maybe they could break free. Maybe they could build something stronger than the empire they had once ruled, something that didn't require bloodshed and fear.

A sudden chime from his phone broke the moment, and Victor's gaze flickered to the screen before he cursed under his breath. Elysia watched his expression shift, the intensity returning to his eyes as he read the message.

"What is it?" she asked, her voice tightening with concern.

Victor's jaw clenched, and he turned to face her, his gaze filled with a mixture of frustration and resolve. "It's from the lawyer. There's a meeting tomorrow, with someone from my past."

Elysia frowned, stepping closer. "What does it mean? What do they want?"

Victor didn't answer immediately. Instead, he pocketed the phone, his eyes locking with hers. "It's unfinished business. The kind I thought I had left behind. But I can't ignore it. Not yet."

Elysia's stomach twisted in anticipation. "Are you going to meet with them?"

He hesitated, the weight of the decision pressing on him. Finally, he nodded. "I have to. It's the last piece of the puzzle. If we're going to leave this life behind, we need to be sure there's nothing left to drag us back."

Elysia nodded, though a part of her hesitated. She had thought they were done, that they had escaped the shadows, but Victor's past had a way of catching up with them. She didn't know if she was ready to face it again, but she knew she couldn't stop him from going. She would stand by him, no matter what.

"Then I'll be here," she said quietly, her voice steady despite the worry gnawing at her. "Waiting for you."

Victor's gaze softened, a fleeting moment of tenderness before he turned toward the door. He stopped, his back to her. "I'll come back to you, Elysia. I promise."

As he walked out into the night, Elysia's heart clenched. She didn't know what the future held, but she knew one thing for certain: the road ahead wasn't going to be easy. Yet, for the first time in a long time, she wasn't afraid to walk it.

25

Redemption

The silence of the old mansion was deafening as the shadows of their past seemed to haunt the grand, empty halls. The faded tapestries that lined the walls, once vibrant with tales of power and blood, now hung like ghosts, witnesses to a time long gone. Victor Lupo stood at the large arched window, his back straight and rigid, his gaze lost in the vast emptiness of the world outside. His fingers brushed against the cool glass as memories of a life filled with betrayal, violence, and power swirled through his mind like a storm.

The house—the house that had been both a kingdom and a prison—no longer felt like home. The walls that had witnessed his rise to power now felt suffocating, as though the very air inside had absorbed the weight of his sins. The echoes of his past, of all the lives he had destroyed, lingered in every corner. There was no running from it. No matter how far he tried to move forward, the chains of what he had done always seemed to pull him back.

Behind him, Elysia stood, her eyes scanning the room, her heart heavy with the burden of decisions she could never undo. The once-powerful mafia queen now found herself tangled in a world that was no longer hers. She had lived through death and pain, and now, in the wake of everything they had destroyed, she found herself searching for something—anything—that could make it all feel worth it.

Her voice, soft and steady, broke through the silence like a lifeline. "Victor, we can't keep running from it." Her words, though calm, carried the weight of everything they had fought for and against. "It's time."

Victor's shoulders stiffened, and his gaze shifted to her, his expression unreadable, but the storm behind his eyes was clear. "You think I don't know that?" He turned away from the window, his voice rough with the exhaustion of years spent in this war of attrition. "I built this empire on lies, on bloodshed… I've taken lives, destroyed families, torn apart everything that might have been good. I can't undo it."

Elysia stepped forward, her bare feet barely making a sound on the marble floors, the faint scent of jasmine from her perfume the only trace of her presence in the otherwise still air. She was no longer the woman who had been pulled into this world by fate. She was no longer the frightened girl who had been forced to choose between survival and morality. She was something more now—stronger, wiser, and, despite everything, more capable of love than she had ever believed possible.

"You can't undo it," she said softly, "but you can change it. You can make it right." Her eyes held a deep sincerity, an understanding that ran deeper than the bloodshed that surrounded them. "I'm not asking you to fix everything. I'm asking you to take responsibility."

Her words hit him harder than any physical blow ever could. He knew the weight of the choices he had made, but hearing it from her—the woman who had seen the worst of him and still chose to stay—tore through him like a blade. How could she still stand by him after everything? How could she want to rebuild with him?

Victor turned fully toward her now, his eyes searching hers as if looking for an answer he wasn't sure he deserved. "What if it's too late? What if we can't escape what we've done?"

Elysia's gaze softened, and for the briefest moment, Victor saw the woman she had been before the war, before the mafia. She was still that woman, somewhere beneath the layers of armor she had built to survive. "It's never too late, Victor. Redemption isn't a destination—it's a journey. And it starts with facing the truth, no matter how painful it is."

The air between them was thick, charged with the tension of their unspoken fears and unacknowledged truths. For so long, they had both clung to their roles in this world, locked in a deadly dance of power and vengeance, each trying to outrun the other. But now, as the dust settled, the weight of their actions finally crashed down on them, and it was no longer just about survival. It was about something more: rebuilding. Reconciling. Finding peace in a world that had never offered them such a luxury.

Victor's breath caught in his throat, his heart hammering in his chest as he allowed himself to imagine what that peace might look like. He had spent years drowning in darkness, burying himself in the lies that kept him safe from the truth. But now, standing before the woman who had seen him for who he truly was and still loved him, a flicker of hope sparked deep within him.

"I don't know how," he whispered, the words tasting bitter on his tongue. "But I'll try."

Elysia reached out, her hand brushing his with the gentleness of a person who had seen too much hurt to ever cause more. Her touch was a balm, soothing the raw edges of his soul, even if only for a moment. "We don't have to do it alone," she said softly, her voice full of a strength that he could only admire. "We face it together, Victor. That's the only way we'll move forward."

Victor stood there, caught in the whirlwind of his own emotions. For the first time in years, he allowed himself to hope—not for revenge, not for power—but for something deeper, something more sacred. Redemption. And it was in that moment that he knew he couldn't do it without her. She was his anchor, his light in the darkest of nights.

"Together," he echoed, his voice steady, the storm in his chest quieting just enough to allow the words to pass through.

The silence stretched between them, filled with the weight of everything that had been said and unsaid. Outside, the sun began to set, casting the room in a golden light, a reminder that even in the darkest hours, there was always the possibility of dawn.

Elysia turned toward the door, her steps light but resolute. "We have a lot of work ahead of us, Victor. But I believe in us."

Victor watched her, the faintest smile tugging at his lips as he followed her toward the exit. For the first time in a long while, he felt a flicker of something more than guilt. It was hope. A hope that maybe, just maybe, they could find redemption after all.

The world beyond the windows was darkening, the last remnants of the day slipping beneath the horizon as the shadows lengthened across the sprawling grounds of the mansion. Inside, the atmosphere was thick, heavy with the weight of unspoken words and unshed tears. Elysia sat at the small dining table, her hands clasped in front of her, the flickering candlelight casting a soft glow on her face, but her mind was far from here.

Victor, standing across the room by the grand fireplace, stared into the crackling flames, his broad back to her. His posture was stiff, like a man encased in armor he could never remove. It had been hours since their conversation, and though they had made an unspoken agreement to start anew, the silence now felt like an insurmountable wall.

She had always known him to be a man of few words—his power lay not in his speech, but in his actions—but tonight was different. Tonight, the distance between them was more than just a space of physical silence. It was a chasm of guilt and regret, of histories they couldn't rewrite.

Elysia's breath caught in her throat, the weight of their shared pasts suddenly overwhelming her. She wanted to reach out to him, to pull him into her arms and tell him that it was okay, that they could move forward, but she knew that words alone wouldn't heal the damage they had done.

"You've been quiet," she said softly, her voice breaking the silence that had become both a comfort and a curse. "Too quiet."

Victor didn't turn immediately. Instead, he let out a long breath, his shoulders sagging under an invisible weight. Then, finally, he spoke, his voice low, rough. "I'm trying to figure out how to make things right. And I don't know where to start."

The words were raw, edged with vulnerability that Elysia rarely saw from him. It was a side of Victor that he kept hidden beneath layers of control, of dominance, but tonight the cracks were beginning to show. The veneer of the mafia king was slipping, and in its place, she saw the man who had been haunted for far too long by his past.

"By starting," Elysia said, her eyes steady, meeting his gaze in the reflection of the flames. "Start by forgiving yourself. And then maybe, we can forgive each other."

The silence that followed felt different from the oppressive quiet they'd shared before. This time, it was filled with the weight of truth, of shared understanding, and the possibility of something more.

Victor finally turned toward her, his eyes locked onto hers, burning with a mixture of gratitude and guilt. "How do you forgive someone who's done things like I've done?" His voice was hoarse, the words almost as much a question to himself as to her.

Elysia stood, her steps slow, deliberate, and walked toward him. She could feel his eyes on her, the intensity of his gaze pulling her closer despite the distance. When she reached him, she stopped, her hand resting just inches from his chest, as if she were afraid to touch him, afraid that any contact might break the fragile connection they were starting to rebuild.

"You start by taking responsibility," she said softly. "You don't run from the consequences. You don't try to erase the past. You face it. With all its darkness. And then… you let go."

Victor's eyes searched hers, looking for something—an answer, maybe, or an assurance that she wasn't asking him to forgive himself too quickly, that this wouldn't be easy. And perhaps it wasn't just forgiveness he needed from her. It was the strength to forgive himself. To face what he had done and accept the man he was, flaws and all.

"And then what?" His voice was barely a whisper.

Elysia's hand trembled slightly as she reached up and placed it against his chest, over the steady rhythm of his heart. "Then we build something new. Something better. You've always been the one to show strength in battle, Victor. But this—this is about finding the courage to be vulnerable. To allow yourself to heal."

The words were almost foreign to him, and yet, as he stood there, letting her touch him in ways he hadn't allowed anyone to, he realized how much he needed this—how much he had always needed it but had buried under layers of pride and control.

"You think we can rebuild?" he asked, the uncertainty in his voice making him sound more human than he'd ever let anyone see. "After everything?"

Elysia nodded, her heart aching for the man standing before her. She understood him more than she let on, understood the darkness that plagued him, but she also knew that if they were ever to move forward, they needed to trust each other completely. The journey to redemption wasn't a solitary one—it was something they had to do together, or not at all.

"I do," she said, her voice firm now, filled with the certainty she hadn't felt in so long. "I believe in us."

The air between them grew thick with tension, but it was a different kind of tension now—charged with hope rather than fear, with possibilities rather than regrets.

Victor stepped closer to her, closing the space that had once felt like an insurmountable distance. His hand reached for hers, his fingers trembling slightly as he wrapped them around her palm, pulling her against him. The warmth of his body, the steady thrum of his heartbeat beneath her ear, was both a comfort and a challenge. He had never allowed anyone to see him so exposed before.

"I don't know if I can be the man you want me to be," he whispered, his voice laced with vulnerability. "But I'll try."

Elysia lifted her face to meet his, her eyes soft with understanding. "You don't have to be perfect. You just have to be real."

And in that moment, standing together in the quiet aftermath of the battle that had been their lives, Victor and Elysia knew that the road ahead would be long. But it would be a road they would travel together, one step at a time, each of them learning how to forgive and rebuild. To leave the past behind—and finally, to find redemption.

The night stretched on, the stars hidden behind the thick clouds that had rolled in as if the heavens themselves were holding their breath. In the silence of the mansion, everything seemed to stand still. The soft click of the front door echoed in the hallway, signaling the end of another day of quiet reflection. Elysia and Victor had spent hours together, unpacking their emotions, shedding layers of guilt and regret, each confession and apology building a bridge toward the possibility of redemption. Yet, as much as they had healed, a lingering uncertainty still danced between them like a shadow they couldn't quite escape.

Elysia stood at the edge of the grand balcony, her hands gripping the cold stone railing as she gazed out at the sprawling grounds beneath the looming trees. Her thoughts were scattered, fragments of the past, of choices made, battles fought, both external and within themselves. She had come so far from the woman she had been when she first met Victor, when their lives had been tangled in lies and bloodshed. But as much as she had transformed, there were parts of her past that still clung to her like the night's cold mist, haunting her, reminding her of what she had lost.

Victor approached from behind, his footsteps quiet, as though he too understood the weight of this moment. Without a word, he stood beside her, his presence a quiet strength that grounded her. For a moment, neither of them spoke. The silence was filled with a thousand unspoken words, things they both knew but didn't have to say.

Finally, it was Victor who broke the stillness. "We can't change what we've done," his voice was rough, as though he had spent the words out of necessity rather than choice. "But we can control what happens next."

Elysia didn't look at him, but she felt his gaze, felt the sincerity in his words, and it made something inside of her ache. The man beside her—this man who had once been her enemy, her captor, her love—was now the one she stood with, the one who, despite everything, still believed in the possibility of something better. It was a strange thing, this love they shared. It wasn't clean, wasn't neat, and it wasn't always kind. But it was theirs, forged in fire and blood, shaped by their shared traumas, and in the quiet of this night, it was more real than anything else.

"I know," she replied softly, her voice carrying the weight of the long journey they had traveled. "But it's the future that scares me the most, Victor. Not the past."

Victor stepped closer, closing the distance between them, his hand brushing gently against hers. It was the simplest of touches, yet it held the promise of everything they had yet to become. "We can face it together. Whatever comes next."

She finally turned to him, their eyes locking in that silent exchange of understanding that only they shared. It was then, in that instant, that Elysia realized how far they had both come. Not just physically, not just in the battles they had fought, but in the transformation of their hearts, their souls. They had learned to trust each other, to heal, and to finally let go of the chains of their past.

Victor's fingers slid gently beneath her chin, lifting her face toward his. His thumb brushed over her skin, the touch tender, almost reverent, as though he were afraid that if he moved too quickly, the fragile peace between them would shatter. "You're not alone anymore, Elysia," he murmured, his voice thick with emotion. "I'm here. Always."

The rawness of his words caught her off guard, and her heart swelled with something she hadn't dared to feel in a long time—hope. She had spent so much of her life running from love, running from the darkness that had haunted her, but now, for the first time, she felt the weight of his love as a shield, as something that could protect them both from the storm they had weathered.

"I never thought it would be like this," she whispered, her breath shaky. "I never thought I could feel safe again."

"You are safe," Victor said, his voice firm and sure. "With me, you are."

The tenderness in his eyes spoke volumes, more than any grand declaration of love ever could. She didn't need him to promise her the world, not anymore. She didn't need grand gestures or promises of forever. All she needed was this moment, this quiet peace that had eluded them both for so long.

Elysia reached up, her hand gently cupping his cheek, the rough stubble beneath her palm grounding her in the present. "Then let's make it count," she said softly. "Let's make this new chapter ours."

Victor smiled—a rare, unguarded smile that softened the harsh lines of his face. For once, he wasn't the mafia king, the ruthless leader, the man who carried the weight of the world on his shoulders. In that moment, he was simply Victor, the man she loved, the man who was willing to risk everything to make things right.

"We will," he promised, his lips brushing against her forehead in a gesture so simple, yet so full of meaning. "Together."

They stood there for a long while, the quiet night wrapping around them like a blanket, the distant sounds of the world fading away as they allowed themselves to simply be. There was no grand resolution, no sudden epiphany, just two people finding peace in each other, ready to face whatever came next with the strength they had found together.

The future, uncertain and ever-shifting, awaited them. But for now, they were free. And that was enough.

26

A New Beginning

The house was quiet. Not the uneasy silence that clung to the remnants of broken trust, but a gentle, soothing quiet that wrapped around Victor and Elysia like a blanket—soft and reassuring. It was early morning, the sky still holding onto the last hues of dawn, as if reluctant to fully wake. The air was cool, a crisp promise of a fresh start.

Victor stood by the kitchen window, his hands gripping the cup of coffee between his fingers. His eyes traced the outline of the garden outside, where the first rays of light broke through the trees, illuminating the wildflowers that Elysia had insisted on planting. There was a certain peace here, something he hadn't thought possible when his life had been nothing but chaos and bloodshed.

The past few weeks had been a blur. After the final battle with the Verrini family, Victor had walked away from the life he knew. He had left the blood-stained streets of the mafia world behind. The mansion that once echoed with the sounds of gunfire and betrayal was now eerily quiet. No more screams. No more lies. No more violence.

But even now, even with the peaceful life they were attempting to build, the past clung to him like an old scar. It was impossible to completely outrun.

He couldn't wash it away, no matter how hard he tried.

Elysia's soft footsteps broke the stillness, and Victor turned just as she entered the kitchen. She had always been the light in his life, even when he didn't deserve it. Her face, unburdened by the world they had left behind, was serene, her smile small but genuine. She was wearing one of his old shirts—he'd given it to her weeks ago, and she'd never taken it off. It was a reminder of the strange but undeniable connection they shared.

"You're up early," Elysia murmured, her voice warm like honey as she reached for the coffee pot. "I thought we'd take a walk this morning."

Victor raised an eyebrow but said nothing as she poured herself a cup. He watched her with a mix of admiration and something deeper, something almost painful—a love so raw it had the power to tear him apart. He had never imagined he would find something so pure in a world of darkness.

"I was thinking about the future," he confessed, his voice low, like the weight of the words was too much to bear. "About everything we've been through."

Elysia's eyes softened, and she crossed the kitchen to stand beside him. She placed a hand on his arm, the simple touch grounding him. "We've made it this far. We can make it further."

Victor swallowed hard, the past trying to claw its way to the surface again. "I don't know how to leave it behind, Elysia. Sometimes I wonder if I even deserve to."

She turned to face him, her gaze unwavering. "You're not that man anymore, Victor. And I'm not the woman who was afraid of you. We've both changed."

He let out a shaky breath, the burden of his guilt pressing harder. "But the damage is done. Can we ever truly escape who we were?"

Elysia's eyes flitted to the window, her expression thoughtful. "Maybe we can't change everything. But we can change what comes next. We have the power to choose."

Her words lingered in the air, and for a moment, Victor allowed himself to believe them. He let go of the past, just for a second, and the world seemed a little lighter.

"Do you ever think about what comes next?" she asked quietly, breaking the silence that had settled between them.

Victor's gaze turned back to the window, the warm sunlight now breaking through the trees, casting long shadows over the garden. It was beautiful here. Simple. Peaceful. He thought of the life they could have. Away from the bloodshed. Away from the betrayal.

"I think about it every day," he admitted, his voice heavy with sincerity. "But I'm afraid of what happens when the past catches up with us."

Elysia stepped closer to him, her fingers brushing lightly against his. "We'll face it together. No matter what happens. That's how we move forward."

Victor looked down at her, at the woman who had somehow become his anchor in a world that had always threatened to drown him. She was the light to his darkness, the calm in his storm. And she was right. No matter what their pasts had been, the future was theirs to claim.

A slight smile tugged at the corners of his mouth. "You make it sound so simple."

Elysia chuckled softly, the sound like a balm to his soul. "It's never simple. But we can make it through."

A NEW BEGINNING

Victor reached out, pulling her into his arms. For a long moment, they stood there, silently, the weight of everything they had been through hanging in the air but no longer threatening to crush them. The world outside might still be waiting for them to slip, to fall back into the shadows, but inside this house, in this moment, they had peace.

And that peace, fragile as it was, was enough. For now.

"You're right," Victor murmured, pressing a kiss to the top of her head. "We'll face whatever comes next. Together."

Elysia pulled back slightly, her eyes searching his. "No more secrets, Victor. No more running."

He nodded, the conviction in his heart stronger than the doubts that had once plagued him. "No more secrets."

The sun was higher now, fully risen, and the world outside beckoned to them. There would be more challenges. More battles to fight. But for the first time in a long time, Victor felt ready. Ready to embrace a future not defined by violence, but by love. By the life he could build with Elysia by his side.

As they walked out into the garden together, side by side, the world seemed to stretch out before them—new, untamed, and full of possibility.

The evening settled over the house like a soft, silken blanket. The kind that wrapped around you, cocooning you in comfort, while outside, the world remained uncertain. Elysia sat on the porch, her fingers grazing the edges of a weathered book, the pages worn with use. She hadn't read in days, her thoughts constantly pulled in different directions by the life they had built together, and the fragile peace they were trying to hold on to.

Victor stood at the edge of the porch, his broad shoulders hunched as he stared into the horizon. His mind was a storm of conflicting thoughts—doubts, regrets, and the lingering shadow of a past that refused to fade. The mafia world had always been his reality, his constant, and now that it was gone, he was left with a haunting emptiness.

"Sometimes I forget what peace feels like," Elysia said softly, breaking the silence that had draped over them like a shroud. Her voice, so simple yet filled with the weight of truth, carried across the space between them.

Victor didn't turn to face her, but his voice came out hoarse, as if the words themselves were heavy. "I don't know if I'll ever truly understand it." He let out a sigh, a long, drawn-out exhale that seemed to release more than just air. He felt a dull ache in his chest, an ache that had only grown since they'd left the life behind.

Elysia's gaze softened, and she stood up, closing the book with a gentle thud. The night air had grown cooler, and she wrapped her arms around herself as she walked over to stand beside him, her presence a quiet reassurance.

"You've always been about control, Victor," she said, her voice gentle, yet unwavering. "But you don't have to control everything. You don't need to control the peace, or the healing. Let it happen."

Her words were like a balm to his wounded soul, but the truth of them stung just as much as it soothed. Letting go had never been his strong suit. He had always been the one to take charge, to make the decisions that carved their fates. But now, for the first time, the stakes were different. The game had changed.

"You're right," Victor murmured, his voice tight. "It's just that I'm so used to being in control. To knowing what comes next. Now… I don't know."

The quiet hum of distant traffic reached their ears, an audible reminder that the world continued to move, even when it felt like they were standing still. Elysia's fingers brushed against his, and he instinctively took her hand, the familiar warmth of her touch grounding him in a way that nothing else could. He hadn't realized how much he needed her until she was there, right beside him, offering him something he never thought he'd find—peace.

"You don't have to know," she said, squeezing his hand. "You don't have to have all the answers. We're in this together. We always have been, even when it didn't feel like it."

Victor finally turned to look at her, his eyes searching her face, the unspoken connection between them stronger than any words could express. The weight of everything they had endured—the betrayals, the battles, the moments when he thought they might not make it—seemed to fall away, replaced by something gentler, something that felt like a future.

Her eyes held his, a flicker of understanding passing between them. "We have time, Victor. Time to rebuild. Time to heal."

He nodded, but the doubt still lingered in his chest. How could they ever truly escape what they had been? How could they make peace with the violence, the lies, the years spent on the edge of darkness?

"It's hard to believe sometimes," he admitted, his voice barely above a whisper. "That I can leave it all behind. That I can be someone... else."

Elysia's lips curved into a soft smile. "You're already someone else, Victor. You've always been more than what the world saw. You just have to let yourself see it."

Victor chuckled, the sound low and rough. "You always know what to say."

She raised an eyebrow, the spark of playfulness returning to her eyes. "I've learned from the best."

There was a moment of quiet between them, the kind that only true understanding can create. In that silence, Victor realized something—something that he had never fully understood before. His past didn't define him. It had shaped him, yes, but it didn't have to dictate who he was going to be. And with Elysia by his side, he didn't have to face that journey alone.

As they stood there, the world around them continued to shift, to grow, just as they were. The house, once a symbol of darkness and danger, had now become a home—a sanctuary where they could be something more than they had ever imagined.

Victor squeezed Elysia's hand tighter, pulling her closer. "I don't know if I can ever fully escape it," he said, his voice filled with an honest vulnerability that surprised even him. "But I know I don't want to do it without you."

Her gaze softened, her fingers tracing the edge of his jaw as she looked up at him. "And you won't. I'll always be here, Victor. No matter what."

The quietness of the night stretched around them like a blanket, wrapping them in its warmth as they stood together in the calm after the storm. But even in this moment of stillness, the future was waiting for them—just beyond the horizon.

"I think we can build something better," Victor murmured, more to himself than to her. "Something worth fighting for."

Elysia nodded, her lips pressing against his in a gentle kiss. "We already have."

As they pulled away, the world felt like it was theirs to command, to shape.

And for the first time in a long time, Victor felt something like hope—an emotion he had long forgotten. A new chapter was beginning, and though the road ahead was uncertain, he knew one thing for sure. They were going to face it together.

The early morning sun crept through the cracks in the curtains, its golden light spilling across the room in delicate rays. Elysia stirred in the bed beside Victor, her movements slow and deliberate, as if she feared disturbing the fragile peace they had found. The sound of birdsong floated through the window, a peaceful reminder of the world outside—the world that, despite everything, was still turning.

Victor lay next to her, his back to her, yet they were as close as they had ever been. His breathing was steady, almost rhythmic, as if he had found a sliver of calm he hadn't known existed before. For so long, his life had been a chaotic, violent swirl, but now, in this moment, everything seemed simpler, quieter. Their future was a blank slate, ready to be written.

Elysia turned over, her hand resting lightly on his back, her fingers tracing the lines of muscle that had always been a symbol of strength—both physical and emotional. But she knew the strength he carried now wasn't just in his body. It was in his heart, in his soul. He had fought for them, for their future, and she could see it in the way he slept—at peace, for the first time in as long as she could remember.

But even now, in their new life, Elysia knew that the shadows of the past still lingered. There were still ghosts they had to confront, and she had to admit that she wasn't sure if they had left everything behind, or if the past would follow them, lurking just beyond the reach of their efforts to move forward.

A soft sigh escaped her lips, and Victor stirred, rolling over to face her. His eyes, heavy with sleep, were still the same dark pools that had held so many secrets. But now, there was something different in them—a warmth, a flicker of hope that hadn't been there before.

"Are you awake?" he murmured, his voice rough from the remnants of sleep.

Elysia smiled faintly, brushing a strand of hair from her face. "I am now," she replied, her voice quiet but filled with affection.

For a moment, they simply lay there, their eyes locked in a silent conversation—one that was not about words, but about understanding. Elysia had always known how to read him, how to feel his moods without him saying a word. And in this moment, she felt the same way. The weight of everything they had survived—the danger, the betrayal, the loss—seemed to have finally melted away.

"We've come a long way, haven't we?" Victor said, breaking the silence that had settled between them. His voice was tinged with something softer than usual, an emotion that felt foreign but comforting all the same.

Elysia nodded, her fingers lightly stroking his arm. "Yes, we have. But I don't think it's the end of our journey. It's just… a new beginning." She looked out the window, her gaze distant, as if searching for something just beyond the horizon. "We've built something here, Victor. And maybe it's enough. Maybe it's all we need."

Victor's chest tightened at the thought, his fingers reaching out to trace the curve of her face. He had always been driven by a sense of duty, by the need to protect and control. But now, in the quiet comfort of their shared space, he realized that it wasn't control he craved anymore. It was peace.

"You're right," he said, his voice quiet, but the conviction behind it was unshakable. "I think… I think we can make it work, Elysia. This time, we're building something that's ours. Something that isn't defined by our past."

Elysia's smile softened, her heart swelling at his words. "And maybe, just maybe, we can let go of what we were, and embrace what we're becoming."

Victor leaned in and kissed her then, a kiss that spoke of everything they had endured and everything they were about to face. It was slow, deliberate, full of meaning—of love, and hope, and the promise of a future where the past would no longer dictate their fate.

As the kiss deepened, Elysia felt the familiar fire ignite between them, a reminder that their love was not just something that had survived the worst of the world—it was something that had thrived because of it. No matter how many battles they had fought, no matter the blood that had been spilled, their bond had only grown stronger.

When they finally broke apart, they both felt something shift, something settle in the air between them. It wasn't just the quiet of the morning or the warmth of the sunlight—it was a feeling of completion, of a chapter closing and another beginning.

Elysia reached for his hand, intertwining their fingers. "We'll keep moving forward. Together."

Victor squeezed her hand, his voice low but filled with certainty. "Always."

As they sat there, their fingers woven together, the past seemed further and further away. The ghosts of their former lives had faded, replaced by the vision of the future they would build together—one rooted in love, trust, and redemption.

But just as they began to breathe in the promise of the new life they had carved for themselves, the phone on the nightstand buzzed, its sound cutting through the peaceful silence like a knife.

Victor's gaze shifted to the phone, his face hardening just slightly. He knew, deep down, that the past never truly left. It had a way of knocking on your door when you least expected it.

Elysia's eyes followed his, her heart skipping a beat as she saw the name on the screen.

It was a name neither of them ever thought they would see again.

The air in the room seemed to still, as if the entire universe was holding its breath.

Victor reached for the phone, his jaw tightening, as he swiped to answer it.

And Elysia, feeling a strange sense of foreboding, knew that their peaceful life was about to be tested once again.

27

The Final Test

Victor stood at the edge of the cliff, his eyes fixed on the horizon. The sea below churned restlessly, mirroring the storm of thoughts swirling in his mind. A storm that had been brewing for weeks, ever since the day he received the cryptic letter. The letter that had shattered the fragile peace they'd fought so hard to build.

Elysia was a few feet away, her silhouette outlined by the fading sunlight. The wind tugged at her hair, sending strands whipping around her face, but she didn't seem to notice. She was staring down at the ground, her posture stiff, her mind miles away.

Victor's gaze softened as he watched her, but the guilt gnawed at him. He had promised her a life of peace, free from the ghosts of their past. But promises were fragile things. And the shadows they had tried so hard to outrun had finally caught up to them.

"I don't know if I can do this anymore, Victor," Elysia's voice broke the silence, raw and trembling. Her words hung in the air between them, as heavy as the storm clouds gathering overhead.

Victor's chest tightened, his breath catching. He knew this was coming—

the final unraveling. He had been prepared for everything but this: the possibility of losing her, the woman who had breathed life back into him. The woman whose love had been his anchor through the darkest of times.

He turned to face her fully, taking a step forward, but she held up a hand, stopping him. "No, Victor. You don't understand. This… this isn't about what we've been through together. This is about the person I've become. The person I was before all of this. I can't keep running, hiding from the truth. I need to know who I am, who I was, before you came into my life."

Victor's heart hammered in his chest. He knew what she was talking about. The truth about her past, the secrets buried deep within her, that had always been a part of her but never fully acknowledged. He wanted to reach for her, to pull her close, to promise that everything would be alright, but the words felt hollow.

"You've always been enough for me, Elysia," he said, his voice low but firm. "You don't have to be anyone else. Not for me, not for anyone."

Her eyes flickered with uncertainty. The wind tugged at her dress, but she stood her ground, unwavering. "I don't think I've ever truly been enough. Not for myself."

The air between them seemed to freeze, as if the world itself was holding its breath. Victor could see the conflict in her eyes, the battle waging within her. He had always known that her past was a wound she carried, but he hadn't realized how deep it went.

The silence stretched, thick and suffocating. The sun dipped below the horizon, casting the world in shadow. It was a metaphor for the darkness closing in around them, the past they could never fully escape. The letter—the one they'd both hoped was nothing more than a threat—had been the final catalyst. The Verrini family had once again set their sights on the

Lupo empire. But this time, it was different. They weren't just after Victor anymore. They were after Elysia too.

Victor could feel the weight of her gaze as she turned to him. There was no fear in her eyes, no anger—just sorrow. "I don't know if I can love you the way I have," she whispered. "Not if it means losing myself in the process."

Her words struck like a blow, and for the first time in years, Victor felt the ground shift beneath him. He was used to threats, to bloodshed, to the brutal game of survival that defined his world. But this? This was something he couldn't fight with his fists.

"I will never ask you to give up who you are," he said, his voice thick with emotion. "But we're running out of time. The Verrinis won't stop until they've destroyed everything we've built. We can't keep living in this limbo. Elysia, you're more than just your past. You're the woman I love, the woman I'll fight for, no matter what it takes."

She closed her eyes, her shoulders trembling. The sound of the waves crashing against the rocks below seemed to echo in the silence between them. Her heart was breaking, piece by piece, and Victor felt every jagged shard.

"I wish I could believe that," she murmured, so softly he almost didn't hear. "But there's a part of me that still belongs to the past. A part of me that's always been tied to it, no matter how far I run."

Victor stepped closer, his hand reaching out. She didn't pull away. Her warmth was a silent invitation, and he took it, cupping her face gently in his hands.

"You don't have to run anymore," he whispered, his forehead pressed to hers. "You're not alone in this. You never have been."

The words were a balm to her wounded soul, but the doubts remained. Could she really leave the past behind? Could she truly step into the light with him, knowing that darkness would always linger in the corners of their lives?

Her breath hitched as she allowed herself a moment of vulnerability, a rare glimpse of the woman she had been before all of this—the woman who had once known peace, before Victor had come into her life and turned everything upside down. The woman who had once believed in something other than survival.

But that woman, that life, was gone. In its place stood someone who had survived unimaginable horrors. Someone who had learned to fight, to endure, and to love in spite of everything.

"I don't know if I can do this, Victor," she said again, but there was something different in her tone. A subtle shift, as though she was allowing herself to consider the possibility. The possibility of a future beyond the violence, beyond the fear.

Victor gently kissed her forehead, his lips lingering. "You don't have to decide right now," he murmured. "But when you're ready, we'll face whatever comes together. As equals. As partners."

The tension in her body eased ever so slightly. She nodded, though the weight of her decision still loomed over them both.

They stood there in the fading light, two souls at the precipice of everything they had ever known, and everything they had yet to discover. The future was uncertain, but for the first time, Elysia wasn't running from it. And for Victor, that was enough.

The night stretched out before them, long and endless, like the darkened abyss of the ocean below. Elysia lay in bed, staring up at the ceiling, her thoughts as restless as the waves that crashed against the rocks below the mansion. The room, once a haven of tranquility, now felt oppressive, as though the walls were closing in around her. It had been a long time since she'd felt this unsettled—this torn between two worlds.

The sound of Victor's footsteps outside the door was the only thing that brought her attention back to the present. He had been quiet, so quiet these past few days, as if he, too, were struggling to hold everything together. The weight of their past had finally caught up with them, and despite his unwavering strength, she knew he wasn't immune to the emotional storm that raged within her.

She heard the door creak open, and his presence filled the room like a shadow. His silhouette was strong against the faint light spilling in from the hallway, his broad shoulders and tall frame casting a shadow that seemed to fill every corner. Elysia could feel the tension between them, thick as the fog that rolled in from the sea. Neither of them had spoken of what happened at the cliff—what had been left unsaid between them lingered like a cloud in the air.

Victor approached the bed, his eyes meeting hers in the dim light. There was a rawness to his gaze, a vulnerability she hadn't seen in him before. He was always the one who shielded her from the darkness, the one who was unshakable. But tonight, it was as if he, too, was a man on the edge of breaking.

"Elysia," he said her name like a prayer, soft and laden with emotion. He took a hesitant step closer, as though afraid she might pull away, but she didn't. She stayed still, allowing him to cross the invisible line that had been drawn between them.

She didn't speak right away, didn't trust herself to say the right thing. Instead, she reached for his hand, threading her fingers through his. The warmth of his touch grounded her, and for a fleeting moment, the storm inside her heart calmed.

"You've been quiet," she finally said, her voice barely above a whisper. The words felt heavy, almost foreign to her, but she pushed them out anyway. "What are you thinking?"

Victor stood there, his jaw clenched, as if weighing his words. He had always been guarded, always calculated in his approach, but this moment felt different. The vulnerability between them was palpable, a thread that could snap at any second.

"I don't know if I can fix this, Elysia." His voice cracked, and the honesty in his words took her by surprise. He didn't hide his pain, didn't pretend to be the unshakable leader of the Lupo family. In this moment, he was just a man—a man who had made mistakes, who had fought for everything but was now unsure of what to fight for.

Her heart tightened at the sight of him like this. She had seen him in countless battles, seen him stand tall amidst bloodshed and loss, but never like this. Never so human, so vulnerable.

"You don't have to fix everything, Victor," she said, her voice steady, though inside, she was breaking too. "You don't have to carry all of this alone."

He knelt beside the bed, lowering himself to her level. His eyes searched hers, pleading for understanding. "But I promised you peace," he said. "I promised you a future away from all of this. And now, everything we've fought for, everything we've tried to build, feels like it's slipping through my fingers."

Elysia reached out and cupped his face in her hands, urging him to look at her, to truly see her. "It's not slipping away, Victor. We're just... we're just being tested. I'm not going anywhere. I never have been."

She saw the conflict in his eyes, the silent battle that raged within him. He was terrified, terrified of losing her, of failing her in the one thing he had promised to get right. He had always been so sure of his power, his ability to control every situation, but this? This was different. It was personal. It was about them, about their future, about the love they had built amidst the ashes of their pasts.

Victor closed his eyes briefly, leaning into her touch as if it were the only anchor in a sea of chaos. When he opened them again, the determination had returned, though it was softer, more tempered with vulnerability. "I don't want to lose you," he murmured, his voice a whisper of raw emotion. "You're all I have left."

Elysia's heart clenched, and she pulled him closer, resting her forehead against his. The air between them was charged with the weight of their unspoken fears, their unhealed scars. But in this moment, as their bodies pressed together, there was a fragile sense of peace—a shared understanding that despite the chaos around them, they had each other.

"We'll face this together," she said, her voice firm, though her own doubts threatened to surface. "Whatever comes, we'll face it together."

Victor didn't reply with words; instead, he kissed her—a kiss filled with all the things they had never said aloud. It was a promise, a vow, sealed with the rawness of their love and the weight of their shared history.

As the kiss deepened, Elysia allowed herself to believe, for just a moment, that they could survive this. That they could move forward, leave the past behind, and carve out a life free from the shadows that had always threatened to pull them under.

But even as the warmth of Victor's embrace surrounded her, the nagging feeling in the pit of her stomach refused to go away. The past wasn't done with them yet. It never would be.

The storm outside raged on, the wind howling against the windows, but inside, the world seemed still. The silence was thick, heavy with anticipation. Whatever came next, it would be the final test. And they would face it, not with the certainty of victory, but with the hope that love, in its truest form, was enough to see them through.

The dawn light filtered weakly through the curtains, casting long shadows across the room. The air felt still, as though the world was holding its breath, waiting for something monumental to occur. Elysia stood by the window, her eyes fixed on the horizon, but her mind was a storm of memories, fears, and the unbearable weight of uncertainty. The events of the past few weeks had worn her down to her core, leaving behind fragments of herself that she wasn't sure how to piece back together.

Victor had been quiet for days, lost in his own thoughts, retreating into a silence that only fueled the anxiety building in her chest. She had seen him at his strongest—his ruthlessness, his ambition, the way he commanded respect without saying a word. But now, she was seeing a different side of him. A side that was vulnerable, shaken by the cracks in the empire he had built and the guilt of dragging her into this world.

Behind her, she heard the familiar sound of footsteps—heavy and purposeful. She didn't need to turn to know who it was. The air around her seemed to thrum with the intensity of his presence, the weight of his emotions pressing against her like a storm gathering on the horizon.

Victor stopped beside her, his gaze never leaving the window. For a long moment, neither of them spoke. The silence between them stretched out like a taut wire, ready to snap at the slightest movement. Elysia could feel the tension in his posture, the way he clenched his fists at his sides as though he were holding himself together by sheer will.

"Do you ever wonder if we're too broken to fix?" she asked, her voice quieter than she intended. Her words were a confession, a question she had been afraid to ask herself for fear of the answer. The life they had built together was fragile, and no matter how much they fought to protect it, she feared that the past, with its violence and betrayal, would always haunt them.

Victor's silence was his answer, and it pierced through her like a blade. He wasn't sure either. They had both come so far, fought so hard, but the scars they carried—both visible and hidden—seemed to weigh heavier with each passing day.

"You know we can't outrun it, Elysia," Victor finally said, his voice low, almost strained. "The past doesn't let go easily. It clings to you. It suffocates you. It's been clawing at me for so long, and I thought I could outrun it. But it always catches up. It always finds a way."

Elysia's throat tightened at his words. The vulnerability in his voice was raw, so unlike the cold, calculated Victor she had come to know. He had always been in control, always had a plan. But now, it seemed like all the power he once commanded had slipped through his fingers, leaving him grasping at something he couldn't hold onto.

"I know," she whispered, her heart heavy. "But I'm tired of running. I'm tired of living in the shadows of what we were."

Victor turned to face her, his expression unreadable, but there was something in his eyes—a depth of emotion that she had never seen before. It was a mixture of fear, guilt, and something softer, something fragile. He took a step closer, his movements deliberate, as though every inch closer to her was a step he was afraid to take.

"Elysia," he said her name like a plea. "I don't want to lose you. I don't know how to fix what's been broken, but I'm not willing to give up. Not on us. Not on you."

Her breath hitched at the intensity of his gaze. He had never been this raw, never bared his soul so openly. It was both beautiful and terrifying, like standing on the edge of a precipice, knowing that a single misstep could send them tumbling into the abyss.

But instead of pulling away, Elysia reached for him. She touched his face, her fingers trembling slightly against his skin. For the first time in what felt like forever, she let herself be vulnerable, allowed herself to believe that maybe, just maybe, they could overcome this together.

"We can't fix everything, Victor," she said softly. "But I believe in us. I believe in what we have. We don't need to outrun the past. We need to face it. Together."

Victor closed his eyes at her words, a heavy exhale escaping his lips as though the weight of the world had been lifted from his shoulders, if only for a moment. When he opened his eyes again, there was a new resolve in his gaze, a strength that radiated from him like a beacon. He was no longer the man trapped by his past, but the man who was ready to face whatever came next—no matter how difficult.

"I'm not afraid of the past anymore," he said, his voice firm. "I'm afraid of losing you."

Tears welled in Elysia's eyes, but she refused to let them fall. Instead, she smiled, a faint but genuine smile that spoke of everything they had been through—of the darkness, the betrayal, and the love that had somehow survived it all.

"We won't lose each other," she said with conviction, the words wrapping around them like a promise. "Not now. Not ever."

They stood there, locked in that quiet, powerful moment, as the first rays of sunlight broke through the curtains, spilling golden light across the room. The world outside was still turning, life continuing on its course, but in that small space, in that fragile moment of peace, everything felt possible. Everything felt right.

But just as they began to let go of the fear that had held them captive, a soft knock at the door shattered the silence. Elysia's heart skipped in her chest, her instincts immediately on high alert. Victor's hand instinctively moved to the gun tucked beneath his jacket, though he didn't reach for it. His eyes locked with hers, a silent communication passing between them.

Without a word, Victor moved toward the door. Elysia followed closely behind, her hand instinctively gripping his arm. She could feel the tension radiating off him as he opened the door, his posture rigid with caution.

The figure standing in the doorway was one they both recognized—someone from their past, someone who had been long gone but whose presence now threatened to unravel everything they had built.

Victor's face tightened at the sight of him. "You," he growled, the storm inside him returning with full force.

Elysia's heart skipped a beat. The final test had arrived.

28

Epilogue—A Love Rekindled

The sun dipped low in the sky, casting a soft golden glow across the rolling hills that surrounded their new home. Elysia stood at the large bay window, her fingers tracing the cool glass, watching the horizon as if it could hold all the answers to the questions she had once asked herself. The air smelled of fresh earth and blooming jasmine, the scent of a life they had built together—a life free from the chains of their pasts. It was a life, she realized, she had never dared to imagine until now.

Victor, standing in the doorway behind her, didn't speak at first. He never did. There was a stillness about him, a quiet understanding that had been forged over the years of struggle and sacrifice. His presence was a comfort—an anchor in a world that had once felt unmoored. She could feel the weight of his gaze on her, the way it seemed to wrap around her like a protective cocoon. And yet, in the silence between them, there was a subtle tension, a reminder of how far they had come—and how much they had left to face.

"Do you ever think about the past?" Elysia's voice was soft, a murmur that barely broke the peace of the room.

Victor's gaze flickered to the horizon, then back to her. His face was a mask of strength, but she knew him too well to miss the faint crease in his brow, the unspoken words that lingered between them. He had always been the one to carry the weight of their shared history, the one who had seen the world through a lens of darkness and survival. She, on the other hand, had come into his life like a shard of light, a beacon of hope amidst the chaos. Together, they had created something that neither of them had believed was possible—a future, not defined by violence and betrayal, but by love and redemption.

"I think about it every day," Victor admitted, his voice low and raw. "But I've learned to live with it, Elysia. The past doesn't define us anymore." His words held the quiet certainty of someone who had fought his demons and emerged victorious. He had come to understand that the scars on his soul were not something to be ashamed of but something to be embraced. They had shaped him, yes, but they did not control him.

Elysia turned, meeting his gaze with a softness that only she could afford him. In the beginning, it had been impossible to imagine this moment—to see them standing here, side by side, as equals, as partners. There had been too many walls between them, too much darkness to overcome. But now, there was only light—a light that had been forged through shared struggle, through the acceptance of their flaws and the healing of old wounds.

"I used to think we couldn't escape it," she confessed, her voice tinged with a vulnerability that surprised even her. "That we would always be trapped in the world we came from. But now… now I see that we've built something different. Something real."

Victor stepped forward, closing the distance between them with a slow, purposeful stride. His eyes softened as he reached out to touch her face, his fingers grazing her skin in a tender caress. His touch was familiar, a comfort, but there was something more in it now—an acknowledgment of how far they had come.

"You were always the one who believed in us, Elysia," he said, his voice thick with emotion. "Even when I didn't. Even when I thought I was beyond redemption, you saw something in me. You made me want to fight for something better."

The sincerity in his words struck her to the core. It was a raw honesty she had never fully allowed herself to embrace, a reflection of how deeply their lives had intertwined. They had been broken, yes, but together, they had found a way to heal. And now, as the weight of the past began to lift, they stood at the threshold of something new—a future untainted by the shadows of their former lives.

"I didn't just believe in you, Victor," she said, her voice steady but filled with a quiet intensity. "I believed in us. In what we could be, if we were willing to let go of everything that tried to tear us apart."

For a moment, neither of them spoke. The silence hung between them like a fragile thread, one that was woven from the love they had shared and the struggles they had overcome. And in that silence, Elysia could feel the warmth of his presence, the steady beat of his heart, a reminder of how far they had come—and how far they had yet to go.

Victor's hand fell to her waist, pulling her close, his embrace both possessive and tender. The way he held her now was different, more grounded than it had ever been. It was as though they had come full circle, and with every step they had taken, they had shed the old versions of themselves that had once seemed so lost. There was no longer any need for walls between them; there was no longer any room for secrets or lies. What they shared now was raw and real, built on trust, respect, and an unwavering commitment to each other.

Elysia closed her eyes as she rested her head against his chest, listening to the steady rhythm of his heart, feeling the steady pulse of his life against hers. It was a sound she had grown to cherish—a sound that symbolized not only the strength of their love but the resilience of the life they had built together. The past, for all its weight, had become just that—past. And in its place was a future that held promise.

"Do you ever wonder," Elysia murmured, "what it would be like to live without the shadows?"

Victor's fingers tightened around her, his breath slow but steady. "I think about it all the time," he replied, his voice a low rumble. "But I also know that the shadows are part of who we are. They shaped us, made us stronger. And without them, we wouldn't be the people we are now."

She nodded, understanding what he meant. The darkness they had once known had forged them into something unbreakable, but it was the light that would guide them from here on out. Together, they had learned to embrace both—light and dark—and through that balance, they had found peace.

As the sun set behind them, casting the room in hues of amber and violet, Elysia felt a deep sense of peace settle over her. The past was no longer a burden, and the future was no longer a threat. They were free. And in that freedom, they had finally found each other.

The soft hum of the wind carried the scent of blooming flowers into the air, a gentle reminder of the beauty that had been created from the ashes of their past. The world around them seemed to hold its breath as Victor and Elysia sat on the veranda, side by side, watching the last traces of the day's light fade into night. It had been years since they first found their way to each other—years since their lives had been defined by chaos, betrayal, and the relentless grip of the mafia world. But now, here in this moment, they were something new. They had become more than they had ever thought possible.

Victor reached for her hand, his fingers slipping easily into hers. There was a familiarity to the gesture, but beneath it, there was something deeper, something richer. It was a connection that had grown beyond the physical, beyond the tumult of their past lives. It was a bond of the soul, forged through trials, through shared tears, through the quiet moments of healing they had shared. And now, sitting here in the stillness of their peaceful home, it felt as if the world had finally allowed them the space to breathe.

"Do you ever think about the future?" Elysia asked, her voice soft but filled with an underlying sense of curiosity. She had always been the dreamer, the one who dared to imagine a life beyond the confines of their past, and now, she found herself looking forward with the same hope she once thought impossible.

Victor turned his head to meet her gaze, his eyes dark, yet soft, as though he could see beyond the moment, to the future they had yet to carve out. "Every day," he replied, his voice low, a slight grin tugging at the corner of his lips. "But I don't need to think too hard about it anymore. I know what I want."

His words were simple, but the weight of them settled in the air between them, filling the space with a quiet intensity. There was no more need for words of grand gestures, no need for promises of a better life. They had lived through the worst of it. Together. And now, it was the everyday moments that held the most meaning. The quiet ones, the shared silences, the soft touches—those were the things that mattered most.

Elysia smiled, a genuine, unguarded expression that mirrored the peace she had finally found within herself. "What do you want, then?" she asked, the words playful but with an undercurrent of something more—a need to hear him speak of the future, of the life they would continue to build.

Victor's gaze softened as he leaned closer to her, his breath warm against her skin. He looked at her as if the very sight of her was enough to give him everything he had ever needed. "I want this," he murmured. "I want to be here. With you. Not just today or tomorrow, but for the rest of my life. I want to continue to grow with you, to face whatever comes our way, together."

For a long moment, Elysia didn't speak. She simply let the weight of his words settle into her heart. There had been a time when she had doubted this—doubted that they could ever reach this place of peace, this place of belonging. But now, there was no more doubt. They had fought their way through the darkness, they had healed the broken pieces of themselves, and now, they were standing on the precipice of something new, something worth fighting for.

The sound of footsteps on the gravel path below the veranda broke the silence, pulling Elysia's attention momentarily away from Victor. She glanced over to the source of the noise, a slight frown tugging at her brow. The figure approaching was unfamiliar, yet the determined pace at which they walked seemed almost too familiar. Victor, sensing the shift in her mood, followed her gaze, his protective instinct immediately kicking in.

"Who's that?" he asked, his voice laced with quiet concern.

"I don't know," Elysia replied, her hand instinctively tightening around his, as though anchoring herself to the present. The peace they had worked so hard to cultivate seemed to ripple, a hint of unease settling over her.

The figure stopped at the edge of their property, just beyond the garden's reach. The evening's shadows seemed to cloak them, but there was no mistaking the determined stance, the confidence that radiated even from afar. As they drew closer, the outline of a man came into focus, his features still obscured by the fading light, but there was something about his presence that struck a chord in Elysia's chest.

Victor stood up, his hand still holding hers, a sense of wariness in his posture. "Stay here," he said, his voice low, though there was no question in it. He wasn't going to let anyone get too close without knowing who they were.

But Elysia, unwilling to hide from the past that had defined them both, stood alongside him. She may have been afraid of what was to come, but she would face it—she would face it with him, just as she always had.

The figure moved closer, and in the last sliver of sunlight, the man's face was revealed. Elysia's breath caught in her throat as recognition washed over her. It was a face she hadn't seen in years, a face she had thought was long gone from her life. The man standing before them was someone from their past, someone whose name she had buried deep in her heart, hoping never to be forced to confront him again.

Victor's stance shifted, his protective instincts kicking in once more. "Who are you?" he asked, his voice commanding, but with a subtle edge of tension. There was something about the stranger that didn't sit right with him, something in the air that made his senses stand on high alert.

The man smiled, a cold, calculating smile that made Elysia's blood run cold. "I'm the one who's come to remind you that the past, no matter how far you run from it, will always catch up with you," he said, his words laced with an almost tangible threat.

Elysia's heart skipped a beat. The past had indeed come for them, but this time, she wasn't running. She wasn't afraid. Not anymore. Because the man before them wasn't the one in control anymore. They were. Together.

And as the shadows grew darker around them, Elysia knew that this final test—the one they had prepared for, the one that would truly prove the strength of their bond—had arrived.

www.ingramcontent.com/pod-product-compliance
Lightning Source LLC
LaVergne TN
LVHW011928070526
838202LV00054B/4539